"Eliza," Jack whispered, and then he did what she longed for. He kissed her.

She went up on tiptoe to meet him, twining her arms around his neck to keep from falling, tumbling down from this dream. He caught her around her waist, pulling her even closer to him.

How well they fit together! Their mouths, their hands, their whole bodies, so right. She parted her lips and felt the tip of his tongue sweep over hers. He tasted of champagne, of something sweet. Light, enticing, and then the kiss turned frantic, hungry, full of burning need.

Until she heard a crash of a door slamming, a burst of drunken laughter, reminding her sharply of where they were. Who they were.

He stepped back, his arms falling away from her. She shivered, suddenly so very cold, so sad, so out of breath and confused. She didn't know where to look, what to say, what to think. She only knew that something, everything, had utterly changed.

Author Note

I hope you enjoy spending time with Eliza and Jack as much as I did! This story means so much to me. It combines two of my favorite things in life, Paris and jazz.

When I was a college student, I was lucky enough to take the History of Jazz class led by Dr. Williams, a man passionate about jazz (he had an enormous walrus mustache, and an equally enormous glittery gold *jazz* belt buckle he wore all the time!). It was the best class ever, fifty minutes of listening to records ranging from Jelly Roll Morton and Buddy Bolden to the Marsalis family while Dr. Williams beat time on his desk. I had a lovely time remembering those days while I listened to records for research. A tough job, but a dedicated author will do it!

I also was excited to get to revisit my very favorite city, Paris, in these pages. I've always dreamed of what it must have been like there in the 1920s, with so many writers and painters and musicians creating all new art forms among those beautiful streets and bridges. It seemed like the perfect place for people like Jack and Eliza, dedicated to their art, longing to be free to be themselves—free to find true love in each other. They were truly one of my favorite couples to step out of my imagination—my "what if *this* happened..."—and onto the pages.

You can find more information on their world at my website, ammandamccabe.com, or email me anytime to talk music, Paris, romance—anything at all! Thanks so much for reading.

AMANDA McCABE

—

A Manhattan Heiress
in Paris

HARLEQUIN
HISTORICAL

Recycling programs for this product may not exist in your area.

ISBN-13: 978-1-335-72380-2

A Manhattan Heiress in Paris

Copyright © 2023 by Ammanda McCabe

Harlequin Enterprises ULC
22 Adelaide St. West, 41st Floor
Toronto, Ontario M5H 4E3, Canada
www.Harlequin.com

Printed in U.S.A.

Amanda McCabe wrote her first romance at sixteen—
a vast historical epic starring all her friends as the
characters, written secretly during algebra class! She's
never since used algebra, but her books have been
nominated for many awards, including the RITA® Award,
Booksellers' Best Award, National Readers' Choice Award
and the HOLT Medallion. In her spare time she loves taking
dance classes and collecting travel souvenirs. Amanda
lives in New Mexico. Visit her at ammandamccabe.com.

Books by Amanda McCabe

Harlequin Historical

Betrayed by His Kiss
The Demure Miss Manning
The Queen's Christmas Summons
Tudor Christmas Tidings
"His Mistletoe Lady"
A Manhattan Heiress in Paris

Dollar Duchesses

His Unlikely Duchess
Playing the Duke's Fiancée
Winning Back His Duchess

Debutantes in Paris

Secrets of a Wallflower
The Governess's Convenient Marriage
Miss Fortescue's Protector in Paris

Bancrofts of Barton Park

The Runaway Countess
Running from Scandal
The Wallflower's Mistletoe Wedding

Visit the Author Profile page
at Harlequin.com for more titles.

To Dr. Williams, of the OU School of Music,
for your love of jazz! Your History of Jazz class
was the best. And to all artists who follow
their own souls and make the world
a more beautiful place.

Prologue

Central Park, 1912

Elizabeth Van Hoeven closed her eyes tightly and knelt down low in the bare, frost-rustling branches of the towering elm tree. If only she could turn into a tiny bird and fly away, invisible to her cousins, her brother, and her fearsome nanny, skating on the ice below! If she could escape their calls to always "have some fun," "be sensible, quit dreaming." She would fly up, up, up into the sky, then down, down, down, to Stratton's Music Store, and play their pianos all day with no one to pester her. It was all she had ever wanted in her eleven years. To be with her music, lose herself in that stream of melody that could take a person out of their old, lonely lives.

To no longer be a Van Hoeven of Fifth Avenue. No more Vacani's Dance School, no more deportment lessons. No more afternoons marching around Central Park.

But she *was* a Van Hoeven. She sighed, and sank lower on the branch. As a Van Hoeven, she always had to be polite and charming, to chat and smile and know how to run a large house—or three of them, as her mother did. Music was fine to practice, even a desirable accomplishment for a young lady, so she could play at parties and charity musicales. But it wasn't meant for all the time. That was tipping dangerously over into being a professional. And she certainly could not play on a concert stage. Even at her age, she was supposed to make friends with suitable young ladies—and their soon to be eligible brothers. Astors, Schermerhorns, Vanderbilts, Whitneys.

Eliza huffed out a breath and kicked her kid boots against the tree. Her pale gold curls, always escaping from under her hat to tickle her forehead, blew out. She never knew what to say to those boys; her shyness overcame her, and when they *did* talk, the boys were usually so dull. They were nothing compared to the piano.

She gazed up into the pearl-gray sky, the sparkling snowflakes falling down to catch in her lashes, and she imagined she *was* a bird. What would her song be like? What notes would she string together? She imagined it in her mind, tapping it against the branch with her gloved fingertips...

Suddenly she seemed to hear a bird's song on the cold wind. Not a real bird, and not something sentimental and treacly like her cousins would play, but something flowing and romantic, deep and stark, full of yearning.

Her eyes flew open at the sound, that song made so real. Was it...? No, it wasn't *her* song, her imaginary birds. But it was real music, beautiful, glorious music, like none she had ever heard before. A horn, yes, but turned into real emotion.

She peeked below her tree, to a boulder at the edge of the ice, half hidden by her own wooden perch. A boy sat there, maybe not much more than her age but much taller, lanky in his worn-out brown trousers and blue shirt, his patched coat. His face was hidden by a wide-brimmed felt hat, but she could see he played a cheap tin trumpet. It was battered and tarnished, yet it made such heavenly sounds. Sweet and rich and true.

She listened in astonishment. She so often heard such things in her own head, and then she couldn't make them come out of her fingers to the piano keys. This boy *could*. He made the celestial real.

She was so wrapped up in that music that she almost tumbled from her perch. Her hand slipped, knocking a small branch to the icy ground at his scuffed boots. The stream of sound abruptly ended, and she felt bereft.

"That—that doesn't sound like Mozart," she dared to call out.

He glanced up, his expression startled, and she nearly gasped before she could catch it. Just like his music, he was astonishingly beautiful, with high, sharp, cutting cheekbones, full lips, and deep, dark gold-brown eyes beneath arching brows.

And he was someone she definitely wouldn't be allowed to speak with, if she was caught. His skin was much too dark. But she somehow couldn't turn away from those eyes.

He flashed a shy smile. "It's not. I don't know much Mozart. It's a Coleman original."

Eliza tilted her head. She knew the work of lots of composers, but no Coleman. Her curiosity, her need to know more about that song, overcame her usual timidness, her fear of speaking to boys. "I've never heard of Mr. Coleman. Did you learn it at music school?"

He laughed, a sound as rippling and deep as his music. "I've never been to any music school. *I'm* Coleman. I just play what's in my mind."

"*You* wrote that? All by yourself?" she said in awe. She was often assigned themes to try and compose little songs around, but they usually didn't go the way she wanted. This boy seemed to be an angel of someplace else, a rare place of music she had never glimpsed. She envied him deeply, but she also wanted to know more and more. All that was in his head. "But you caught the way the birds sound exactly right. The way the birds feel."

His smile widened, and he nodded. "It's just like that. I want to make feelings real."

"But if you don't go to music school, however did you learn to play like that? I go to lessons and practice all the time, but I can't do that."

"You play the trumpet, miss?"

Eliza laughed. "The piano. A horn wouldn't be *ladylike* to even try, so my mother says."

He laughed, too, and she swung her feet happily to know she was the one who made him do that. She could go on listening to that sound all day. "Good thing I'm not a lady, then, because you could never fit a piano in my ma's parlor. I like to hide in the stairway at Roseland and listen, when they don't kick me out. Listen and copy and read. That's how I figured out solfege."

"You just—listen? And then can follow the tunes?"

He frowned in puzzlement. "Sure. It goes into my head and turns into a tune. Isn't that how you do it?"

Eliza shook her head. It certainly wasn't. "What was the name of your song? I've never heard anything like it."

"'Flight.' I guess that's not much of a title, but it's what it's about. How it feels to fly. To not really have a home."

So that was why she sensed the sadness, the sweetness, the longing in the song. She nodded, and was about to ask him more, ask him his first name, when a sharp, unwelcome cry rang out. "Miss Elizabeth! Whatever are you doing up there? Come down at once! Your mother will be most displeased."

Eliza sighed, and glanced up to see her nanny striding toward her like a battleship sailing on the horizon, large and billowing and strict and fearsome. Eliza scowled in frustration and worry. Why couldn't she be allowed to do as she liked, talk to who she liked, for just two minutes without getting scolded at, yanked away?

She looked back down at the music angel, but he had vanished. It felt like something hollow, and cold as the ice of the skating pond, opened inside of her. She was alone again.

Chapter One

"**O**h, do come out with us, Liz! It will be wicked fun, you'll see." Elizabeth's cousin, Mamie Van Hoeven, glamorous and Titian-haired in her sea-green chiffon, flopped across Eliza's bed. "The Stork Club is the very latest thing."

Eliza laughed and waved her composition book. She had moved her studies to her dressing table, wedging her notebooks between bottles of perfume and crystal powder pots because there was no room left on the tiny desk her mother allowed her. "I have to study. I'm leaving for the Paris Conservatoire in just two weeks. And you're a terrible influence."

"But you're already accepted. They can't chuck you out now. You've been studying for decades by now. One night of fun won't change that."

Mamie was right. Eliza *had* been working hard, sitting at her piano whenever she could ever since she was three years old. Music was everything to her, the one thing that was her very own. Being accepted at the Conservatoire was everything she had dreamed about. It had taken so long to be accepted, for the war to be over, for her parents to be persuaded to let her go. They still didn't like it; it was only because some of their friends declared a daughter to be in Paris as "prestigious" and "modern" that they reluctantly agreed. She couldn't give them a reason to change their minds.

Fun never really entered her mind. Surely music was meant to be her fun?

Mamie ran her red-lacquered nails over Eliza's blue brocade bedspread. Mamie was the opposite of Eliza, and always had been: "fun" was her reason for being. But she was Eliza's favorite cousin, full of laughter and yet so kind. So different from anyone else in their family. "Come on, Liz. Just this once. Your work will always be waiting for you. And I'm really a fabulous influence. Even your mother thinks so!"

"Only because you know all the eligible young men on Fifth Avenue, and she thinks I'll catch one of your castoffs," Eliza said with a laugh. She'd decided long ago not to marry at all; music was all she needed for the future. "If I want to win the Prix de Rome, though…" She would have to work twice as hard, ten times as hard, as any male student. It had always been that way, even at her earliest recitals.

Even though she had only once found a boy better than her, better than anyone else she had ever met. That boy in the park, with his battered old trumpet. She sometimes heard his song still, deep in the dark stillness of a sleepless night, and wondered if he had even been real.

"And you will win it!" Mamie said blithely. "The Stork Club is all about music, too. They're famous for that new group, Mel Johnson's Hot Seven. Consider it research."

Eliza smiled. She *was* a bit curious, she had to admit. She'd read about the new Stork Club, said to be the most luxurious in town, in the society pages. And a band called the Hot Seven had to be interesting. "And I guess you think Charles will be there, hmm?"

Mamie pouted. Charles was her on-off suitor, a Payne who she had once declared she would marry. Hadn't happened yet, though. "I don't give a snap if he is. There are a lot more handsome men in Manhattan than Charles Payne. Please, Liz darling. One night of fun before you leave? I won't see you for months and months! I'm sure Daddy won't let me near Paris until I'm old and gray. Not after that little matter at the Versailles Club."

Eliza shook her head. The "little matter" at the Versailles had landed Mamie in the papers, and not in a good way, after its dance floor was raided and she was found dancing with one of the Harlem bass players. It had been a family uproar, a scandal that had only just now faded. If it had been Eliza, she would still be locked in her room. But Mamie's father was different, more indulgent. A little more, anyway.

"He can't still be steamed about that?" Eliza said.

"Of course he is. His daughter dancing with an African bass player? A bass player who never wrote to me again, I must say. Dad always wishes I was more like you. Accomplished and serene, never getting into scrapes."

"I think my mother wishes I could be more like you. Flirty and sociable." She glanced at her reflection in the mirror, her pale gold curls unfashionably long, her wide blue eyes that always looked so startled and skittish. Her small, thin figure.

To tell the truth, she maybe wished deep down that she could be a little more like Mamie, too. To feel comfortable in herself, in her own world, to be able to laugh and chat and flirt without a fear. But she was just Elizabeth. Shy, day-dreamy, music-bound Elizabeth. That piano would always pull her back.

One night out, though. It surely couldn't hurt. Mamie was on her good behavior after the Versailles Club scandal, and Eliza had heard so much about that band.

"I don't think I have anything to wear to a place like that," she said, tucking away her book. She looked at her wardrobe, the carved doors hiding rows of pastel debutante silks and organdies. She had to smarten up for Paris, or she would look ridiculous in front of the French gentlemen.

Not that she would ever care about what the French men thought. She'd only ever cared what one male thought of her, that boy she met so long ago in the park—and she had so wanted the chance to impress him with her music.

Mamie clapped her hands, sure of some fun now. "No trouble at all! I'll loan you something gorgeous. You'll love it at the Stork Club, I promise."

* * *

She did rather love it.

Eliza just stood at the top of the marble steps leading down into the ballroom and stared like a Dumb Dora for a long minute.

Crystal chandeliers, sparkling high up on a domed ceiling fresco with images of laughing, couture-clad partygoers just like the ones below, cast a soft, golden glow over the scene, along with pink silk-shaded lamps on every damask-draped round table. The tables ringed a parquet dance floor, where couples circled to the recorded music playing a foxtrot. The stage where the band would play later was still empty, yet there was so much to see. So much life and beauty to take in.

Eliza carefully smoothed her gloved palms over the dress she had borrowed from Mamie. Sunset-pink satin, beaded with silver sequins and seed pearls, draped with tulle over the shoulders and shorter than any of Eliza's own frocks, almost to her silk-stockinged knees, with a matching beaded headband that held back her blonde curls. It was a gorgeous, fashionable thing from Doucet, easily as pretty as anything all the other sparkling, chattering ladies wore. And it wasn't as if she was a complete bluenose. She'd been going to parties since she was a toddler; teas, Newport regattas, the opera whenever she could, dances since she was a deb. Her brother even took her to nightclubs once or twice. But she'd never really been anywhere like this.

Mamie turned back to her from the foot of the steps, where she had already gathered a circle of admirers. "Come on, silly boots! There's champagne waiting."

Eliza laughed, and hurried to join her. The air smelled like flowers, the towering arrangements of lilies and white roses and carnations in tall silver vases, the perfumes of the women. A lady in silver star-spangled black velvet and pounds of diamonds wandered past, her alabaster-white, perfectly oval face clearly recognizable from the movie screen. Eliza tried not to gawk.

A portly, mustachioed man in an expensive evening suit bowed low to Mamie. "Miss Van Hoeven, so lovely to see you again at our little establishment. Your usual table?"

"Of course!" Mamie said merrily. "Liz, this is Mr. Berardinelli, manager of the Stork. Mr. B, my cousin, Elizabeth Van Hoeven. It's her very first time here."

"Then we must make it a very special one," Mr. Berardinelli said with another bow. "Do you enjoy dancing, Miss Van Hoeven?"

"She likes music," Mamie said. "She's going to the Paris Conservatoire!"

"Indeed? Then I hope you are in a for a treat tonight," Mr. Berardinelli said. "If I do say it myself, we have one of the finest bands in all of Manhattan. They will be on momentarily."

"I look forward to it," Eliza said. She thought again of that gorgeous boy and his old trumpet, the song that captured so perfectly the flight and longing of a bird. She hadn't heard much of the new music, jazz or blues, but if that was what it constituted, she wanted to hear more and more.

"Let me show you to your table. Very close to the stage, of course."

As Eliza followed Mamie and her admirers, she saw more people she recognized—a Shakespearean actor who had recently gone onto the movie screen, along with his third wife; an oil company heiress; even a prince from some tiny mountain kingdom, drunk as a skunk. She almost laughed as he fell from his chair, tearing the hem of his peroxide-blonde companion as he went. Luckily it was quieter at their own table, set off to one side of the dance floor with a good view of the stage, just as Mr. Berardinelli promised. Champagne appeared in chilled buckets, uncaring of Prohibition, as well as a silver platter of caviar-laced hors d'oeuvres.

"I told you that you'd like it," Mamie said.

Eliza took a sip of her drink, delighting in its fizziness on her tongue, its golden taste. "It is very pretty. Is that Olga Malinovskaya, the opera singer, over there?"

"Of course! She comes here often. If she has enough champagne, she might sing some arias later."

Mamie was distracted by her suitors who had joined them, and Eliza gazed around the ballroom as she drank her champagne. The gowns all seemed to blend into a sparkling, beaded, diamond-lashed rainbow as their wearers spun around the dance floor, set off by the backdrop of their escorts' perfectly tailored black suits. She couldn't help but notice that the dancers, the people at the tables, were all white, a crowd she could easily see at her parents' dining table, but the cigarette girls and the waiters were much darker.

The chandelier lights slowly dimmed as a spotlight came on the stage, bright as a full moon. The band had appeared there while she was distracted, and their instruments gleamed in the new light. A woman in a gold and white dress on the piano; a clarinet, guitar, drums, a tuba, trombone, trumpet. Like the waiters, the band members were all black, though clad in tuxedos like the clientele. Mr. Berardinelli stepped forward and threw his arms open.

"Ladies and gentlemen," he announced, "Mel Johnson and his Hot Seven!" Applause burst out, and the first song, a raucous, swinging melody started with a flourish. Eliza found herself swaying in her seat, her toes tapping in her strappy silver shoes, longing to move to that infectious rhythm.

Then the trumpet player stood up and raised his horn to his lips. What came out of that horn was incredible. Faster than she ever would have thought possible from a mere mortal and a small trumpet; rapid-fire repeated notes and delicate echoes; dazzling arpeggios. Complex beyond belief, but with such a light touch no one would ever know the great difficulty of it. The spotlight landed squarely on him, gleaming on his high cheekbones, his dark eyes.

"That's—no…" Eliza whispered. Could that really be the boy she met in Central Park all those years ago? Grown-up now, and *how*. Beyond handsome, with those chiseled features and sensual lips, those velvet-brown eyes. And his tuxedo, though a bit shabby at the cuffs and the fabric a little shiny, stretched perfectly over his broad shoulders and narrow waist as he played. He had been skinny when she last saw him; no longer.

And his playing. Eliza stared, wide-eyed in amazement. He had been good in the park, so good she had never forgotten it. Now he was super-human. An angel of music indeed.

He seemed completely absorbed in his song, lost in a soulful moment as she often was at the piano. A slow, dreamy passage that made her sigh. But then he grinned, and launched into a gleeful-sounding bridge, fast and twirling like a dancer, spinning higher and higher, quicker and quicker. Applause rang out from the tables around her.

"That's what, Liz?" Mamie asked her.

Eliza had forgotten she gasped aloud. "Oh—I just wondered if I'd heard that trumpet player before. He's marvelous."

"We've been trying to get the Hot Seven to record for us," one of Mamie's admirers, some sort of music promoter, said. "Coleman there is going to be big. As big as King Oliver, maybe. So far no luck with them, though."

Coleman—that was what the boy had said he was called. Eliza nodded, watching as he played on toward the denouement of his song.

"You should get Liz to talk to them," Mamie said. "She knows all about good music, and if she thinks he's that talented…"

Another of Mamie's admirers, a drunk young stockbroker, laughed loudly, harshly. "He would be so dazzled by her, he wouldn't be able to talk."

Eliza felt her face turn hot, her hands shake with anger. She knew exactly what he meant…. She turned sharply away from him, staring hard at the stage. A waiter, his dark eyes impassive, poured out more champagne for them.

Coleman sat down, and the band swung into a popular dance tune as people swarmed back onto the floor.
Their playing as a group was fine, even fun, but it made
Eliza realize just how far Coleman's trumpet could
transform the sentiments of a cheap tune into genuine
emotion. It was a rare talent.

"Jack 'Baby Sweets' Coleman, everyone," Mel Johnson said, waving his baton. So now she knew his name.
Jack Coleman.

Mamie refused to dance with the apple-jacked stockbroker, and took to the floor with the music promoter.
Eliza certainly didn't want to stay at the table with the
boozy fella. She wandered away, listening to the music,
watching the dancers. Everyone seemed to be having a
good time, but no one seemed to realize what had just
happened right in front of them. The music she had
just heard had sent her skyrocketing, and she couldn't
quite climb down.

The band changed to a straightforward dance group,
playing for a more raucous Charleston, and Eliza noticed Mr. Coleman standing in the stage wings, watching them as he smoked a cigarette and leaned against
a stage prop. His eyes were narrowed as if he didn't
quite approve of the tune. She didn't blame him one bit.

Unable to help herself, she hurried up the side stage
steps, in the shadows where no one would notice her. It
was most unlike her to ever be so bold, yet she had to
do it. Something powerful seemed to push her forward.
"Mr. Coleman," she said. "I just wanted to say—well,
that your playing was utterly gorgeous. Those glissan-
dos…! And I would never have imagined a top note

like that possible. Though I'm sure you hear that all the time."

He stared at her in silence for a long moment. *Too* long. His eyes were wide, and he seemed frozen. She started to feel very, very silly. "You're on your break. I'm sorry…"

He pointed his cigarette at her before crushing it out in a nearby ashtray stand. "You're the bird girl."

Eliza was startled. She glanced down at her borrowed dress: no feathers anywhere. "I'm the what?"

"From the park. The girl up the tree."

Eliza laughed in shock. "You remember me?"

"Sure. Not every day a girl in white fur throws a stick at you from a tree." He stood up straight, a slow smile growing on his lips. "You were a musician, too. Still play?"

"Oh, yes. Some." She wanted so much to tell him all about the Conservatoire, about her discoveries about herself, about people and life and flight, all learned at her piano keys. She really was behaving strangely; she barely even knew herself. But there was something about him, something warm and fascinating, an easiness in talking to him, that drew her closer.

Anyone who could play like that must know so very much about—everything. Not to mention how beautiful those eyes were, even though up close she could see some trace of hardness around them, of watchful sadness.

"I can't play like you, though," she said instead, feeling even sillier. "My cousin's friend says you're going to be as big as King Oliver."

He smiled again, a wide, white slash of a grin, and he looked so young again, those traces of some old sorrow around his eyes vanished. "Is your cousin's friend a clairvoyant?"

Eliza laughed. "No, a music promoter of some sort."

"Even better. Well, from his lips to God's ears, as my ma would say." He tucked his hands casually in his jacket pockets. "You play the piano, yeah? Mozart?"

"Chopin mostly, these days. He's my favorite."

The *Étude Number Three* had been her favorite audition piece. It was called *Tristesse* sometimes. Like this man's birdsong.

"Why is that?"

"Well, I suppose because it's challenging in a technical way, but so emotional and true. I can put my own secrets into it."

"I like Rachmaninoff. *The Piano Concerto Number Two.*"

"I can see that in your playing. The fullness and texture of it, the complexity, the improvisational quality." She glimpsed a few of the other members of the Hot Seven, standing in the shadows of the other side of the stage, passing around a bottle and laughing. "I'm afraid I'm keeping you from your friends."

Coleman glanced at them, his eyes narrowed. "Those cats drink so much, then they goof around, can't keep tune, can't hit their notes. I take my music seriously."

He sounded oddly as if his defenses had come out, his expression, so smiling and interested only an instant before closing. Serious about his music. Surely anyone could see that he was. "Of course you are. I've never seen anyone more serious. And I had a lesson once with Maestro Caetani, so I know serious."

His expression relaxed again. "Yeah? How was that?"

"Quite hideous, really. He smelled like claret and menthol drops and made me horribly nervous. I kept dropping notes. He even rapped me on the knuckles! Just like my old nanny."

He laughed, the sound so warm and sweet, like a fire on a winter's night, or a sparkling sip of champagne. It went all the way down to her toes. "I remember that nanny of yours. Terrifying."

"She really was. I've grown out of her, luckily."

His expression softened as he seemed to study her closer. "I can see that," he said quietly. "Miss…"

Eliza felt her cheeks turn hot again, this time with embarrassment that she had completely forgotten to introduce herself. "I'm sorry, I'm being terribly rude. I'm Elizabeth Van Hoeven, how do you do."

She held out her gloved hand and he took it lightly, his bare fingers long and elegant and warm. "Jack Coleman."

"Yes, I know. The famous Jack Coleman."

"Liz!" Mamie called, and Eliza glanced over her shoulder to see her cousin hurrying toward them. She looked avidly curious, but luckily her admirers weren't with her.

"Mamie," she said, straightening up. Mamie wasn't nearly as scary as the nanny, but she was just as intimidating with her knowing expressions. "This is…"

She started to introduce Jack Coleman, but when she turned back to him he had vanished, just like he had once in the park. Too quick for her.

"Was that Baby Sweets Coleman you were talking to?" Mamie said. "My, my, Liz, you *are* getting brave! Maybe your scandal will be in the papers like me at the Versailles."

For some reason, Eliza felt her anger flare up at her cousin. It seemed ridiculous to talk about a man with Mr. Coleman's rare talents as a "scandal"! "I was talking to him about music."

"Mm-hmm. Well, why don't you come back to the table? We're going to order some supper. Or maybe we could go somewhere else? I don't think the, er, music is going to be as good for the rest of the evening."

Eliza glanced at the stage, but he was still gone. She felt a sinking, hollow sensation in her stomach. She was sure she would never see him again now. Maybe one day she would listen to a record, though, one of his records, and remember how he made her feel for those too-few moments.

Chapter Two

To Jack's surprise, the apartment on 125th Street wasn't dark and silent, as it usually was when he got home from a gig at three in the morning. His family, his parents and sister Katie, all had to be up early for work. Tonight, a light burned, low and smoky, in the kitchen, and his mother sat at the table, a pot of tea in front of her and mending in her hands.

For an instant, she looked worn and exhausted, her once-beautiful face lined and thin, her hair graying at the temples, her shoulders hunched in her quilted, flowered robe. The kitchen looked tired, too, the linoleum peeling on the floor, the wallpaper barely the sky-blue it was when he was a kid, faded to silver. Jack studied the scene for a moment, resolving again to do right by his family, to see that they had much more than this.

She looked up and smiled, her face radiant again. "Sweetie, there you are."

"Ma!" he exclaimed, coming into the kitchen to kiss her cheek. She smelled of violet powder, the scent that always made him think of home. "What's wrong?" His mother did love her kids dearly, but she didn't wait up for them. Not when she had to be at work at the dress-making shop by seven.

"Does something have to be wrong for me to sit in my own kitchen, then?"

"Of course not. But you usually don't at this hour. Where's Dad and Katie?" His father and sister usually went to bed as early as they could, especially Katie with her hat shop job plus her night classes in typing and shorthand.

"They're asleep, perfectly fine. And I don't usually sit in here all night because nothing good happens after midnight. You hungry? I'll make you a sandwich. Got some nice potted ham from the grocery today."

"Sure," Jack said, still wary as he slowly sat down. His mother was right—nothing much good happened after midnight. And she hadn't told him why she was there. But he was hungry. They weren't allowed to eat at the club, and cigarettes and one shot of gin wouldn't take a man far. "That sounds good."

She stood up, taking a letter from the pocket from her robe as she did. She slid it across the table to him, and went to the small icebox in the corner to start making a sandwich. "This came for you. Looks important. All the way from Paris."

"Paris?" A spark of burning hope rose up in him. Finally! He'd been waiting ages for a response to his letter to Monsieur Galliard at the Club d'Or, ages of working for Mel Johnson and his tyrannical ways and tiny paychecks. He reached for the envelope, studying the postmark as if it was some kind of trick.

"One of your old army friends, then?" his mother asked, slicing bread. "I always knew you would go back there. The way you look when you talk about France…"

"Ma, it was a war. Nothing good." But he knew that wasn't quite true. Sure, there was mud and shooting and fear. There was the way his own army treated its black fighting men—worse than he got on the streets at home. And there was the disaster of his romance with Emily, a disaster that had him swearing he would never get involved with a girl not his own kind again. But then there was Paris, and that had made it all worthwhile. Music and lights and fascinating people. People who treated him and his friends like they were people, too.

"All that battle stuff you never tell me. But I've got eyes to read the papers, I know what happened in those trenches. I don't mean that part. I mean *your* Paris. The way you look when you talk about it. The Eiffel Tower, the Seine, the paintings and music. Blowing your horn in the clubs in—where was it?"

"Montmartre."

"Yeah, that. Music all hours, you said."

Jack turned the letter over in his hands, remembering. "Paris was the first place where people just looked at me as if I was a person. A man. A man who was good at his music. They appreciated it. That's all." Just like the bird girl he met again tonight, the girl whose sky-blue eyes had haunted him for years, comforted him in those trenches. Elizabeth, her name was. He'd had to learn very young to judge people right, and fast. It could mean the difference between walking away safe and a beating, or worse. And when Elizabeth looked at him, smiled at him, talked about music, she wasn't cruel or dismissive or condescending. She was just talking to *him*. He hadn't come across that often in Americans.

And she was so pretty, with her elfin face and golden curls. Her sweet smile.

"White people, you mean," his mother said.

"I knew in Paris that all white people aren't alike, any more than we are." Maybe that was why, tonight, he could see Elizabeth, too. A woman. That was all. "There, I wasn't just some worthless black man."

His mother slammed down the plate. "Don't you say that, Jonathan Peter Coleman! We don't say such things in here."

He nodded, contrite. "Sorry, Ma."

She stared out the window, at the fire escape of the building next door, the windows where a few lights were going on. "So that letter's about a job? In Paris?"

Jack opened the envelope and scanned the lines, hastily written half in French and half in English. It *was* from Galliard, and it was exactly what he had been hoping. "Yeah, at a club. The Club d'Or. I met Monsieur Galliard when I was there in nineteen, before they sent us home." The army had sent its black troops home last, but Jack hadn't minded. The longer he had in the Paris *arrondissements* the better. But it couldn't last forever, not then. "He's got an open place for a trumpet player. It's a nice club, Ma. Real class. You'd like it."

She was very quiet, staring out that window. "I guess it would get you away from Leo."

Leo was Jack's cousin, running wild lately with a bad crowd, a mob numbers-running crowd. His uncle was frantic. Jack and Leo had once been good friends, when they were little kids loitering on the street corners, listening to music from open windows. They hadn't talked much lately, since Jack refused to use the Stork to help Leo's "work." Now he just loaned money to Leo sometimes, money he knew he wouldn't see again. "Leo isn't such a bad guy, he's just—lost right now, I guess. He'll come around."

"I hope so. My sister, rest her soul, would hate what's going on with him." She put the plate in front of Jack, watching until he took a bite. She nodded, and went to wipe the counter. Her kitchen was always spotless. "Doesn't mean you have to be mixed up in his trouble, though. Or those clubs downtown. Everyone knows it's the mob behind them, music or not." The rag went still in her hand. "Paris is a long way away."

"Sure is."

They were quiet for a long moment, the sirens from the street and echoes of the neighbors arguing the only sounds. Finally his mother nodded, and briskly shut the cabinet doors. "Just don't bring any of those *mamzelles* home, you hear me?"

He shook his head, and thought of Elizabeth Van Hoeven, her golden curls and impossibly wide eyes. Her diamond earrings and high-heeled shoes. What would she think if he somehow brought her into his mother's kitchen? "No *mamzelles.*"

"I'm going to bed, then. Get some sleep, Jack. You'll have to pack soon." She kissed his cheek and hurried off, leaving him alone in the gray early hours.

After he finished his sandwich and cleaned up the kitchen table, he carefully put away his tuxedo and his precious horn and went up to the roof to read his letter again by the glow of a streetlamp. It didn't seem quite real yet, that he could be actually going back to France. His mother was right; it was a long way away, and not just over an ocean. It seemed like a different planet, a place where he could find himself. Make his way.

Be as big as King Oliver. He remembered what Miss Van Hoeven said, and he laughed. She'd looked as if she believed it, though. Maybe he could believe it, too.

He glanced at the building across the alley, where his uncle, Leo's father, lived. Jack couldn't fall into a life like that, not ever. Paris was far from all that, too. Here, a man like him could be a criminal or, like his own father, work in a factory that would break him. That life wasn't for him. He'd make sure of it. And he would take his family with him.

And a girl like Elizabeth Van Hoeven was a danger to all that, just as Emily had once been. He had to stay away from her, if he didn't want his plans to end. But there were those blue eyes of hers…

He remembered that night, just hours ago, at the Stork. His gaze had fallen on a girl gliding across the crowded ballroom like a spotlight had fallen on her fair hair and her beaded pink dress, making them sparkle— and he couldn't see anything else. His breath, and heart, stopped, and he wondered where all the air in the place had gone. Then she walked right up to him…

Jack shook his head and took out a cigarette and a light. The match flared in the night, brief and shimmering. He'd remembered her for so long, like a dream. The little fairy girl, the bird, high up in the tree above his head. She'd been like Paris in a way, something distant and shining, a dream. Tonight, she'd become real. The way her hand felt in his, her smile, her laughter.

And now she would be a dream again.

Chapter Three

"*The Baltimore* is heaven, Liz! You're going to Paris on cherub's wings! It's *so* much nicer than the poky old *Valor* I crossed on last time," Mamie cried, bouncing from a velvet-cushioned armchair to the neat, cozy single bed bunk tucked in a little vestibule along the cabin's pink-painted wall. "Oh, I'm *beyond* jealous, you horrid lucky girl."

Eliza laughed as she watched her cousin revel in the mound of rosy satin pillows. "It is a pretty swell ship, I admit." And aboard the *Baltimore*, she was free! *Free*, for a glorious crossing of five days, and Paris waiting at the end. No parents, no protective big brother, not even a maid since she'd persuaded her mother that hiring a French maid at the end of the journey would be far more elegant. She could do whatever she liked.

It was thrilling. It was terrifying.

Eliza sat down in the armchair and kicked off her court-heeled shoes, fine ox-blood leather to match her deep red travel suit and hat. "I wish you were coming with me, Mamie. I don't know what I'll do in Paris without you to tell me what's the cat's meow in fashion."

"*I* wish I was going, too. It'll be dull as tombs without you here."

"I doubt anything could ever be dull around you, Mamie darling," Eliza laughed.

"I think my father is going to ship me off to Tuxedo Park or Newport this summer, where I can just listen to the birds, or hear the trees growing or some such thing, and get serious about studying something like you do with your music."

"Music can be fun, too, you know." Eliza thought of the Stork Club, of Jack Coleman and his enchanted horn, the beauty and joy and misery in his notes. "Fun" seemed a weak word for something so profound.

"Oh, I do know." Mamie slid off the bed's satin counterpane and went to the Victrola on the round table just under the porthole. It had been a present from Eliza's father, so she could listen to Mozart and Puccini and Chopin in her studies. And she had records of all this, of course, piled up in her valise, but she also had…

"Jelly Roll Morton? The New Orleans Rhythm Kings?" Mamie said as she sorted through the discs. "Jeepers, but you have become modern, Liz."

Eliza felt her cheeks turn warm, and she snatched the Morton record away. "I enjoyed the band that night at the Stork Club, and thought I'd listen to a few more like that." None of those musicians came close to Jack, though. None of them had even an ounce of his complexity of playing, the raw emotion in their notes.

Mamie sighed. "They were the bee's knees, weren't

they? I heard the Hot Seven broke up after that night, though. Not even the Stork will be the same now."

Eliza sat up straighter. "Really? They aren't there anymore? What happened?" Ever since that magical night, she'd been busy getting ready for the journey, studying, shopping, but she'd avidly read all the local papers looking for news of the Hot Seven. No wonder she hadn't been able to find anything.

Mamie shrugged. "Whatever happens with all these musicians? They're always traveling around. Artistic differences, I guess."

Eliza sat back, her stomach sinking. It was silly, of course; there was no way she could go back to the Stork, not from Paris. But now it seemed as if Jack had vanished without a trace again. How would she ever manage to track him down? "That's too bad."

"Hmm, yes." Mamie glanced out the porthole at the busy pier beyond, the smaller vessels bobbing in the gray water of New York Harbor, the rows of buildings in the hazy distance. "Well, while I am perishing of boredom in the woods, you'll be dancing your way across the ocean!"

"I'll be studying my way across the ocean."

Mamie spun around with a horrified expression on her face beneath the beribboned edge of her Reboux hat. "You absolutely can't shut yourself away in here with your dusty books, Liz! I forbid it. Why, this ship has the Veranda Café, a swimming pool, squash courts, deck tennis. Not to mention all those handsome fellas we saw when we came aboard. I swear the whole Yale lacrosse team must be here! They couldn't keep their eyes off you."

"They couldn't keep their eyes off *you*." Eliza giggled to remember all those golden-haired, sunburned boys in their white suits and boaters, ogling Mamie like they'd never seen such a hotsy-totsy before. "And they're probably just as boring as all those boys my mother made me dance with at my deb ball at the Waldorf. I bet they're the *same* boys, in fact."

"You just wait, Elizabeth Van Hoeven. One of these days you'll fall hard for a handsome man, and you won't care one bit about your fusty old piano scores."

Eliza thought again of Jack Coleman, his smile, his delicious brown eyes, the way his hand felt on hers. The way his music seemed to wrap all around her and pull her closer and closer...

A brisk knock sounded at the cabin door, and Eliza felt a wave of relief that she didn't have to talk about "romance" anymore. That she could turn away and cover her too-warm cheeks. "Come in!"

It was a stewardess, small, compact in her neat navy-blue uniform, redheaded and with friendly gray eyes. "Good afternoon, Miss Van Hoeven. I'm Violet, stewardess for this deck, and I thought I would just make sure your cabin is quite satisfactory."

"It's quite glorious, thank you," Eliza said.

"The ashore bugle will sound soon, but I thought you'd like to see this," Violet said, handing Eliza a printed sheet with the *Baltimore*'s etched drawing and monogram at the top. "You can see some of the amenities, and all the activities for the next few days. Whist games, swimming lessons in the pool, the Turkish baths, dance classes..."

"Oh, she won't need any of that!" Mamie said merrily. She grabbed the paper and tossed it onto the table with the Victrola. "Miss Van Hoeven will be studying her music every day."

Violet looked bemused. "Well—the staff of the *Baltimore* do want their passengers to do whatever pleases them. I could find a piano for you, if you like, Miss Van Hoeven. Someplace quiet if you need to practice?"

"That would be absolutely wonderful," Eliza declared. She'd been afraid she would have to draw a piano keyboard on her dressing table and hum along with the imagined keys.

"Of course," Violet said. "And shall I bring a dinner tray later, or would you like to dine in the à la carte restaurant or the main dining saloon? There's dancing after, the ship has a new band they say is very good."

"That sounds delightful," Eliza said. "I'll be in the dining saloon."

"Very good, Miss Van Hoeven. Your table assignment is printed on the back of that page. Just let me know if I can do anything else, the bell is just beside your bunk."

As Violet left, Mamie said, "See, Liz? It's music all the time with you. You'll just hole yourself away with some piano and miss all the Turkish bath and whist."

Eliza laughed. "I'm sure it won't be *all* studies. That deck tennis sounds jolly."

The bugle sounded, and Mamie had to go ashore. They found their way up to main deck where visitors were making their way down the gangplank to the crowded docks below. Couples embraced one last, tearful time, parents admonished their Yaley sons, whistles sounded and streamers drifted on the wind.

Mamie hugged Eliza. "Oh, Liz! Just promise me you will make time for some fun. You'll be in *Paris*, after all!"

Eliza hugged her back hard, feeling the flutter of nerves. She was going to be alone now. "I will, I promise. Write to me?"

"You will be my bright spot in the wilderness. *Au revoir*, darling!"

Mamie hurried off through the crowd, and Eliza leaned on the polished rail to watch for her cousin to emerge on the dock. The alarm sounded, deafening, and the ship slipped its moorings and glided slowly away. The gleaming buildings of lower Manhattan slid past, and Eliza waved her handkerchief at it all madly.

She stayed there until they passed the Statue of Liberty, staring stolidly off into the distance as Eliza headed towards the Lady's birthplace in France and left her home behind. It was really gone now, all she had ever known. She was by herself in a way she'd never even dreamed of before. The other people on deck drifted away as the cold sea wind blew over them, but Eliza stood there until the city had completely vanished and there was only the gray waves between her and Paris. That salty, chill-edged wind grew stronger, and she caught at her hat before it blew away, shivering in her new suit.

This was it, she realized with a frightened little thrill.

For the first time in her life, no one watched her. No one would tell her what to do next. She could do whatever she wanted—and she had no idea what that was.

Seabirds wheeled over her head with black-tipped wings. She stared up at them, and suddenly she heard music in her head. That song Jack once played in Central Park, the one about birdsong. *Flight.* She remembered just how it made her feel, the exhilaration of freedom, the fear of it all. The wonderful possibilities in the next moment.

"Thank you, Mr. Coleman," she whispered. She reached out her hand, as if she could grab onto his music itself, the glissando of real freedom, and she laughed.

"Not bad, huh?" Tony Green said, peering out the tiny porthole.

Jack looked around the little cabin he was sharing with Tony, the ship's band's trombone player. It was tiny, but clean as a pin, with a white linoleum floor, iron bunks one on top of the other, a sink and desk. A lot better than the steerage he'd been expecting.

"Not bad at all," he said. He thought he'd be bunking with a dozen others, tucked away in the fish-smelling belly of the *Baltimore*, but this was unexpected luxury. He'd just been grateful when Monsieur Galliard at the Club d'Or got him a paying gig to take him to the job in France, but this was more. Things were already looking up in the world.

The shiny floor under his feet gave a lurch, and the hum of the ship's engines revved. Jack peered past Tony's shoulder out the porthole, and saw they were almost even with the gray sea. The city was sliding behind them, and there was just the world of the ship left. A world between worlds.

Jack thought of all the things he left in New York— his parents and sister, his cousin Leo and his problems with crime, uncertain jobs, uncertain paths. And what was ahead in Paris? He didn't even know. Hopes, that was all really. Hope for a career, respect, security. Hope that looked like old cobbled streets, and misty ancient bridges over the Seine, and swanky clubs full of new music and cafés that smelled of baguettes and strong coffee where he could sit wherever he liked and talk to whoever he wanted. Best of all, he would be walking through all of that like a free man. A musician, that was all. He could be himself.

Hope that looked like blue eyes and a shy smile…

He shook his head, trying to banish that image of Elizabeth Van Hoeven that had come into his mind much too often lately. The dimple in her pale cheek, the sweetness in that smile, her frank admiration of his music. The silver bell sound of her laughter.

As he stared out at the sea, the sea he'd crossed once before maybe to die in a war and now crossed to finally find his life, he knew he couldn't let dreamy romantic thoughts get in his way. Not now. Not when he was so close.

Tony threw himself down on the bottom bunk and crossed his feet on the iron headboard. "Should be a fun week, huh? Ladies on a ship like to loosen up their corsets, I hear, and they do sure like a musician. Saw some pretty ones on deck."

Jack shot an amused glance at his bunkmate. Listening to Tony was like listening to his cousin Leo in the old days, full of bluster and teasing and romantic silliness. Before Leo lost his way in the world, lost himself to gangsters and gambling and drugs.

Jack sure wasn't sad about leaving that sort of thing behind. Paris was a fresh beginning, away from trouble. He just hoped Tony could manage to stay disentangled before they got to Cherbourg. "Ladies don't even wear corsets anymore," he said, opening his trumpet case to check on his precious horn.

Tony frowned. "They don't?"

"Don't need them under these new style dresses, do they? That's what my sister Katie says." He remembered Elizabeth and her sunset-pink dancing dress at the Stork, light and rippling over her slim shoulders, her tiny, surely corset-free waist. The prettiest thing he could ever remember seeing. "Katie says women are emancipated now. Short skirts, short hair..."

"E-man-ci-pated, huh? That sounds just fine to me," Tony said. He slid a cigarette out of a crumpled packet and then tossed it to Jack. "You have a sweetheart, Baby Sweets Coleman? Or maybe a doll you're running away from back in New York?"

"Neither one. No time." He frowned as he thought of Emily, so long ago, the boyish dreams he'd had of her during the war—and how they came crashing down, crushed by their differences. He'd avoided romantic ideas of any sort, happy with short flings, until he saw Elizabeth Van Hoeven gliding across the Stork Club, all gleaming in a silvery spotlight.

"Me, too. Free as a bird, me. Good thing, too! Did you see that little Irish stewardess? Yummy as an apple dumpling, I'd say."

"I think I'll be too busy for any spooning on a moon-lit deck," Jack laughed. "You saw what all we have to do. Play for luncheon, play for tea, play for dinner and dancing…"

"They did say you were a serious one." Tony lit up his cigarette and blew out a plume of smoke, gray as the mist outside. "I get it. We all have to make a living. But we're not in New York now, man. We don't have to keep our heads down all the time."

Not in New York now.

And didn't Jack know it. He could hardly believe the dream of Paris, the dream of freedom, was so close now. He wouldn't do anything to lose that.

"Think I'll get some air before we have to change for dinner," he said, and he left Tony reading a dirty magazine in the cabin as he made his way up to the boat deck. His thoughts swirled fast and furious as he hurried up stairs and along winding corridors, thinking about the music he had to play at dinner, the club that waited in Paris, the family behind him in their Harlem apartment. Dreams, plans, ideas, all mixed up in a jumble.

He emerged at the top of the last flight of stairs into the chilly air of the deck—and suddenly froze at the image that appeared on the polished planks that were dark against the painted white lifeboats. An angel in red, the golden waves of her hair bright in the gray day, staring out at sea with a cameo-soft profile.

Elizabeth Van Hoeven.

He rubbed his eyes hard, sure he was imagining it all. The bird girl, the angel, right there in front of him where she definitely shouldn't be.

Her rare beauty, her delicate gold and creaminess, the sweetness of her, made his knees suddenly weak, made him want to fall down in front of her and ask her not to vanish on him again. Which was foolish in the extreme, but there it was. There *she* was.

When he looked again, half-sure, half-afraid she would really vanish into the sea mist, she was really still there, turning toward him with her wide blue eyes.

She smiled suddenly, sunlight bursting from behind the clouds. "Mr. Coleman!" she cried, her voice full of silvery delight. "Is it really you? I can hardly believe it! I was just thinking about that song, your song, the one about the birds."

She hurried toward him, seeming to glide, her red skirt floating around her. His sister was right—ladies didn't wear corsets now. She was as slim and graceful as one of those birds, all on her own.

She landed lightly right in front of him, smiling up at him. Her eyes were even more blue than he remembered in his dreams. "But how very extraordinary to see you again, here of all places. How wonderful."

Wonderful. For one giddy, ridiculous, unreal moment, Jack was sure it was wonderful, too. Wonderful— and all for a lady he shouldn't, couldn't, be thinking about at all.

Chapter Four

"What is this club like, then? Where is it? Is it like the Stork?" More questions poured out of her, even as Elizabeth knew she was chatting away like a magpie, firing off inquiry after inquiry ever since Jack told her he was on his way to Paris for a job, but she couldn't seem to stop herself. It was Jack Coleman—right there in front of her! So close she could touch him. Oh, how she wanted to touch him, she had to curl her gloved hands into tight fists to hold back. He was on his way to France just as she was.

It was so startling, yet so, so—right. As if *of course* he was there beside her now, as if he had been there ever since she saw him at the Stork. The two of them, bound for a Parisian life of music.

They'd made their way further onto the boat deck and leaned on the railing half tucked between two lifeboats suspended from their davits, blocked from the cold sea wind. It was still gray now that they were well away from the city, the sky roiling with clouds and the white-tipped waves choppy. The planks under her shoes were damp and slippery. Yet she saw none of that, didn't feel cold at all. Something warm and golden had been fizzing in her veins like champagne ever since she saw him. She could almost swear she was floating.

He laughed, and it sounded like music, too, deep and sweet and luscious. "I really shouldn't even be up here, Miss Van Hoeven. I'm the hired help on this voyage."

"Oh!" Eliza was startled. He'd said he was playing in the ship's band, paying his way to the new job in Paris, yet she hadn't even noticed where they were going as she fairly skipped along beside him.

He nodded at a sign posted at the head of the staircase: *First Class Passengers Only in This Area of Deck.*

She glanced the other way and saw no one at all. The chilliness had driven them inside.

"Looks like the deck is all ours right now," she said, hoping beyond hope he wouldn't leave her there. Wouldn't disappear from her life again. "Or we could go down those stairs! I'm quite aching to hear more about this Parisian club. What kind of music will you play there? Can anyone go? Where is it? What is Paris *really* like?"

He laughed even harder, and leaned his forearms on the railing. He was just as handsome as he'd been at the Stork. No—even more. So distinguished, elegant, gleaming as if he'd been polished. He had a new suit, she noticed, cheap dark gray fabric but fashionably, sharply cut, fit perfectly across his strong shoulders, the line of his back, over his slim hips. He would look perfect whatever he wore, drat him.

"It's called the Club d'Or, the Golden Club," he said, his golden-brown eyes narrowed as he stared out over the waves, like he could see the Eiffel Tower itself from there. "It's in Montmartre, tucked in among those winding, steep streets, where the art studios and theaters are. Not a big joint at all, really, they serve local wines and Madame Galliard makes cassoulet for midnight suppers, but the music's always the best. Whatever anyone wants to play that night—jazz, mostly, and the blues, but sometimes your Chopin, too. Dancing; beautiful art on the walls. Lots of conversation. You'd like it."

Eliza sighed happily. She could just picture it all— his glorious music in the air, the smell of garlicy cassoulet and rich red wine, the hum of chatter about art and philosophy and poetry, dancing feet, laughter. And best of all, jack's glorious trumpet, winding those deep emotions around everything. "It sounds just as I've imagined Paris in my dreams."

"Haven't you been there before?"

"Oh, yes—technically speaking."

"Technically?"

"It was before the war; I was really young and my mother took me with her. I got to see a few lovely things—the Louvre, the Jardin des Tuileries, Nôtre-Dame and Sainte-Chapelle, a day trip to Versailles. But mostly it was just going with Mama to fashion ateliers and waiting for her to be fitted for her spring wardrobe. Not at all like I've imagined it since. I'm sure there's this whole other Paris, hidden from me behind an invisible wall. Now I can look for it."

He smiled wistfully. "I imagine my own Paris, too. Every night."

Eliza turned and leaned her back against the railing, watching him, wondering what images went through his head before he fell asleep. If he longed for something just beyond his reach, like she did. "You've been there, too?"

"Right after the war. They didn't bring us home for several months after Armistice, but aside from missing my family I didn't mind at all. I'd have stayed there forever. Couldn't believe it was a real-life place. The lights on the river, the music that played all night. The wine and bread! After the trenches…"

His voice trailed away, and he looked very far away in that moment, a crease appearing between his eyes as if he didn't like what he saw there in his memory. Her heart ached to see that. Jack was surely a man who saw the real beauty in life, art and music and old, hallowed places, just as she did—she'd known that about him from the first time she saw him, in Central Park. His beautiful bird song. To imagine he had been in the mud and blood and pain of battle…

She laid her hand gently on his, without thinking. His fingers tensed under hers, and he stared down at her hand for one long, frozen instant. She knew she should draw away, yet she couldn't. It felt too *right*, too warm and safe, to touch him and feel him with her. To try and let him know that she saw, she understood.

His fingers suddenly relaxed, and he turned his palm up, laid against hers. The tips of his fingers were a bit rough where he played his horn, but his palm was smooth and warm as satin. It made her smile like a fool to feel it.

"You were in the war?" she said gently.

"Not for long, luckily. I was in Paris a lot longer than I was in the trenches. And the Huns were too tired by then to give me much trouble."

Eliza wasn't sure that was true. Her parents had tried to keep her from hearing much about it all, but when the flu swept through New York they also kept her closed up tight at home. She had nothing to do but play her piano and sneak around reading all the newspapers. She knew the Germans had a big, last-ditch push to try and snatch a hopeless victory, taking too many soldiers with them.

"It must have been awful," she said. "My brother almost went, but we were so lucky he only got as far as a camp in New Jersey before Armistice. He was terribly disappointed, but I was relieved. I couldn't do without Harry."

He smiled at her gently. "Your only brother?"

"Only sibling. Older than me, and so lighthearted and fun. Not a bit like our parents. When he's at home, he makes us all—makes everything—so much *easier*. If he was gone, if he wasn't there to sometimes stand between me and my mother, I don't know what I would do. I just…"

She stopped suddenly, startled. She'd never said such things aloud before, hardly dared think them. To fully look at how stultifying her home was. She loved her family, but they didn't really see her, didn't know her, and didn't want to.

And she still held his hand, leaning lightly against his shoulder as if it was the easiest, most natural thing in the world.

She peeked up at him, and caught her breath all over again at how very handsome he was. And the way he looked at her—no one else had ever quite watched her in that way before. Her family only saw her to make sure she was *correct*, that she fit into their image. But Jack's brown eyes, so serious, so serene, seemed to really *see* her. To care what she said, and felt. Just as she did for him. She wanted to know everything about him.

Yet he was so hard to read. Controlled, careful. He made her feel so silly, so young, and she envied him his ability to hide behind his own eyes, to conceal what he was thinking. She envied the light confidence he wore like a cloak.

She slid her hand away and turned to stare out at the sea again. "Do you have a brother, too?"

He shook his head. "Just a sister. Katie. My baby sister. She lives with my parents and works at a milliner while she learns to be a typist."

"How clever she must be! I turn all thumbs when I try to use my mother's secretary's typewriter, it's incomprehensible."

"Can't be any harder than a piano, surely."

Eliza laughed. "Well, it *looks* rather similar, but it all makes no sense at all. Not like musical notes."

"I can see that. Those letters aren't even in order! And Katie *is* clever, a lot smarter than me. And pretty, and bossy as the day is long. It's always been easier just to go along with her than try to argue with her."

"Sounds like she and my mother would get along splendidly, two peas in a bossy pod." Eliza studied the choppy, frothy white break of the waves far below, glad all over again they were carrying her farther and farther away from New York. "Won't you miss Katie? And your parents?"

The corners of his lips turned down pensively. "Course I will. I'm so lucky to have them. But I can make my way in Paris, really get somewhere with my music, like I can't in Harlem. What was it your cousin's beau said? Bigger than King Oliver."

"Yes, and I know he was right. You're *much* more talented than Mr. Oliver. Paris sounds just the place for you." She still watched those waves, and suddenly realized they weren't just taking her away from something—they were taking her towards a chance to make her ideas and dreams come true. Just as he did. "I hope I can do that, too—make something new of myself. Without my parents always looking over my shoulder, I can see what I can actually do myself at the Conservatoire." She laughed and nudged his shoulder with hers. "If I had champagne right now, Jack Coleman, I would toast to our lives in Paris."

He smiled down at her, a real, dazzling smile of pure light and delight. It made her fizz all over again. "To Paris then, Elizabeth Van Hoeven! May it give you all you want."

"Yes," she whispered. "All we want." She wasn't sure even Paris could give her *all* she wanted, though, because in that moment what she really, really wanted was him. His smile, his laughter, that understanding, watchful look in his eyes. His music. His touch.

Maybe even his kiss? Oh, yes, above all she wondered what his kiss would feel like.

A loud bugle sounded, and she jumped, laughing nervously at her own thoughts. Her own crazy desires. "I guess I haven't gone too far from home if a dressing gong follows me. I should be going."

"And I've got to fetch my horn. We're playing for the dinner, and dancing after."

"Then I'll see you in the dining saloon? Hear you play again? How wonderful." She remembered his song at the Stork Club, the impossible technical brilliance of it, the wild emotions, and she longed to hear it all, feel it all, again.

"You'll hear me, yeah, but not quite like at the Stork," he said wryly. "Mel Johnson's not exactly what you'd call 'experimental,' but he likes to be thought modern. A ship's band, though…" he took her hand and spun her into a dancing box step. "Hope you like a foxtrot, Miss Van Hoeven."

Eliza laughed as he picked up the tempo, swirling her around and into a quick dip, making her head spin. It was amazing, how he could go from making her feel serious and contemplative and filled with longing, to laughing and light and giddy. "Wonderful!" she cried, gasping as the wind snatched at her hat and he caught it before it could fly away. "Because I absolutely adore a good foxtrot…"

Chapter Five

Eliza studied herself carefully in the cabin's dressing table mirror, turning her face this way and that in the pinkish glow of the small lamps. It had been a bit trickier managing without a maid than she'd expected, but she knew she had to get used to it since she had no intention of actually finding a French maid. She didn't want to give up even an ounce of her newfound freedom! And she didn't think she'd done that bad a job.

But was it good enough for Jack to notice her? To think she was pretty? She felt like such a silly, fluttering schoolgirl, like the boy-crazy teenager Mamie used to be, for worrying about it at all when she'd never worried before, but there it was. When he looked at her so intently with those serious, watchful eyes, she *did* want to seem pretty.

She carefully touched one of her blond curls. She was no use at *coiffure*, so she'd just pinned it up simply and bound it with a silver ribbon and bead bandeau. It was still the same slippery, fine curls as usual, though, and there wasn't a lot to be done with it. She thought of some of the glam ladies at the Stork Club, the stylish women in their small cloche hats coming aboard the *Baltimore*—they'd all had short hair. Glossy, swingy bobs, daring shingles like caps close to their ears, or fringes brushing their plucked brows. Even the piano player with the Hot Seven at the Stork had bobbed hair.

"I look absolutely Victorian," Eliza muttered, patting the upswept loop of her long hair. Maybe, just maybe, if she was very daring, she would find a Parisian hairdresser to lop it off for her. Who would stop here there? Her family was further away every minute.

"I'll do it!" she declared. It felt as if somehow, by talking to Jack, being herself with him for those precious minutes, spinning around him in a foxtrot under the gray sky, had given her a jolt of pure courage.

She stood up and examined her frock in the mirror. There hadn't been time to buy much before leaving, and her mother had been very doubtful about the styles Eliza wanted until Eliza coaxed her with the hint that French men—possibly even *ducs* and *comtes*!—would meet her in Paris. And they would want a stylish lady. This was one of her new favorites, a sky-blue silk and chiffon that went with her eyes, with a low waist and pearl beadwork around the softly draped neckline. The hem was a bit higher than her old dresses, showing off her new silver satin shoes.

She gave a little spin, feeling very daring, and hummed a bit of a foxtrot tune.

A knock sounded at the door, and she froze in midspin. "C-come in," she called, half afraid it could be her mother, hidden aboard to suddenly spring out at her and berate her for behavior unfit for a Van Hoeven lady.

But it was Violet, the friendly-looking stewardess. "Good evening, Miss Van Hoeven. I just came to see if you needed anything before dinner. Oh, you're already dressed! I could have helped you with that."

"Thank you, Violet, but I'm quite bally excited to do it myself for once! These new dresses really are the bee's knees, so light and simple, I'm surprised we didn't demand them earlier. I could use help with this necklace, though, the clasp is always so stubborn." She held out her double strand of pearls, and Violet stepped up to loop it around Eliza's neck and fasten the ruby clasp.

"Of course, though," Violet said with a little laugh, "if fashions keep on like this, I may be out of a job."

"Have you worked on the liners very long?"

Violet tidied up the pile of clothes Eliza had left on the chair, gathering up the red suit to be taken to clean. "I've been on the *Baltimore* since just after the war, when she came back into civilian service. I nursed during the fight, and before that I was on the Australia passage, back and forth five times."

"Heavens! You don't look as if you could have been working so long."

Violet laughed. "You're ever so kind, miss. It must be all that sea air. Good for the complexion, they say. I've also been to Tahiti and Hawaii, ever so many islands. I'd like to work around the Mediterranean, too, one day."

Eliza sighed at the image of glorious, blue-sky islands, far away from the real world. "I *am* jealous. I've never really seen anything at all."

"It's hard work, but interesting, always changing. And I like the people I meet. Once I got moved into first class, I waited on Princess Mary once. She didn't have such nice pearls as you, I must say. You find out people are all just the same underneath."

Eliza laughed. She liked Violet's attitude, so different, so modern compared to everyone back in New York. "Has it all changed much since you started? My grumpy old great-aunt says travel has 'come down shockingly' since *her* day. Of course, in her day they went under sail with Queen Anne!"

Violet laughed, too, and Eliza found she enjoyed getting to just have a friendly chat with someone. "I bet I waited on your aunt a time or two. It's changed a bit, sure. There are more amenities now, the stuff people want, like a place for tennis and a nice swimming pool, room for dancing. The new sort of music. The *Baltimore* is an old-style liner, but even she has to keep passengers coming back. We even have a new band on this voyage! The other stewardesses are hoping they play some of the latest songs—like *Some Other Day, Some Other Girl* or *An Orange Grove in California*."

Eliza thought of Jack, of how his music wasn't like any she'd ever quite heard. "New bands?"

Violet examined Eliza's travel shoes to see if they needed cleaning. "It used to just be fusty old waltz orchestras. Now they even have..." She leaned closer to Eliza, her eyes wide with wonder, and whispered, "*Colored* musicians! Never thought I'd see that on the *Baltimore*. Moving along with the times, we are." She looked down thoughtfully at the suit draped over her arms. Eliza wondered if her fashions weren't 'moving with the times' enough. "One of the musicians is *awfully* handsome, if I dare say so."

Eliza wondered if she meant Jack, who was indeed "awfully handsome." Of course other ladies would notice that. "Then I definitely need to hear this band."

Violet frowned. "Mind you, some here don't like it at all."

Eliza frowned, too, though she knew what Violet referred to. She'd heard it all before, of course; her parents' friends weren't shy about sharing their opinions of everyone "not like us." How lazy and stupid and destructive everyone was towards people they considered to be different. It never made her less angry about it all, though. "Jeepers! It's 1924, not 1824."

"Try telling that to some of our regular passengers. The world moves too slow, I'd say."

"Indeed, Violet. Too slow by half." She caught up her gloves and beaded bag, suddenly determined not to let *her* world be slow. Not any longer. She was in charge of it now. And she wanted to see Jack again.

The dining saloon of the *Baltimore* was just as grand as the rest of the ship, if a little old-fashioned. It reminded Eliza of English country houses in books, all carved wood paneling surmounted by gilded Tudor roses, soaring up to a skylight dome high above that seemed to let the night sky inside. The round tables, draped with crisp damask cloths and lined with gold-edged china and crystal, heavy silverware and jade-hued vases filled with fragrant white lilies and roses, were ringed with scrolled chairs upholstered with dark green leather that matched the thick green carpet underfoot, so heavy they wouldn't roll in a swell and didn't need to be bolted down.

As Eliza followed the maître d' to her assigned table, she glanced around for the band's dais, tucked behind a polished dance floor at the far end of the room. She did hope the music was about to begin, and that she could discreetly wave to Jack. But it was still empty, shadowed by green velvet draperies, and she bit her lip in a little, sharp wave of disappointment. Luckily, she found herself at a table near the edge of the little stage, so she could watch for him without blatantly twisting her neck about.

As she settled into her seat, she nodded at her fellow diners. She knew from the passenger list Violet left her that one of them was a French Comtesse, along with a Pittsburgh steel magnate and his mother, a honeymooning couple, and Mr. and Mrs. Smythe, who sadly knew her parents. No fun and frolics at this table, or she'd be reported quick-time to her mother.

Mrs. Smythe raised her old-style, pearl-framed lorgnette to study Eliza. Eliza tried to smile sweetly, demurely, as if she was only ever occupied with the most ladylike of thoughts. No jazz for her, no sirree.

"My word, but isn't this Margaret Van Hoeven's girl?" Mrs. Smythe said, the pearls draped over her pigeon-bodiced purple satin dress trembling. "All alone, my dear?"

Her husband impatiently tapped his wineglass for a refill, even though the soup course hadn't been served yet. Eliza couldn't blame him. "Don't you remember? She's going off to study painting or music or some such. Aren't you, m'dear?" he said.

"Indeed?" Mrs. Smythe said, one of her silvery brows raised. "Oh, yes, I have heard you play the piano at a charity musicale. Very sweet."

"Thank you," Eliza said, hoping her teachers at the Conservatoire wouldn't dismiss her as "very sweet."

"I've been accepted to the Paris Conservatoire."

"And you are going *alone*?" Mrs. Smythe tsked. "Whatever can your mother be thinking? To not even send your brother with you! Or a proper chaperone."

"My brother is terribly busy with his new job, he's working as a stockbroker," Eliza answered. She smiled at the waiter as he carefully served the Consommé Sevigne into the shallow, gold-trimmed bowls.

The woman Eliza was sure must be the French Comtesse du Lac, because she was frightfully chic in an emerald-green silk Patou gown, diamonds looped through her raven-black bobbed hair, laughed as she fitted a cigarette into an amber holder. So shocking, she wasn't even in a smoking lounge! Mrs. Smythe scowled at her. "Ah, *madame*, but no one requires chaperones now! It is so *de trop. Mademoiselle* looks perfectly capable of looking after herself. Aren't you, *ma chère*?"

"Oh, yes, indeed I am," Eliza agreed. She did like the Comtesse already.

Mrs. Smythe gave a loud huff that set her pearls trembling again. "Perhaps where *you* are from, *madame*, young ladies are allowed to run quite wild. In New York, we believe in manners and civility. At least in the New York I was raised in, before such vulgarians as the Vanderbilts took over all that was fine and decent."

The Comtesse smiled. "Ah, *oui*. Paris is a land of—how do you say? Barbarians. No manners whatsoever. Wiping fingers on table linens, trampling tulips in the park—pah! Louis XIV would be shocked, I say."

Eliza pressed her napkin to her lips to hold back a laugh. The Comtesse turned her smile onto Eliza. "You look quite well-mannered to me, *ma chère*, even without a nanny peering over your shoulder."

"I hope so, Madame la Comtesse. I was followed by governesses and their lessons for years. It's been drilled into my very soul."

"Call me Chloe," the Comtesse said with a laugh, and waved over one of the white-jacketed waiters. "Champagne, *s'il vous plaît*, for my new young friend and me. Tell me, *ma chère*, do you know many people in Paris?"

Eliza glanced over at Mrs. Smythe, wondering if she should moderate her words very carefully, but the iron-haired lady was busy berating her husband now. "Almost no one, I'm afraid. The professors I auditioned for, of course, and I have a few letters of introduction to people in St. Germain who know my mother…"

Chloe waved this away with her cigarette holder. "Pah, but I am sure you won't want to see them, whoever they are! So dull, surely directly out of Proust. You must come to my house. The Conservatoire will keep you terribly busy, I'm sure, but I have my salon every Tuesday evening. You might find some of my guests amusing, I have many musicians who visit, painters, writers. There are so many amusing American *artistes* in Paris now!"

Eliza took a happy sip of her champagne. Like Jack's club, the Comtesses's salon sounded exactly like the Paris she was seeking. "I would love that! I adore art, and books. Have you met Mr. Fitzgerald? I read he was going to France, and I so enjoyed his *This Side of Paradise*."

"Oh, yes, he has sent a card to me, I would enjoy meeting him and his wife. Though I've heard one must keep him far away from the bar cart!" Chloe studied the plate of oysters being placed on the table. "*C'est bon*, then, it is settled! You shall come on Tuesday as soon as you are free. Tell me, where will you be staying?"

As they chatted about what must be seen in Paris, where Eliza should go for clothes, new art exhibitions, and the fish course of poached salmon in mousseline sauce was served, Eliza heard a few notes of music, and glanced at the dais to see the band had arrived while she was distracted. Jack sat near the end of the small stage, dressed in his tuxedo again, elegant and handsome, his horn held lightly between his fingers. She gave a tiny wave, and he smiled at her, making her toes tingle.

As the table chatted about music, about the opera in Paris, gallery shows, and the lobster Newburg and chicken Lyonnais was served, a newcomer joined their table, a tall, pale-haired, toothy young man in an expensive evening suit.

"Sorry I'm late, Auntie, do forgive me," he said as he slid into his seat, giving the table a wide smile. His eyes widened when he saw Eliza.

"Miss Van Hoeven, perhaps you've met our nephew, Henry Smythe?" Mrs. Smythe said with a fond smile at the pomaded young man. "He is studying law at Yale now, such a clever boy, and has a position waiting for him at a fine old firm. We always have said he will go very far in the world."

Eliza studied Henry without much interest. He looked like so many men who'd stumbled through dances with her in her deb season—tall, skinny, damp pale skin, a mustache struggling to grow. He was the same right down to the arrogant gleam in his eyes, the knowing little smile as he looked her up and down. They usually thought she'd be so grateful for their flat tire attentions, while all they could chatter about was cricket and polo horses and cars—it all made her want to run straight back to her piano bench and stay there. She never had anything to say back to them.

In fact, the only young man she could think of who had ever been more interesting than the piano was Jack.

She glanced over at the stage again. He was playing a few warm-up notes on his horn, but he watched her with those inscrutable, brown eyes. Watched her talking to Henry Smythe.

"I think we met at the Oelrichs' tea dance last year," Henry said, his careless tone saying *of course* she would remember him. "Billy was so amusing when he fell into the fountain! You must recall, we danced a tango."

"How thrilling that must have been for you, *mademoiselle*," the Comtesse said, and Eliza had to cover her mouth with the napkin again to conceal another choking laugh.

"Oh, yes, I remember," she managed to say. And she did. While he thought he was playing Valentino, jerking her all over Mrs. Oehlrich's parquet floor, he'd ruined her new pair of pink kid shoes. "It's nice to see you again, Mr. Smythe."

The band launchéd into the song *Blossom Time*, which of course was a foxtrot, and Henry held out his hand. "Would you do me the honor of a dance, Miss Van Hoeven? I know you remember how well we moved together!"

"I—well…" Eliza glanced desperately around the table. Mrs. Smythe beamed, while her husband called for more port. The Comtesse arched her brow, clearly amused by the quandary, and Eliza knew she was caught. *Drat.*

"Of course," she said through gritted teeth, and took Henry's hand. He led her onto the dance floor, his touch soft, doughy, clammy. Her mother liked to bemoan the newfangled lack of men's gloves at dances, and for the first time Eliza wholeheartedly agreed with her. She was afraid for her pretty dress when that damp clasp pulled her close.

She had to concentrate very hard on her feet, as he was not a very coordinated dancer, and he smelléd rather strongly of gin beneath his cologne. She backed up with a grimace as he stepped on her new shoe again.

"You're definitely the prettiest girl here, y'know," he said in a low voice, one he probably thought was seductive but just sounded like he had a sore throat. "I couldn't believe my luck when I saw you sitting there!"

Eliza peeked up at him. He was smiling down at

her smugly. "Really, Mr. Smythe? How—kind of you to say so."

His smile widened, and she saw he had spinach between his teeth. At least he'd started on his entrée; her sirloin was surely getting cold at her table. "I meant to send a note after the tea dance, but, well, you know how busy life is for a man like me."

"I am sure it must be quite frantic," she murmured.

"I'm finishing up my studies, and have a position lined up at a nice firm, they'll rely on me so much. And everyone does try to matchmake fellas like me!"

"Hmm," she hummed, and tried to keep her new shoes away from his trampling patent pumps.

"But here we are, on the same ship for days and days." He pulled her even closer, throwing her off balance. "I'd say it's fate, wouldn't you?"

Eliza struggled to right herself, to move away from the press of his body, but he held her too tightly. She felt a cold touch of panic deep in her stomach, a smothering claustrophobia. "Fate? How—how so?"

"An ocean voyage, perfect for a little romance, eh? Lots of hidden nooks, long days with nothing to do. Smooching in the moonlight. What d'you say?"

Eliza's brain said she wanted to scream. To slap this bruno into next week, and then run screaming from the dance floor. She knew she couldn't; any hint of scandal would fly right back to her parents, and her Paris life would be over before it began. Everyone would say she led him on. As if any girl would! His roaming hands felt like slimy snakes slithering over her.

That icy panic grew, like an ocean wave sweeping

over her. She *had* to get away from him. Without even realizing what she did, she glanced desperately toward the band dais. That desperation must have shown on her face, because she glimpsed Jack's appalled, furious expression just before he covered it again.

He started to put down his horn, half rising from his seat, and she shook her head frantically. If he came to her, lost his job because of her, the whole situation would be a hundred times worse. As she wriggled in Henry's ever-shifting grasp, she saw Jack lean forward and whisper a few words to the band leader. The man nodded, shifted his baton, and sent the waning foxtrot into a Charleston, fast, swingy—and danced side by side.

As the couples around them separated and burst into the leg-flinging steps, Eliza tore herself free. She was able to breathe again, and she sucked in a deep gulp of air. She had to resist the powerful urge to wrap her arms tightly around herself.

"I—I don't know these steps, sorry," she choked out.

Henry scowled. "Then let me see you back to your seat," he said, swaying back and forth as if his gin-imbibing had caught up to him. "Or even better, we could just slip out onto the deck together…"

Eliza thought that was a capital idea—but certainly not with him, the slimy slug. "No, thank you. I—I have to…" He reached for her again, and she fell back a step. "Lady problems!" she yelped, and gave into her urge to flee at last.

There were several people strolling the glassed-in promenade deck outside the dining saloon's staircase, couples giggling together, men sneaking a smoke, officers keeping an eye on the ship. Eliza forced herself to stroll slowly past them, nodding and smiling, instead of pelting away full force. She made her way up to the boat deck, which was almost deserted under the stars, and hid away between the davits like she had with Jack. *The wine-dark sea*, she remembered some old poem calling it, and it certainly looked like that now, inky and mysterious. The distant echo of music and laughter disappeared over that endless darkness.

The wind off the waves was cold, and she'd run away with no coat or wrap over her filmy dress. The tulle of the neckline fluttered against her skin, tickling, and she wrapped her arms around herself. She closed her eyes, and sucked in a deep, bracing breath of the delicious salty air.

"I *have* to do well at the Conservatoire," she whispered fiercely. She just *had* to! It was the only way she could escape a lifetime of men like Henry Smythe, of marrying one of them and becoming her mother. If she could do well at her music, use it to find a career for herself, she never had to go back to that at all. If she failed…

She heard a rustle, a footstep, behind her, and she whirled around, her stomach tense with that "fight or flight" feeling. What if Henry followed her? What if he grabbed at her with those raw dough hands again?

"Oh," she sighed in profound relief, when she saw it was Jack there. So tall against the backdrop of diamond stars, all dark and light in his tuxedo, his eyes narrow with concern. "Jack. I—the music…"

"It's fine, the band's taking a break while the passengers eat their dessert, after all their efforts at that Charleston. A bit faster than their usual waltz." He stepped up to the rail beside her, slow and careful, deliberate in his movements, watching her closely as if he didn't want to spook her.

But Eliza didn't want to run at all now. Unlike Henry and his stale gin reek, Jack smelled delicious, of lemony cologne, soap, the soft wool of his jacket. He felt so warm and strong beside her. She'd felt so very alone on that crowded dance floor with Henry Smythe, cut off from any escape.

She didn't feel alone at all now.

"You okay?" he said gently. "That bruno dancing with you. You looked a little…"

"Desperate? Disgusted?" Eliza gave a shaky laugh. "Sure I was."

He laid a soft, fleeting, reassuring touch on her hand. "I wanted to go all Sir Galahad out there. Run out and slap him with a glove, you know, get a duel going like they do in old novels."

Eliza laughed some more, lighter now, feeling much more herself. The ground, or deck, was solid under her shoes again. "'You impugn the lady's honor, sirrah! Pistols at dawn!' So Victorian of you."

He laughed, too, that deep, rich, satiny sound. "Okay, so I haven't shot a gun since the war, and I don't really want to again, but I might have wanted to duel there. Just a little bit."

"But you *were* Sir Galahad! I saw you get the band to play a Charleston so Henry had to let go of me. I got away from him without a scene." She stared down at the inky water, so far away. High up there, she felt like she was floating free, just the two of them up, up, up in the sky. "I do hate scenes. Hate people staring at me."

"You get used to it," he muttered, his voice suddenly distant. As if he thought of something different entirely.

Eliza glanced up at him, at his chiseled profile against the white of the boat cover. "Do you often have—scenes?"

He gave her a rueful smile. "I play music in nightclubs. I look like—well, like myself. Can't ever get out of this skin. Of course scenes happen. I avoid them as much as I can. Usually."

Eliza was intensely conscious of that *usually*. What happened when there was no avoiding it? But Jack fell silent, and for long minutes they stared out at the night together, quiet, comfortable. She was able to gather up again the shredded remains of her dignity.

"Well, thank you a *lot* for doing that for me," she said. "I'd thought I'd shriek if he moved any closer. Like one of my old governesses whenever she saw a mouse." She shivered as a chilly breeze rushed past them again, and without a word Jack shrugged out of his tuxedo jacket and draped it over her shoulders. She was surrounded by the warmth and scent of him, wrapped up tight, held safe. And yet not safe at all, because that heat and lemony trace of cologne was more intoxicating than any champagne.

"My ma just chases the mice down with her broom," he said.

Eliza tucked his jacket closer under her chin. "Does she? The women in your family do sound marvelous."

"They are. But then, they have to be." He reached over and slid a packet of cigarettes out of his jacket pocket. She felt the brush of his fingers through the fabric, and it felt—completely unlike the revulsion and fear when Henry Smythe touched her. It felt all hot and tingling, sparkly like the stars overhead, and she had to clench her fingers over the railing to keep from leaning closer, from grabbing onto him. "Want one? You look like you could use it."

"I rather could, yes," she said, glad her voice sounded relatively steady after the electric shock of his touch. "But I don't smoke, and I wouldn't like to look like a fool in front of you, choking and gasping."

"You're right. It's a foul habit no one should get into." He tossed the pack overboard, making her give a startled laugh, and he took out a battered silver flask from the pocket instead. "How about this? It's the good stuff, no bathtub gin."

"Thanks." She took a long, fortifying sip, and studied the silver in the moonlight. It was a bit battered and tarnished, but etched with twisting vines and leaves, and monogrammed: *To J. From L.* A gift from a lady? "This is pretty."

He took it back for his own sip. "My cousin gave it to me. A long time ago."

"Cousins can be good friends." Eliza thought of Mamie, of how she wouldn't have ever met Jack again without her cousin taking her to the Stork Club.

"Sometimes, yeah." He took another sip, the muscles

of his throat shifting above his bowtie. "Sometimes not so much. Do a lot of fellas like that one in there court you in New York?"

Eliza blinked at the sudden question. Why did he care? Could he be, just a tiny, teensy bit, jealous? She bit back a smile at the thought. "Not *court*, though I'm sure my mother would like that. I'm too busy with the piano usually, but at dinner parties and teas and such..." She remembered her deb balls, the painfully dull struggle for conversation, the tepid punch and bad music, and shook her head. Boring those parties might be, but they were proper, too. "Most of them don't behave like that. Too many people watching. He seemed to think he gets a free pass because we happen to be on a ship. And because people like him always seem to think they get a free pass when they want it."

"Sure. I know the type."

Eliza nodded. He probably saw lots of yahoo college lad sorts in his work, all on their worst behavior drinking in clubs. "I've never had a real romance. When I feel like I did there on that dance floor, well, I just wonder if *romance* is overrated. No one seems to mind it all in those novels my cousin Mamie reads. Or Mamie herself, she loves to be in love."

He glanced down at her with a bemused smile. "Not like in books, huh?"

"Have you ever read *The Sheikh*?"

"Can't say that I have."

"Well, there's this English lady, Diana, she wants to have an adventure in the desert, and is captured by Ahmed. The sheikh. He, well, seduces her, and eventually they fall in love, though they don't want to admit it to each other. So there's much running away, and swooning, and shrieking, until they fall in true love forever. Or something like that. I suppose Mrs. Hull the author has better models of manhood in front of her than the Harvard-Yale football game can offer."

Jack gave a choked laugh. "Models of manhood?"

"What else can I call it?" she demanded.

"Eliza Van Hoeven, you *are* funny."

"Am I? No one ever thought so before." Eliza wondered if "funny" was good. She doubted Diana of the desert was ever funny. "I don't mean to be, but I guess I don't mind it. If you don't?"

"I love it." He turned sideways, one elbow on the railing, facing her, so close. So wonderfully, deliriously close—and much too far away. "I'm glad you're feeling better now."

"I am, much," she said, and realized it was true. Henry Smythe seemed like a distant bad dream now. All she had in that moment was this wonderful night, the stars and moon and water and Jack. "If you don't mind me asking, have *you* ever had a romance? A real one?" She deeply doubted he ever rudely grabbed a girl on the dance floor. But surely he had ladies lining up just to get him to smile at them.

He turned back to face the sea, staring at the empty distance. "Once, I guess. It didn't end so well."

Eliza pushed down a jealous pang. "No? I am sorry. What a chump she must have been."

"A chump?"

"To pass up a man as handsome as you. Oh!" She

pressed her fingers to her lips, not believing she had actually said that aloud. "Sorry. It must be too much of your lovely flask."

He flashed her a crooked smile. "If you don't mind being funny, I don't mind being handsome. I guess she and I were both chumps. Knew from the start it could never work out, but I jumped in anyway. I learned my lesson."

Eliza nodded sadly. No matter what, she knew she and Jack could never, ever "work out" either. Not that he seemed to think about her that way, even if he was being so very kind. "I think I'd rather not have to learn lessons like that." The wind shifted, carrying a few bars of lilting music their way. Eliza turned and stared at the flashing lights of the distant party floating up the stairs from the dining saloon. So near, but so far away from her cozy, precious, fleeting world with Jack. "*Pale Moon.* I like that song."

"I like it, too. *'Speak to thy love forsaken, thy spirit mantel thrown...'*"

"Ah, so you know the lyrics! You must be able to sing as well as play."

"I can't. But in my line of work, you have to try to be flexible." He flashed her a wide grin, as wide and shimmering as the moon in the song. "I can dance, too."

"Can you?" She laughed, remembering the quick foxtrot he'd spun her in earlier.

"Certainly better than that masher in there. My ma taught me to be a gentleman." He gave a low, flourishing bow, and held out his hand.

Eliza smiled shyly, and took it with a curtsy. His

touch was nothing like Henry Smythe's clammy grab, his fingers were long and tapered, elegant, slightly callused where he played his horn, his touch gentle. He turned her in a circle, making her laugh again, before he swirled her into his arms and led her in a graceful waltz step. She leaned close to him, her cheek brushing his linen-covered shoulder.

He hummed along with the song against her hair, the sound vibrating through her. He was right—this was *nothing* like dancing with a grabber like Henry. It was like drifting on a cloud, their steps moving perfectly together, so intimate.

She stepped even closer, her heart pounding so loud she couldn't hear anything else, not the distant laughter or the wind. This was *Jack*, Jack Coleman, he was right here, holding her close. She wasn't about to let him go now.

They moved into the slower steps, finding their rhythm together. As his arms held her close, she rested her head on his shoulder and closed her eyes, the music languid and sensual. She let those intoxicating notes slowly wind around her as his warmth seeped deep into her heart and she didn't know anything but him.

She'd never felt so safe in her life, and she didn't want it to stop. Their steps slid together perfectly, their bodies fitting like the long-missing pieces of a puzzle. *This* was the way dancing should always be. It was what she'd been waiting for during all those dull deb dances—waiting for him.

The song ended all too soon. There was a distant

burst of laughter, as if people were leaving the dining saloon, drifting out onto the deck, and Jack let her go.

Eliza stepped back, feeling shaky and fragile all over again. But not in the same way she had on the dance floor with Henry. No, this was very different—different from how she had ever felt before.

"Th-thank you, Sir Galahad. You are indeed a fine dancer. And a gentleman."

He nodded, his light smile gone, that serious veil dropped again. Eliza felt like it was one step forward, another back with him. "My ma would be glad to hear it."

"I should write and tell her." That laughter and chatter was louder now, and Eliza said quickly, "Violet, the stewardess on my deck, promised to find me a piano someplace quiet where I can practice. I've heard *you* play…it only seems fair you listen to me, too. Can we meet tomorrow? If you're not too busy, of course…"

She felt suddenly shy, her cheeks turning embarrassingly warm at asking. What if he thought she had no talent at all? What if she wasted him time, put him on the spot? But he smiled again, and nodded, almost as shyly as she felt herself.

"I—sure, yes, bird girl. I'd love to hear you play. I have rehearsal after lunch. Maybe in the morning, after breakfast? Meet here?"

Eliza nodded eagerly. "Yes! I'll see you then." She reluctantly handed him his jacket, and the night felt cold all over again.

"*Mademoiselle!* There you are! You quite vanished," a merry voice called.

Eliza glanced over her shoulder to see the Comtesse coming up the stairs, two young men to either side of her and another following. The Comtesse smiled, but her eyes were narrowed as if in curiosity. Eliza turned back to introduce Jack—but he had vanished all over again.

Chapter Six

Jack lay back on his bunk, hands propped under his head, staring up at the ceiling so close, and wished he hadn't thrown away that cigarette packet. For some ridiculous need to impress Elizabeth Van Hoeven with his vast willpower, his devotion to healthfulness? He laughed at himself. As if he could impress a lady like her. Elizabeth Van Hoeven—even her name was filled with history and effortless wealth. Of Fifth Avenue and debutante dances and afternoon tea in silver pots. Of the old pearls around her beautiful swan neck.

Not that she was stuck-up, stuffy. Those were the last words that could describe her. She was beautiful, true, all gold and roses, but a bit awkward, enthusiastic, like a foal galloping through the world, wide-eyed, unsure of its own elegance.

She was—Jack stared up at that watermarked ceiling, trying hard to grasp at the right word for her. She was *good*. Not "good" like old Mrs. Hornby, their neighbor when he was a kid. She'd been a Sunday school teacher at her church, and never let anyone forget it. Always preaching, dolling out bits of hard candy to kids when they said a prayer perfectly. Eliza didn't do that sort of thing at all. No lectures, no pretending to be kind. She was just funny and light and concerned and interested—and good.

She was so innocent, unaware, like no one else he'd ever known. She had no mask to hide behind, not like he did. In his world, you couldn't let your real feelings show. Life would fix some of that fast enough for her, now that she was beyond the feathery shelter of her family. He hoped so very much, and even felt pretty sure, that it couldn't change her so much, change who she was deep down inside.

Maybe that was why he'd felt so furious when he glimpsed the desperation on her lovely face there on the dance floor as that masher grabbed at her. He'd really wanted to be Sir Galahad then, storming the floor with a lance and shield to whisk her to safety and deck the villain. He'd seen injustice, bullying by men like that, men who knew full well they'd never have to answer for mistreating a woman or someone like him... He'd seen that too many times in his life. When he saw it with someone like Eliza, someone gentle and defenseless, it made him burn with anger.

But he'd also known that giving into dreams of knighthood would do no one any good. If he slugged a passenger, he'd lose his job, the Paris future he was counting on for everything, not just for him but for Katie and his parents. A scene like that would ruin Eliza's reputation, too, bring her family crashing down on her just as she took her first steps into the world and ending that tiny hope for freedom he saw in her eyes when she talked about the Conservatoire. The freedom they both craved.

He wouldn't ever ruin that, no matter how satisfying the crunch of his fist would be on that man's pasty nose. But neither could he ever leave Eliza out there looking so frightened, not for anything. All those years of daily dealings with people like that, of getting out of tough situations and finding back door justice, could come in handy. He'd told the band leader, a man who seemed reasonable enough, that several of the younger passengers had urgently requested some newer, more fashionable songs, and since that crowd was the vast majority on the dance floor surely they should give them what they wanted. Like the Charleston.

Luckily, the man knew he'd hired some modern musicians for just those reasons, and quickly launched into a fast number. Eliza broke away from those grabbing hands, and shot Jack a grateful smile that made him feel like a real Sir Galahad. Like he would do anything to make her smile again.

And that was surely dangerous. The way she made him feel was dangerous. Her buoyant enthusiasm, the glow of sheer delight in her eyes, made him feel happy, too. His usual caution flew away when he was with her.

Jack shook his head. "You're in trouble now," he muttered. He'd made a mistake just like that once before with Emily, and it ended in such a crash. Eliza was so much more, deserved so much more. And now he had promised to listen to her play the piano! If she was a good musician, as well as beautiful, sweet, and funny...

He'd be a goner. If he was really smart, he'd stand her up, avoid her, mind his own business, remember all the ways their worlds were too far apart. How they had to *stay* apart, for the good of both of them.

He sure wasn't feeling too smart right then, though. He felt giddy and dizzy, wanting only to see her again.

No mamzelles. He heard his mother's words in his head. Saw her disapproving eyes if she knew he was becoming infatuated with a Fifth Avenue *mamzelle*, out of all the girls in the world.

Yet—the *Baltimore* would arrive in France in just a few days, and then he'd probably never see Eliza again. Paris was big; Montmartre jazz clubs and the marble halls of the Conservatoire were a long way apart, in every way. She's appeared three times just where he happened to be—Central Park, the Stork Club, the deck of this ship. Three strikes, surely there were no more. Not for them.

The ship felt like a moment out of time, a world floating above the real world where he and a Van Hoeven could never be friends. That was all, he told himself; it was just the power of the sea, the feeling of being in a dream, which made everything so very different. It would fade soon enough once they docked.

Another memory flashed into his mind. His father, not usually a man given to sentimentality, drinking a beer on the apartment roof and talking about how he'd met Jack's mother. How he'd glimpsed her across the room at a dance, a slim beauty in white organdy, and lightning flashed through him.

"Fate gets you sometimes, Jackie, no doubt about it. You can't escape it if it wants you then. Your mama, she was too pretty and sweet and smart for me, but fate wanted us together no matter what, and here we are. You watch out for that crafty old fate, you hear?"

Jack thought it was more likely his mother than fate who wanted then together no matter what.

"Handsomest man you ever did see," she'd say with a gleam in her eyes. *"He still is. I knew right there he was the one for me."*

Jack was sure fate was a lot of bunkum. But now, now he didn't know. Those wide blue eyes of Eliza's, they hit him somewhere deep inside, somewhere soft and vulnerable, somewhere necessary.

"Nertz," he cursed, and really wished again for one of those lost cigarettes.

"You talking in your sleep?" Tony muttered from the lower bunk.

"Sorry," Jack answered. He rolled over and pulled the wool blankets up around himself. A man could surely outrun fate, if he was quick and clever enough. If he stayed sharply aware. And with a lady like Elizabeth Van Hoeven, running away was the only option for a horn blower from Harlem. The trouble was, fate with sky-blue eyes and a laugh like a harp song was mighty hard to *want* to run from at all.

Chapter Seven

He wasn't going to come. She just knew it.

Eliza paced again along the top of the stairs, stopping to bounce up on her toes as if she could somehow glimpse him that way. It was a gray, misty, chilly day, and there weren't many people on the boat deck, but she hoped she might see him behind those coat-bundled figures. She glanced down at the slim gold watch on her wrist. Three minutes since she'd last checked.

Okay, he wasn't so very late. She'd just been early. Dressing and breakfast seemed to take a decade, when all she'd wanted to do was run out here. At least her table in the dining saloon had been empty that morning, no Mrs. Smythe to quiz Eliza about her horrible nephew, no Comtesse to tease her. She'd been able to gulp her coffee and nibble her toast and eggs, alone with her thoughts.

But how those thoughts plagued her, spinning around and around in her head! Jack's smile, his laugh, the touch of his hand on hers, the way she went all spinny with delight when he twirled her around under the stars. She'd barely been able to sleep remembering it all. She was sure that silly Diana in *The Sheikh* had nothing on her.

She spun around again now, and smoothed the skirt of her morning dress under her mink-collared coat, wondering if she should run back to the cabin and change into something more daring, more eye-catching. The problem was, she didn't really *have* anything more daring. The navy blue, drop-waisted frock, with its white ribbon trim, square neckline filled out with her pearls, and long, sheer sleeves was new and pretty, if a bit dull, perfect for playing the piano as it allowed her to move.

She also rather liked how it made her eyes more blue, since her mother frowned on mascara—though Eliza fully intended to procure some as soon as she arrived in Paris, and some red lipstick, too.

And she feared that if she ran off to change, Jack would appear on deck, think she'd stood *him* up, and leave for good. She just had to be patient. This was a long symphony, not a short nocturne.

Eliza tapped the tip of her blue-and-white spectator pump against the damp deck. She'd always considered herself very patient. You had to be in the Van Hoeven house. The ormolu clocks there ticked slowly, counting down mealtimes and dressing times and music practice times and bedtimes. Since escaping on her own, though, her hidden *im*patience was just bursting out all over. She wanted to run now, to laugh and dance and shriek! Or maybe she just longed to talk to Jack again, to see his understanding smile, the glint in his beautiful eyes that told her he saw her, understood her. That they understood each other.

She glanced down at her watch. Three minutes again!

"Oh, Mademoiselle Van Hoeven!" a voice, high and lilting, definitely not Jack's, called. "You are out quite early."

Eliza turned to see the Comtesse strolling toward her. Shockingly, she wore *trousers*, tailored white pants with a nautical blue sweater and matching beret, a tennis racket swinging from her hand. Two men, not the same ones as last night, trailed behind her, watching her avidly. Eliza wished she knew her secret. Women like her and Mamie were a fascinating enigma, and Eliza longed to be more like them. "Madame la Comtesse. I didn't see you at breakfast."

The Comtesse laughed merrily. "Oh, I am quite sure I asked you to call me Chloe! Shipboard is no place for formality, and I sense we are going to be good friends. And a breakfast tray in one's cabin is quite the way to do things. I was up much too late playing poker in the lounge with these lovely *gentilhommes*." She glanced around, that racket lazily swinging. "Are you waiting for someone?"

Eliza felt her cheeks turn warm in a ridiculous blush. She'd never be mistaken for a French woman at this rate. "No, I—I'm just going to practice the piano."

"Ah, yes. You cannot fall behind at the Conservatoire. They are so strict, one hears." She glanced around, almost as if searching to be sure Eliza didn't have a beau hiding behind the davits. "Do have tea with me in the

Veranda Café this afternoon. I am quite sure we'll have much to talk about, *n'est-ce-pas*?"

Eliza wasn't sure what *she* could have to say that would interest a glamorous woman like the Comtesse, but she nodded. She was truly curious about life, real life, in Paris. She needed so much help, so much advice about romance and such things, and she could never dare go to her mother with such things. Maybe a friend like Chloe was just what she needed. "Thank you, Madame la—Chloe. I'd like that very much."

"Until later, then." Chloe linked arms with her escorts and strolled away, laughing merrily with them.

Eliza turned, bemused, and saw Jack at last. He looked different than she'd seen him before, younger, in pale trousers and a knit vest, no coat despite the crisp day. He smiled widely, the corners of his eyes crinkling, a tiny, enticing dimple flashing low in his cheek. Eliza longed to place her fingertip just there, and she had to push her hands into her coat pockets quickly to hold them still.

"Jack!" she called happily, bouncing up on her toes to wave. "Over here."

He waved, his smile dimming, turning cautious, and she suddenly realized people might be watching them. She sank down flat on her shoes, feeling chilled.

But as he reached her side, that smile, that dimple, was back, and she smiled joyfully in answer.

"I have rehearsal later, but I can get away for a couple of hours," he said.

"Oh, good! Violet found me a piano in a little sitting room, just an old upright, but she said it seems to be in good tune," Eliza said. She felt a tense flash of nerves at the thought of him hearing her play.

They hurried toward the staircase that led to the lower decks, moving easily together. Even though he was much taller, he measured his steps to hers, keeping stride with her. "I can't wait to hear a Conservatoire student play."

Eliza laughed. "I'm afraid you'll be disappointed. My music isn't nearly as creative as yours. I'm just a—a practicer, that's all. An imitator."

He gave her a startled glance. "Are you kidding? They say the Conservatoire only takes three percent of their applicants. They wouldn't take just some scale-practicing machine."

She remembered the auditions, the large crowd of tense-faced students clutching their sheets of music at Carnegie Hall, the raw nerves and fear. The knowledge that out of that whole group, only one or two Americans would be allowed. "The judges at my audition *were* pretty fierce-looking. They just scowled at everyone who dared cross the stage in front of them! They probably scared away the ninety seven percent with just a frown."

She led him into the little sitting room off C-deck, just past a staff dining saloon. Violet said a few of the stewards liked to use it after their teatime, for gossiping and a bit of music, but it would be empty in the morning. It was a smallish, windowless, stuffy space, but it did boast that piano, as well as a few well-upholstered chairs and hassocks, and a Victrola and stack of records.

Eliza could see it would be a nice hidey-hole from demanding so-and-sos like Mrs. Smythe.

Hopefully, she and Jack could hide there a while, too. Wrap themselves up in music, just like that time in Central Park, and let the rest of the world fly away. They might be seen as too different to ever meet out there, but in music they were the same.

She only hoped she could play well enough not to embarrass herself! Maybe even impress him, just a tiny bit. She'd never been so nervous about someone hearing her before, not even those prune-faced Conservatoire judges.

She sat down on the narrow piano bench as he settled in one of the armchairs next to the instrument, slightly behind her so she couldn't see him and feel nervous all over again. She took a deep, slow breath, and ran her fingers over the keys. It was in good tune, the ivory giving and warm under her touch, familiar.

She played the soft first notes of one of her favorite pieces, Liszt's *Consolation Three*. As she always did with music, she soon lost herself in its streams of rhythm, its emotions, and they became her own for those moments.

As the last notes drifted away, light as a fluff of lace, a bit of starlight, Eliza rested her wrists on the edge of the keyboard and closed her eyes. She heard nothing from Jack, not even a breath, and she wondered if he had left. If she had been so dull, so terrible, he gave up in musical disgust.

She peeked over her shoulder and saw he did still sit

there. His face was very still, stunned. He ran his hand over his face, and she saw it shook a bit.

"That was beautiful," he said simply, hoarsely, and those words were the loveliest she had ever heard.

She bit her lip and stared down at the keys, that familiar formation of black and white she'd long seen as her best friends. Her refuge. Her outlet for everything she couldn't say. "My mother thinks Liszt makes me too sad after I finish."

"It would, wouldn't it? It's so dreamy and gentle, so tender."

"Oh, yes, exactly! A true consolation when things are sad. I can't do what you do with music—play with it, change it, make it my very own. I can only find my own feelings in what's already there."

"But that's what music *is*! That's its deepest meaning, its purpose," he said passionately. "It connects us to people who are long gone, as well as people who hear us. It helps us find out *what* we're feeling, helps us show that to others. Right? Then we can know we're not really alone, no matter how empty or lonely it feels right then." As if overcome with his thoughts, he reached out and covered her hand with his, his touch connecting them as firmly as music did.

Eliza twined her fingers with his and held on tightly, so tightly she hoped he could feel the rush of her emotion, that he would never really leave her. "Yes, yes! That's it exactly. In my family, I never could find words to show them who I am, not really. And I doubt they would care anyway."

"Me, too. The war, what happened to me there—and

what it was like when I found Paris. I can't put those things onto my family. Here, I'll show you."

He slid onto the bench beside her, so close his warmth seemed to wrap all around her, holding her safe in that moment. He did smell wonderful, of that lemony cologne he wore, of the salty sea air, of Jack. She leaned lightly against his shoulder, wanting to be closer and closer.

His long, elegant fingers drifted over the keys, coaxing out a bright, dancing sound, like sunshine on water.

"You play the piano, too?" Eliza said in delight.

"Not much. Not Conservatoire-like. But Lil taught me some."

Eliza bit her lip to hold back a twinge of jealousy. "Lil?"

"She plays piano with the Hot Seven sometimes. And I worked once in a while at Heinrich's Music Store, demonstrating new sheet music. I can pick out a bit of a tune." He played a few bars of the Liszt.

Eliza had to laugh. She'd practiced hours a day, for years and years, and he demonstrated some sheet music in a store and could do that! It was infuriating—and marvelous. She wished she could see music as he could, the sound of it transforming into notes in his head and then back into music, but changed and made personal, made only his.

"You caught so much wistfulness, such loneliness in this part—I thought I'd surely start bawling and embarrass myself," Jack said, playing a bit of the *Andantino*. "I've never heard anything so achingly beautiful before, bird girl. I can't do that. I play something sad, something melancholy, and I can't stand it inside for very long. I have to jump out of it."

"So what would you do with Mr. Liszt here?" she asked.

He frowned in thought for a moment, those beautiful hands drifting over the piano like butterflies' wings. Light and airy and heavenly. "Maybe—this?" He played the opening, repeating, low D flats, but they sounded lighter than usual, like a soufflé rising. "Or you could go like this. Jumping up onto a cloud, see?" His fingers skipped over the keys, coaxing out a sunny, happy sound.

Eliza laughed. It *did* sound like jumping onto a fluffy, candy floss-pink cloud, buoyant and weightless and sun-dappled.

She ran her own fingertips over the keys, winding a new, almost singing line around his sunshine, the tune chasing higher and higher. Jack let out a whoop of delight, and they played and played, perfectly in sync with each other. Birds singing in the summer sunshine.

They crashed down on the crescendo, the music floating away. Eliza fell against his shoulder, both of them gasping with laughter. She'd never felt so wild with joy before, her music set free into the wind. She'd never felt so very *with* another person.

She glanced up at him. He watched her intently, and his bright smile slowly faded, leaving the air around them tense and crackling.

His head bent towards hers, and for one breathless, sparkling, taut moment, she was sure he would kiss her. She tingled all the way to her toes, wondering how he would taste, how his lips would feel on hers, how his touch would wrap around her…

Her stomach tightened with a sharp pang of disappointment when he drew back. He stood up, not looking at her, and the moment of sheer exhilarated delight faded like a firework vanishing in acrid smoke. Everything changed, even the very air around them. It was all cold again. He shrank away from that flash of rare intimacy, and banged the shutters down between them.

She turned away, and busied herself with closing the piano case. She felt hot with embarrassment, and couldn't believe how she had misunderstood that moment. How much she had longed for his kiss; how bitter the world seemed without it.

He must think she was the biggest idiot ever.

"I—I've kept you too long. Your rehearsal…" she said. She sounded too bright and jolly, even to her own ears, but it was better than bursting into tears.

"Yeah, I should get going," he said, not looking at her. His hands were balled into his pockets.

"Of course." She smoothed her skirt and folded her hands in her lap, staring down at them. She couldn't help but ask, though… "What did you think of my playing? Would you hire me for your band at the Club d'Or?"

A tiny, reluctant smile flashed across his face. "In a minute. But can you sing, bird girl?"

"Not a bit, I'm afraid." She took a deep breath, and burst out in her thin mezzo soprano, "*All the nice girls love a sailor, All the nice girls love a tar, For there's something about a sailor... Well, you know what sailors are, Bright and breezy, free and easy..."*

"Okay, okay," he said with a laugh, and she was relieved to hear that sound again, relieved everything between them wasn't ruined by the almost-kiss. "No singing, just the piano. You won't get paid much, though."

"Oh, that is too bad! Did they make you sing for extra pennies in the Hot Seven, then?"

"No, but then you have to remember I'm just as bad." He sang a few bars, "*Bright and breezy, free and easy, he's the ladies' pride and joy..."*

Eliza exaggeratedly clapped her hands over her ears. "All right, I give in, I won't request *All the Nice Girls Love a Sailor* tonight."

"Thanks for that." He turned away, then hesitated an instant. "And thank you for playing for me today—Eliza. It was an honor."

Flustered, Eliza knocked a piece of sheet music off the piano. "Oh, no, not at all..."

"I mean it. I can brag about this when you're headlining at Carnegie Hall, when you're a great concert pianist." He glanced back at her, his eyes unreadable again. "See you in the dining saloon?"

"Yes, of course. Hopefully no need for an emergency Charleston tonight."

"I'm there if you need it." With one more lovely, quicksilver flash of a smile, he slipped out of the little room and the door clicked behind him.

Eliza faced the piano again, and played a few notes of the Liszt. But it wasn't at all the same now.

* * *

"Coleman! You missed that chord again," the band leader shouted, his voice even louder in the vast, empty dining room, dark and shadowed during rehearsal. "What are you thinking? Galliard said you were the best. And the passengers of the *Baltimore* expect the best!"

"I'm sorry," Jack muttered, wiping at his forehead with a handkerchief. Tony grimaced at him in sympathy.

"Try again," the band leader said, waving his baton. "A one, a two…"

Jack raised his horn to his lips, wondering in a fit of remorse where his head was. But he knew all too well where it was—with Eliza Van Hoeven, enraptured by her music. By her smile, her perfume—by *her*.

Her playing was truly exquisite. Technically perfect, but still filled with sheer, raw, passionate emotion that called out to something deep inside of him. Something he'd thought dead and buried with his old romance with Emily. Something that made him feel so very, very *alive*.

He played his section of the song, glad it was just a simple dance piece because there was no way he could truly play right then, not with Eliza taking up all the space in his head. Just his luck—the most beautiful girl he'd ever seen, the finest musician, and she was a rich white girl.

He glanced at the music propped on the stand in front of him, glad of the notes, all ordinary. He knew what those meant, where it led, orderly and proper. It was just like breathing for him, and always had been.

Women, especially women like Eliza Van Hoeven, that was something else entirely. He couldn't read them at all.

So he'd closed off his heart after the war, after Emily. It had been for the best that she'd left him. He'd concentrated only on his music, his future, and that was enough. That filled his soul. Until Eliza smiled at him at the Stork Club. Until he held her in his arms.

He couldn't afford any distractions, no matter how intriguing, how elegant they were—no matter how beautiful the music that flowed out of her was, and it was achingly beautiful. No matter what electrifying effect she had on him. No dance was worth that kind of trouble, and he couldn't bring trouble to her, either. It was clear she was innocent, sweet. He'd seen too much in the world to let it touch her.

He picked up his horn again, and lost himself in what he could do, and that was play his heart out.

Chapter Eight

The Veranda Café reminded Eliza very much of her mother's conservatory at home. The airy space was all white wicker furniture with green-striped cushions, a thick green carpet underfoot, and walls painted a sunny yellow and lined with paintings of verdant English gardens. Trellises draped with climbing ivy made the watery sunlight diffuse and pale, enclosing them in a foresty bower. Even the delicate china tea service was painted with green leaves and daffodils.

Eliza took a sip of Earl Gray and looked around at the people gathered around the white-draped tables as she listened to the music. It was a string quartet today, not Jack's band, playing a serviceable Schubert, and the ladies gathered around all wore their most fashionable hats and fluttering silk frocks, laughing and whispering over scones.

Yes—just like a tea party in her mother's conservatory.

But her companion was not like any she'd ever met

around her mother's table. The Comtesse wore a purple brocade, kimono-like coat that matched the purple and green scarf tied loosely over her hair, her emerald earrings swaying and sparkling as they caught in the scarf's bow. Her lips were a bright ruby-red that Eliza envied, smudging on the fussily flowered china.

Chloe took a tiny cucumber sandwich from the tiered tray. "And of course, *ma chère*, you will have to take a lover as soon as you arrive in Paris."

Eliza choked on her tea. "Will I? As soon as?"

"Certainly! It is expected of all the chic ladies." Her gaze swept over Eliza's afternoon frock, white muslin trimmed with blue ribbons, her wide-brimmed white hat. "And I will give you the names of some good modistes as well. You are too young for such fusty styles! It's not 1882, you are not your *grandmère*. You should see the delicious things Monsieur Patou is doing now! And Mademoiselle Chanel, such simple lines. Perfect for a pretty *jeune fille*."

Eliza thought of those long, dull days with her mother in designer ateliers. "I won't have very much extra time for shopping, not with my studies."

"You will be at a *French* school! They will expect you to be fashionable, to be your loveliest self. It will help you to progress in your career, I assure you." Her eyes narrowed. "You are planning a career, I think?"

Eliza glanced down into her teacup, thinking of all those hopes and ambitions and dreams she'd never dared talk about. "I do hope to be a concert pianist one day, yes. Playing the piano is all I've ever really wanted to do, all I'm good at really. The alternative…"

Chloe nodded understandingly. "The alternative is to marry someone your parents choose, *oui*? Someone like that horrible boorish young man you danced with, I imagine."

Eliza shivered to remember dancing with Henry Smythe, his clammy hands and boozy breath, that feeling of not being able to escape. Not at all like dancing with Jack, which was just as she imagined it would be to float on a cloud.

Luckily, Henry hadn't appeared at dinner last night, and she could eat her lamb chops with mint sauce in peace, except for Mrs. Smythe's incessant chatter about her nephew's great prospects. She'd been able to listen to Jack play for the dancing, though she hadn't been able to catch his eye and share a smile. The evening without him seemed rather lonely.

"Yes," Eliza said, "get married, run a household, join charity boards, and never have time for the piano again. Or be able to go to Paris alone."

"Oh, I don't know, *ma chère*." Chloe reached for a tiny éclair. "I gained much more freedom when I married than I had in my parents' home. My mother always made me have a chaperone! No one cares what a married woman does, as long as she is discreet. But I think it might be rather different for American ladies."

"Yes," Eliza said with a sigh. "If only we could do as the French do."

"But you can! You shall be an honorary Parisian, and learn all our ways."

"And that would include taking a lover?" Eliza said with a laugh.

"*Certainement*! It makes life much easier, and more fun of course, to have someone for escort to the opera, the races at Longchamps, and going to the jazz clubs. They are all the rage now, and a lady must have a dance partner! And to fully experience life—I assume you have not been able to do that in New York?"

Eliza felt her cheeks turn hot as she imagined wandering all over Paris—with Jack. "If you mean…er… physically…um…experience…" Her words faltered.

"*Ma chère*, please! I am not of your *maman*'s charity boards set. We both know what I mean."

Indeed she was not Eliza's mother's type. Chloe was vivid, adventurous, free, completely herself, and Eliza wanted to be more like her. She remembered the few kisses she'd received at home, behind potted palms at dances or walking in the park, pale, pallid, quick things that felt like a sad trombone note. Nothing at all like she imagined Jack might kiss her, with heat all the way to her toes, fireworks shooting off overhead.

"And I do mean physically, as with all other things." Chloe poured out more tea. "It is quite a natural part of life."

"I have—well, I've been kissed a few times. It didn't feel inspirational at all."

Chloe laughed. "Then you have gone about it all wrong! Or rather, your chosen partners have. I have long suspected as much of American men. They have no— primitive essence. They do not *like* women, as French men do. Many of them, anyway."

Eliza shook her head. "I think you are probably right.

At least most of the American men I've met, which aren't a very extensive cross sample at all."

Chloe reached out and squeezed her hand. "I must tell you, Paris will be very different from what you're used to. You will have so many more options, especially now that you're out from under your *maman*'s eye. When I married and left my parents' house, I was amazed at how many avenues were suddenly open to me! How I could choose whichever of them I liked. And they have only grown more open since then. We are in the nineteen-twenties now!"

"What do you mean?"

"There are rules, yes, expectations. And as the Conservatoire is so important for your career ambitions, *ma chère*, you must maintain a spotless reputation with them. Yet it is not like your New York. Everyone should have fun; everyone is *expected* to have fun! We lost so very much in the war, and we are alive now. Paris has changed since I was a girl. The music, the champagne, the clothes! You are young and pretty. These times were made for you."

Eliza felt a tingle of excitement, of anticipation, all the way down to her toes. This was what she hoped when she read about the cafés and parties of Paris, what she hadn't quite dared to believe could happen. That she could start to make some choices for herself. "I do love dancing. And jazz music! I would probably like those new cocktails, too."

Chloe gave her a sly smile. "And the people who play jazz, too?"

Eliza laughed, and felt that silly blush creeping back into her cheeks. "What do you mean, Comtesse?"

"The very handsome man you were talking to on deck. The one with the trumpet? He does not look like—your usual cross sample. What heavenly eyes! And hands. And how you looked at him…"

Eliza was mortified to think her feelings toward Jack were obvious in any way. She fussed with her napkin, not daring to look at Chloe. "I do think he's handsome, yes. But I hope you won't say anything to anyone else, Chloe. I never want to get anyone in trouble."

Chloe made a zipping motion across her red-painted lips. "When it comes to romance, *ma chère*, I am the soul of discretion! All my friends confide their little *amours* to me, and I never repeat a word. A ship is like a chatty little village, everyone is—how do you say? In each other's business. Such judging little eyes, like your Madame Smythe. Paris, you will find, is different. They may see, they never say."

"How so?"

Chloe leaned closer. "I have seen a bit of the American way of seeing people like your jazz musician. Of seeing anyone slightly different at all. I do not like it, not at all."

Eliza thought of separated bus seats, of sudden flares of anger, of wary eyes. "Nor do I."

"In Paris, there will be people who think like that, I am sorry to say. But there will be far more who do not. All Parisians really care about is music, art, life. If you are good at those things, they love you. And look at Mademoiselle Baker! France adores her, and she has many, many white lovers. You would not have the same deep worries, I assure you, Elizabeth, if you were seen dancing, holding hands, even kissing by the Seine in the moonlight, as all Parisians are practically required to do! People would remark on your beauty, for you are two exceptionally handsome people, but nothing else."

It sounded too lovely to be true. "You do make Paris sound like a paradise, Chloe."

"Pah! It is far from that. Yet it has its beautiful moments. If you wished to pursue a little romance..."

"I'm not sure *he* would be interested in—a little romance. With me."

"How could he not be? Bring him to my salon, *ma chère*, and we will show him how life in France can be. We will be rid of that caution I see in his lovely eyes."

"I think he knows about life in France. That's why he's going there now." She told Chloe what little she knew of Jack's life in Paris after the war, the way he talked about it, the hopes he said waited there.

"Very wise of him. I've seen many men like him in the last few years, men who fought bravely in the war coming back to us. They have made the city so much more fun! Their music and art." She squeezed Eliza's hand. "You will remember what I've said, *oui*? Enjoy your life in France. You remind me of myself when I was your age, when I was so excited, so uncertain, about what was before me. I am always happy to give you any advice."

"I do appreciate that, Chloe, more than I can say." And she *did* appreciate it. Chloe had given her so much to think about. To look forward to.

"Now, let us talk more about your clothes! You really must visit Chanel, and Patou. Poiret, if you're feeling adventurous," Chloe said. "And let's order some champagne, I've had quite enough of tea for the afternoon."

They chatted about the new, smaller styles in hats, about the ballet and opera, galleries Eliza had to see in Paris, until the light grew pinker between the trellises and the tea things were cleared away. As they gathered their gloves and handbags, the first officer approached them with a bow.

"Miss Van Hoeven," he said. "I have heard you are a very fine pianist."

Eliza was suddenly worried. Had they heard about her sneaking in to play the piano, and gotten Violet into trouble? "Yes," she said slowly. "I do enjoy it."

"She is far too modest," Chloe said merrily. "Mademoiselle Van Hoeven is on her way to study at the Paris Conservatoire."

The officer smiled. "Then I am even more hopeful you'll agree to honor us with a performance at the passenger concert."

"Passenger concert?" Eliza asked.

"A tradition on the *Baltimore*. We hold it on the second to last night, as a fundraiser, and any passenger with a talent is asked to perform. So far this crossing, we have a magician, Gilbert and Sullivan overtures, a flute solo, and a whistling solo. It is quite fun, helps lift the doldrums near the end of a journey."

"You should ask her to play *Fur Elise*. It is arranged for piano and trumpet, *n'est-ce pas*?" Chloe said mischievously.

Eliza shot her a glance. They weren't in Paris yet! But she certainly *would* love to play with Jack, to hear their music meet and twine and feel as one. "I would be happy to play for your concert, of course. A bit of Chopin, maybe?"

He beamed. Perhaps he'd been afraid it would be all whistling solos. "Excellent! I shall put you on the program right before the ship's band plays the finale." He bowed and left, off to recruit more acts, and Chloe laughed.

"Not Paris yet, *ma chère*," she said teasingly. "But very close indeed."

Jack paused in the rehearsal for the passenger concert and studied the program—it wasn't very challenging, playing a dance number or two, accompany a Gilbert and Sullivan sing-along. And then there was Eliza's name at the bottom.

A Chopin Nocturne by Miss Elizabeth Van Hoeven of Manhattan and Newport, recent student at the Paris Conservatoire, making her SS Baltimore debut.

Miss Van Hoeven of Manhattan and Newport. He had to remember who Eliza really was. He might like her a lot, too much; might long to kiss her, but she would never be serious about him. She wasn't at all like the other white girls he sometimes met, slumming it in Harlem clubs, looking for an "exotic" lover. But she *was* a lady of Society.

As he studied the sheet music for their first number, he noticed a flash of green from the corner of his eye, parrot-bright. He turned to see a woman gliding toward him, all vivid red hair under a stylish cloche hat trimmed with peacock feathers, green silk swirling around her—and a wide smile on magenta-painted lips.

He looked around to see who she smiled at, but she came right up to him. Her fingertip brushed over his sleeve, and he instinctively stepped back, sensing danger if someone was watching.

"You're the one who plays the trumpet, aren't you? So very *divine*," she purred, a touch of England in her accent. "I'm Lady Ashley."

"How do you do? I'm Jack Coleman. Glad you enjoy the music," he said politely, briefly shaking her hand.

"I've always been a bit of a musician myself. Do you give lessons?" she said, leaning closer.

"Not on this voyage. They keep us pretty busy."

She pouted. "Oh, too bad. Well, if you'd like a drink later, just look for me. I hope you will." She drifted away, tossing a sultry smile back over her shoulder. "Toodle-loo for now!"

Jack let out a rough breath and shook his head.

"Some Miss Anne, huh?" Tony said with a laugh.

Jack frowned. A "Miss Anne" was a woman exactly like the one he'd just been thinking about—rich white ladies looking for a bit of a thrill. Just the sort of lady Eliza clearly wasn't. "Just someone who appreciates music."

Tony laughed louder. "Some guys have all the luck. Like that blonde you were talking to earlier. And now some redheaded English lady."

Jack was shocked to hear he'd been seen with Eliza, which was foolish. He had to be vigilant all the time, he couldn't believe he'd let his guard down. "I don't mess with dolls like that. Too much trouble."

"You're one cool cat, Jack. But a ship isn't like the streets at home. We can have some fun here. Live a little!"

That was the problem. When he was with Eliza, he felt more alive than he ever had before. And that was the real danger.

Chapter Nine

Eliza glanced at the concert program again as she half listened to Miss Carlisle's celebrated "Whistling Solo." Luckily, Miss Carlisle needed no accompaniment for her whistling, and Eliza had a few minutes to just sit quietly at the piano. So far, she'd played for Gilbert and Sullivan selections, a bit of polka music for background to the magic tricks, and the *Dance of the Baby Swans* for Miss Petrie's ballet number. Her fingers already ached, and she hadn't even played her own piece yet! She was glad the next bit was the Comic Patter, which presumably would be all spoken.

She had to admit it was all a lot of fun, though. Her parents would *never* have allowed magic tricks or whistling, or even *Three Little Maids*, in their house, and in rehearsals Eliza had met so many interesting people. It made her even more eager to see what life in Paris could hold, when she was free to talk to anyone at all. When she could play *For He's Gone and Married Yum-Yum* whenever she wanted.

It also gave her a fine excuse to avoid Mrs. Smythe and her handsy nephew as much as possible. She'd seen them from afar, strolling on the deck and playing whist in the Lounge, and had been able to wave her rehearsal sheet music and duck away. Quite pleasant.

The only drawback to rehearsing so much was that she hadn't seen much of Jack, just smiled at him as he played with the band. He had nodded back, but then quickly turned away.

The band was setting up now for the finale of the program, at the other end of the stage. She peeked over at them, pretending to rearrange her sheet music. He sat at the end of the front row, impossibly handsome in his tuxedo. He seemed to shine even in the shadows, smiling and nodding as he went over the music, so filled with enthusiasm and energy and confidence—more alive than anyone else.

But he wasn't alone. Several ladies clustered around him, including Miss Carlisle of the recently concluded whistling solo, and two ballerinas in their tutus and tights, as well as a red-haired English Ladyship. They were all giggling as Jack showed them his trumpet, trying to edge each other farther away in order to be closest to him. Miss Carlisle even reached out to touch the horn's bell, blushing prettily.

Eliza studied Jack to see how he reacted to so much flirtatious attention. He was smiling, nodding at something one of the dancers said. He did look happy, at ease, but not overjoyed at so much attention. Maybe he just wanted to be left alone to get ready for the show? Or maybe that was just how Eliza *wished* he looked.

No wonder he seemed to have backed away from their budding friendship. He probably had so many women running after him all the time—women more beautiful than her, more sophisticated, far less awkward. He probably thought she was boring, a silly bit of skirt okay to occupy a quiet minute. How could it be otherwise, with his looks and talent?

Eliza bit her lip in uncertainty. It hadn't *felt* that way, though, when he talked to her, played music with her, danced with her. Looked at her for that one sizzling moment when she longed for him to kiss her. She'd been so sure he really saw her, heard her, that they understood each other on some special level. That he really wanted to be just there, with her.

But what did she know, really? She'd always been alone at her piano, no romances besides clammy dances and a few sad trombone kisses behind potted palms at parties. She didn't know much about men at all, or even about people in general. She could so easily have read Jack wrong all along.

As she glanced over at him again, saw the ladies staring at him raptly, she felt a sharp pain, deep inside. She wanted so much for what she had believed of him to be real, to believe there were people like him in the world. Kind, handsome, so filled with glorious music. If it was all an act, a facade just like her parents' world…

She felt a weight over her, an old, unbearable weight that only went away when she was with him.

Eliza blinked away the sting of tears and shuffled the pages of the music again. Some of them fell to the floor, and she pressed her palm to her hot cheek.

"Miss Van Hoeven? You're up next," the ship's offi-cer, chairman of the show, whispered from the wings. "Two pieces, yes? Then the band plays, and we start the auction pool."

"Yes, of course. Thank you." She had to push away those distracting emotions, as she always did. Present a smooth smiling face and play her music. Music al-ways came to her rescue; it was always the one thing that was always there, never changing. Jack had seemed to believe that, too, to live his life by those transcen-dent notes.

She dared to glance over at him once more. His circle of admirers had gone, and to her surprise he watched *her*. Intent, close, slightly frowning. He gave her a little nod, and she smiled back.

The comic act ended, and the chairman stepped for-ward to introduce her. "And now a true treat, ladies and gentlemen! A young lady of one of New York's finest families, on her way to study at the Paris Conserva-toire. She has agreed to honor us with one of the first of many concert performances."

Eliza sighed. *New York's finest family.* She glimpsed Mrs. Smythe in the audience, her lips pursed, surely considering what she would write to Eliza's mother when this was over. She wished the man had just said "And Miss Van Hoeven will delight us with a piano selection!" instead of so much snobby nonsense. But she couldn't worry about that, or even about Jack. She just had to play.

She took a deep breath, and plucked out the first notes of Chopin's *Nocturne Number Two*. That always seemed to be a favorite at New York musical evenings. Short, pretty, plus she just liked it. It was like slipping into the dark velvet of the night with its rich, dark tone.

She certainly wouldn't worry if Jack liked it, too. She would *not*. All she would think about now was finishing this concert and running away.

But as the Chopin faded away and applause sounded among the audience, the officer stepped forward and said, "That was beautiful, Miss Van Hoeven! I am sure we can see that you will have a great success in your studies. And now, everyone would love an encore!"

Eliza swallowed hard. "I—I didn't plan on…" What on earth could she play now? Her palms itched with nervousness.

She heard a rustle of movement from the other side of the stage, and glanced up to see Jack stepping closer, his horn raised in his hand. He arched his brow, nodded, and she smiled, suddenly feeling confident, reassured. This concert was supposed to be fun; why shouldn't she do that?

She smiled back at him, and raised her hands to the keys again. *"'All·the nice girls love a sailor!'"* she played, singing along as loudly as her thin voice allowed. Jack took his trumpet to his lips and played along, with trills and arpeggios that carried the song along. *"'For there's something about a sailor, well you know what sailors are…'"*

At the end of the song, the two of them playing around each other like a dance, like a twirl in a sunny meadow on a summer day, applause and whistles burst out in the lounge. Eliza laughed, and rose to curtsy as

Jack bowed. She caught a glimpse of Mrs. Smythe in the first row, her lips pursed, and for an instant Eliza worried her mother would soon hear of this. Her daughter, a *Van Hoeven*, playing risqué songs with a trumpet player in public!

But then she caught Jack's eye, saw his grin, and nothing else mattered at all but the two of them and their music. She curtsied again, and waved happily. If only every concert could be just like that!

Eliza stared out at the inky ocean from her perch high on the boat deck, gathering the collar of her velvet evening coat closer around her throat against the chilly night. It was very late, but the after-concert cocktail party was still going on in the lounge. She'd fled when she glimpsed Mrs. Smythe and Henry headed her way.

She also hoped, hoped beyond hope, that Jack might find her there. It was almost the last night of the voyage, after all, the last chance for them to talk together quietly. Maybe she even hoped he would ask to see her in Paris, ask her to come to his club.

Paris was the place where a lady could take lovers, the Comtesse said. It sounded much too sophisticated for Eliza, but also—intriguing. She was headed into a new, heady, strange life; it would be nice if she had one friend waiting for her there.

Yet what if he was too busy drinking and flirting with Miss Carlisle and his other admirers to seek Eliza out? What if he saw the Parisian future very differently than she did?

"It doesn't matter," she told herself firmly. She would

make her new life no matter what. But, oh, it would be so much brighter if Jack could somehow be a part of it all!

At last, just as she was sure she was being silly and should go inside where it was warm, she heard footsteps on the staircase behind her.

She turned, and her heart gave a little, joyful stutter when she saw it was really Jack. Casually elegant in his tuxedo, his hands tucked in his pockets, a tentative smile on his face very different from the bright flirtatiousness she glimpsed on the stage.

"Thanks for playing along onstage," she said.

"Hey, it's *our* song, right?" he said teasingly. "I couldn't let you take it alone."

"We sound good together, don't we?"

"Of course. You're a great improviser." He came to her side, leaning on the railing as he stared out at the sea with her. "You should try playing some jazz."

She smiled, thinking of playing like that with others, following along, leading, seeing where the waves of notes might take them. "Should I really?"

"Sure. You're looking for something new in France, right? What could be more 'new?' Put some Chopin into the blues!"

Eliza laughed. "I think I would enjoy that. But I'm not sure I have the right training."

He shrugged. "Music—it's all just a feeling you build. Whole, natural, a flow, yes? Jazz, it can take darkness into light if you let it. It has some of its roots in slave music."

"Does it?" Eliza asked, fascinated.

"Sure. Music was one heritage the slaves could keep. Optimism, despair—they could sing in the field, play at night. Gave some hope then. Now it gives some of us a livelihood. Music can always give hope, movement, freedom. You can do that, too. You already do it."

Eliza slowly nodded. As she'd grown up, she had never thought about race. It was invisible in her family, not something discussed or considered. Now she heard things Jack told her, thought of things she read, and she couldn't fathom the irrational hatred that was all too real. "I always wanted to do something, be something, besides my family."

A frown flickered over his face, and his fist clenched. She wondered if he wished for those cigarettes he'd tossed overboard. "My great-grandfather, my dad's family, he was a slave. They were on a plantation in Georgia, I think, that's all I really know about them. I did know my great-grandma for a while when I was a kid, she was a lot younger than her husband and he met her after the Civil War. She said he always had terrible nightmares, even when he was old. We can't ever go back to that. Can't ever let anyone steal the humanness of us. Our choices, our dreams, our *lives*. I owe it to them to succeed. To be happy."

Eliza swallowed past a hard, dry lump of tears in her throat. "Yes," she whispered. "You can be happy in Paris?"

He curled his fingers over the railing. "I think I have a fighting chance there. I glimpsed it there before, after the war. The way people talked to me, looked at me— just like I was a person. I'd never known that before.

Nothing's perfect in the world, but at least I can try. And so can you. People like us, people who have music to hold onto—we can try anything."

Eliza had never felt like that before, never believed she could be strong, make her own choices, try and succeed and find a happy life. With him, with his smile and his words, his warmth so close to her, she started to think it really could be that way.

A song drifted up to them from the open windows of the lounge, a waltz tune, and Jack gave his head a little shake and smiled down at her. "Shall we dance, Miss Van Hoeven? Last chance for a waltz with the ocean under our feet, bird girl."

"Yes, I believe we should," she said, something poignant and bittersweet piercing her heart. He took her hand and twirled her into the dance, smooth and natural and perfect, just like before.

As the music ended, they swirled to a stop, the stars a glittering blur over her head. He raised her hand to his lips. She reached up with her other hand to touch his face, marveling at his rare beauty. He made her feel so safe with his quiet strength, even as she was dizzy with so many strange feelings—feelings she'd never had before, never even imagined except in music.

"Eliza," he whispered, and then he did what she longed for. He kissed her.

She went up on tiptoe to meet him, twining her arms around his neck to keep from falling, tumbling down from this dream. He caught her around her waist, pulling her even closer to him.

How well they fit together! Their mouths, their

hands, their whole bodies, so right. She parted her lips and felt the tip of his tongue sweep over hers. He tasted of champagne, of something sweet. Light, enticing, and then the kiss turned frantic, hungry, full of burning need.

Until she heard a crash of a door slamming, a burst of drunken laughter, reminding her sharply of where they were. Who they were.

He stepped back, his arms falling away from her. She shivered, suddenly so very cold, so sad, so out of breath and confused. She didn't know where to look, what to say, what to think. She only knew that something, everything, had utterly changed.

"It's getting late," he said gently, his voice a bit rough.

She looked up at him, at his golden-brown eyes, and he seemed so terribly unhappy. Surely he regretted kissing her, regretted being there with her. And she couldn't bear that at all.

"Yes," she said. "I—I should be going." She backed away.

He half raised his hand. "Eliza…" he said, still so gentle. But she didn't want his pity. That was the last thing she wanted, never from him.

"Good night!" she said, and fled down the stairs, hoping she could make it to her cabin before the tears fell.

Jack sat awake on his bunk for hours that night, feeling the pitch and roll of the sea beneath him, seeing Eliza's beautiful face in his mind. The way her large blue, blue eyes went so soft with desire when he kissed her hand, the smile that curved her lips. He'd dared to think maybe he could indulge in the joy that watching her brought him, just a little, just for a moment, but then he feared he would never want to stop. Not with her.

She smelled like flowers in a summer rain, so delicate, and she wasn't just beautiful. She had a rare, special talent, a feeling for music that was the same as his, that he understood so well. He could see his own dreams in hers, and he wanted so much, more than he'd wanted anything except that music, to watch her dreams come true. Watch her talent flourish and take flight, like the elegant bird she'd once seemed to him. But he knew that was not possible.

Jack laid back and stared at the dark ceiling, thinking of the redhead who'd flirted with him. Eliza was nothing like that, nothing like anyone else he'd ever known. She had an innocence about her, a sensuality that was just a part of her. She deserved so much, the very best. How he wished he could be the one to give her that!

Since Emily, since the war, he had given up on any kind of romantic happiness. The future, his work, that was the only key. And he and a woman like Eliza, even more so than with Emily, were so far apart they might as well live on the moon and on Mars. He knew how people could be, how terrible, and he wouldn't let a spirit like hers be smothered by it.

He closed his eyes and reminded himself that he had been foolish once. He couldn't afford to be foolish now.

Chapter Ten

Eliza sat with her back to a collapsible lifeboat, staring up at the night sky. She'd never seen a sky quite like that, alive with diamond-sparkling stars, seeming to move and shift. She only wished Jack was there to share it, one last time.

The music and laughter still went on from the after-show party, despite the very late hour, a muted, blurry roar in her hiding spot. Despite the merriment, she felt all too sharply that this was the last night at sea. The last night of that delightful sense of floating above that being on a ship gave. The feeling that she was coming down into herself at long last, finding the world beyond her parents' house.

She drew the fur collar of her evening coat closer against the brisk wind and thought of everything that had happened in those few short, momentous days. A lifetime, yet also the mere snap of fingers. Kisses, dances, music, meeting Chloe and hearing about the wide world waiting. Seeing that world in Jack's eyes, his smile. Thinking of the choices she suddenly had she'd never realized before.

And it was all thanks to Jack, really.

She'd come back to their place on the deck, hoping he'd look for her there, one more time. She knew she could march into her new life in France with confidence, carrying the memory of his smile with her. But she'd been waiting and waiting!

Finally, she heard a footstep, a rustle, and he sat down beside her in the shadows. She could smell his lemony cologne, feel his warmth, and that bright flash of joy rose up in her. She dared to snuggle next to him a bit, the two of them alone again.

"Thanks for coming to my rescue again, there on stage," she said. "You were a big hit!"

He gave a low, soft laugh that rumbled through her and made her shiver. "*You* were the big hit. I just gave a bit of accompaniment."

"I wouldn't say that at all." Eliza frowned as she remembered all the ladies who flocked to him. "You'll be swarming with fans at your Paris club."

He laughed again, and to her thrill his arm came around her shoulder and drew her closer. She laid her head on his shoulder and sighed happily.

"I'd be happy with a few people who just like what I'm doing with my music," he said.

"You'll have so much more than that, I know it," she said, and she really did. Jack had greatness in his talent, more than anyone she'd ever seen before. "You won't remember us poor music-lovers who knew you before."

"Nah, you'll be the one who forgets us on your concert stage," he teased.

She closed her eyes and tried to picture it, the secret dream she'd nurtured for so long. An image emerged, of Jack in the front row. Applauding, beaming with pride. Pride in *her*. It was amazing.

"I will send you an invitation to my debut," she murmured, and half hoped he would ask her to his club once they were in Paris.

He squeezed her shoulder. "I'll hold you to that."

Eliza looked up at him in the starlight, and found he watched her, too, intently, solemnly, searching as if he wanted to read her very thoughts. She was sure he was going to kiss her, and she couldn't breathe, couldn't move, couldn't think. It was everything she wanted, that kiss.

But in the end, he turned away, and she shivered as she felt the cold breeze all over again.

"Tell me what piece you'll play first in your big debut," he said, and Eliza curled her hand into his jacket, as if she could hold him with her. Just for that one last, precious moment.

Jack stared down at the top of Eliza's head, gleaming like silver in the night, as he held her in his arms. How he'd wanted to kiss her! It had taken everything he possessed to hold back, to try and do what was right… but, oh, how he hated it.

She peeked up at him, her eyes huge and gleaming blue, and bit her lip. She looked uncertain, just as he felt inside, all those new feelings boiling up around them.

But then she smiled and cuddled closer, and he was afraid he was lost. Never to be found again.

This was some wild dream, and all too soon the light of day would come over the horizon of the sea and he would have to snap out of it. He had to pull himself out before he drowned in this lust.

No—no, this wasn't lust. He admitted that now, just to himself. It was no mere fleeting need. When she danced with him, kissed him, something seized hold of him. Something warm and soft, full of longing, like a perfect piece of music. Something he'd thought long dead in him, after the war, after Emily, after all those years living in his own skin in New York.

It was—tenderness. A great, aching tenderness. For her, her beauty, her humor, her rare talent, her enthusiasm and sunniness. For Eliza.

And that was so dangerous. He let go of her, practically thrust her away from him, and stood up to run his hands over his face, waking himself up before he helped her stand beside him. He had to stop this, to make it right, but how? He felt so swept away by her. But she deserved so much, she deserved everything best in life.

"You made this crossing a lot better than I expected it would be, bird girl," he said. Those words seemed much too small for what she'd done, yet he knew he couldn't give more. Couldn't say anything that was really in his heart. He held out his hand as if to shake hers, like she was a bandmate, a colleague.

She looked startled, her eyes filled with hesitation as she studied the offered hand. To his surprise, and probably hers too, she hugged him instead. He smelled her light, flowery perfume, felt the soft warmth of her against him, and it nearly drove him crazy. That tender longing seemed to close over him like the ocean, swallowing him whole.

He only wanted to taste her lips again. He was a starving man, given one little taste of nectar, but now it was going again.

"It's been wonderful, Jack, truly," she said as she stepped away. She smiled, but her eyes glowed as if with tears. "And tomorrow we'll be in France! How strange it will all be."

"You'll do wonderfully there, I know it," he said. "And I'll be reading about you in those music mags soon."

Her smile widened, and she looked away. "Of course you will! Maybe we'll see each other tomorrow, before we get to Cherbourg? It's a bit of a journey on the tender."

"Maybe," he said, but he knew they wouldn't.

She nodded, and hurried away, the click of her satin evening shoes fading on the steps, vanishing into the music from the party. Jack let out a deep breath and leaned over the railing, staring at the sea that brought them closer and closer at every moment to a new life. But he knew he'd never feel quite the same again, not after her.

Eliza stared across the gangplank at the tender that would carry her off the ship and into Cherbourg harbor. To France, and the next step on her journey. She had longed so much to cross it for so long—and suddenly she wasn't so sure.

She glanced back over her shoulder at the crowd swirling behind her, passengers in their travel suits and dark coats clutching valises and flowers and lapdogs, pages fetching last-minute items, the officers with their checklists shepherding everyone along. The noise and chaos and clutter. She'd hoped Jack would be there, that she would catch one more glimpse of him, have one more word. After last night, that wondrous kiss under the stars, the way they parted so suddenly—she just wanted to touch his hand, look into his eyes, and know it had really happened.

Which was silly, of course, as he would be disembarking from a different deck, a different class. Still, she stretched up on her toes, straining to peer through the crowds.

"Must be going now, miss," one of the officers said, polite but clearly impatient. "The tender has to leave before the tide turns."

"Yes, of course."

"Miss Van Hoeven! You forgot this," a voice cried, and Eliza turned to see Violet dashing toward her, a peacock-blue scarf in her hands.

Eliza smiled at her. "You keep it, Violet. The colors would look so much better on you, and you've been such a fine friend on this journey."

Violet beamed. "That is ever so kind! You've been a fine passenger, too."

Eliza laughed. "I hope so!" She leaned closer and whispered, "Did anyone happen to leave a note at the cabin, or—or anything like that?" She held onto that tiny shred of hope, that maybe Jack had written to her.

But Violet shook her head. "Nothing at all, miss. Were you expecting something?"

"No," Eliza said softly. "No, nothing."

A whistle blew sharply, and Violet gave her a little nudge. "Time to go, miss. Maybe I'll see you when you go back to New York!"

Eliza would love to see Violet again, certainly, but she hoped it would be a long time before she left France again! She turned and started toward the gangplank, clutching the valise that held her music. She glimpsed a man beside the railing, his back to her, tall and lean in a faded, gray overcoat, and for an instant her heart lightened, wondering if it could possibly be Jack.

But when he glanced over his shoulder, she saw it was another man from the band. She nodded at him, and said as she passed by, "I have so enjoyed the music on this voyage!"

He looked startled for an instant, but then he smiled shyly and nodded. "That's kind of you, miss. I'm Tony."

"Oh, yes. The trombone. I think you played next to that wonderful trumpeter, yes?"

"Jack. He's a talent all right. And the ladies enjoy his music lessons.

Eliza froze. "The ladies?"

"He was walking off with that English lady this morning." He shook his head ruefully.

The officer urged Eliza onward again, and gave Tony a quelling look that sent him hurrying away. She stumbled up the gangplank, barely seeing where she was going. The tender was like a miniature *Baltimore*, she saw as she walked automatically toward the salon. Cream and gold settees, Louis Quinze writing desks, deck chairs and porters offering cups of bouillon and tea. She tried to shake off some of the vague, chilly disappointment she'd felt since Jack had vanished. The journey had been such a wonderful dream! Music and dancing and kisses, the world flowering before her in a way she'd never imagined. She'd even begun to hope it might all swing into a whole new life.

Now everything looked just as it had begun. A brocaded salon, a facade of manners and luxury, her true self locked away. A true self only Jack had really seen, really understood. And it looked like Jack was moving forward without her. That their gorgeous moments together had meant only that, a moment.

She glanced around at the people who laughed and chatted over cups of tea and glasses of champagne. Just as always. She straightened her hat and made herself smile. She'd been doing that her whole life; it should be easy. Yet it wasn't. She'd had a taste of being herself, being *seen* for herself, and truly seeing someone else in return. It wouldn't be easy to go back.

Across the salon, Eliza glimpsed the Comtesse, and she started toward her and her group, hoping to be distracted from the sadness of not seeing Jack again. Mrs. Smythe, swathed in a dark mink, stopped her with a gloved hand on Eliza's arm.

"My dear," Mrs. Smythe said. "I shall look in on you as soon as we are in Paris."

Eliza was overcome with horror. "Oh—how very

kind, Mrs. Smythe! I shall be so busy with my studies, and I wouldn't like to take your time…"

Mrs. Smythe emphatically shook her head, the feathers on her velvet toque hat trembling. "I insist. I owe it to your mother." A chilly smile touched her lips. "And I know Henry will be delighted to see you again. He can speak of nothing else!"

Afraid Henry would pop out at her, Eliza glanced around frantically. She could only nod and make her escape across the room.

They were out on the water, the tender swaying as they made their way to France. Away from the golden time with Jack, and into whatever the future held. She prayed it was *not* Henry Smythe.

Chapter Eleven

Jack paused on the street across from the Club d'Or, studying it from under the brim of his hat. In the daylight, in the middle of the working world, it didn't really look like much for being one of the most popular jazz clubs in the city. A two-story building, pale stone, with shuttered windows and a dark red awning shading it from the cobbled street, a small sign, gold letters on a white background, above the black door: *Club d'Or. Music. Dancing.* On one side was a café, quiet at that hour with just a few lingering over coffee, or, for the mid-morning brave, pastis, at the wicker sidewalk tables. On the other side a milliner's shop, with glassed-in artists' studios above.

But Jack knew that at night, the club, the whole street, would burst into sparkling life.

He glanced around, taking in the neighborhood, the close-packed buildings, the gray mansard roofs, the people hurrying past on their errands, the dogs doing their business on the sidewalk for ladies to dodge around in their heeled shoes. In the distance, towering above them all, the wedding-cake-white dome of the Sacré-Cœur church. The air, still touched with a morning chill, smelled of coffee, paint, cigarette smoke, the tang of the nearby river, of flowers from the florist's shop and perfume, of baguettes at the bakery. It smelled, wonderfully, of Paris.

"Pardon, monsieur," a man said casually as he hurried past with a little terrier on a lead, not giving Jack a second glance, a resentful shove for being a black man daring to stand on a sidewalk. Everyone, in fact, just walked past as if he *should* be there, except for one lady in a lacy raspberry-red dress who smiled at him boldly. Just an ordinary, everyday, glorious morning.

He glanced up at the sky between the slate roofs, the blue flower boxes overflowing with red and yellow and coral-orange. The light was pinkish, glowing, Parisian light, and he could hear the faint echo of music coming from somewhere nearby.

It all felt like a dream, hazy and rosy gold. Paris was all that he had remembered from after the war, beautiful, shabby, old and new at the same time. Ever since the train deposited him at the St. Lazare station and he set off walking, walking and walking through parks and gardens and past shops and museums and ancient churches, he hadn't been able to get enough. After years of memories, he was really there again. The narrow streets, the sparkle of the river in the light, the cafés, the lilting sound of the language, the music that drifted out of windows to catch at his ears—it was all his.

He couldn't quite believe it.

If only Eliza was there, an idea that flashed into his mind more often than was comfortable. When he strolled through the Jardin du Luxembourg, he thought of her there amid the flowers, her wondering blue eyes taking it all in; he would see her delighted smile at carousels and crepe stands. He wanted to hear what she thought of it all, how she saw the colors and heard the songs. To dance with her to the accordion music on the quay, run up the stairs of the Eiffel Tower next to her to see her take in the whole city spread far below, sit on the steps of the Sacré-Cœur and study the city below. To pretend *he* had given her that city, given her everything she could ever want.

He'd thought of her all the time since he left the *Baltimore*. Even though he'd avoided her at departure, hoping she could step free into her new life, he'd replayed every moment they had together in his mind—every touch, every look from those sky eyes of hers, every kiss, every song they played together.

A bird suddenly took off from a balcony across the street, soaring into the sky, making him think of her all over again, his bird girl. Flying free into her future. Eliza Van Hoeven was the most truly *alive* person he'd ever seen; she glowed with wonder at everything around her. But the more he wanted to be near her, to bask in her joy at life, the greater he had to resolve to stay far away from her. His emotions were always wrestling with themselves now. Even as he craved her sweetness, her inner peace, her soft touch, just like some of those cats in the jazz clubs craved cocaine, he knew very well he wouldn't be good for her. She deserved so much more. She deserved everything fine and good in the world.

And he was so close to all he'd dreamed of...all he'd worked for. He couldn't be distracted by something no working, no dreaming, could achieve.

The club door swung open, and Monsieur Galliard appeared there. Tall, stout, his black hair neatly oiled to match the sharp ends of his mustache, just as Jack remembered him. He stretched as he studied the street, a broom in one hand, an apron over his suit.

"Monsieur Galliard, *bonjour*," Jack called.

Monsieur Galliard glanced up, and his frown turned to a beaming smile under the swoop of his mustache. "Jacques! *Mon ami*, you are here at last."

Jack crossed the street to meet Galliard's outstretched handshake. "I can't tell you how happy I am to be here, *monsieur*. And how grateful I am for your offer, and the job on the *Baltimore* coming over."

"*Non, non*, not at all—the ship's band leader owed me a favor. And I'm grateful to *you* for taking my offer. It is a long way to come for a job. I remember how you played back in nineteen." He kissed the tips of his fingers. "An angel! Angel of music. I'm sure you've only gotten better. We will have more customers than we can ever handle once word gets out."

"Your lips to God's ears, *monsieur*."

"He will be sure to hear your horn! But come in, come in. Your lodgings are fine, I hope?"

Jack nodded. The two little rooms in a narrow old building only a few streets away were better than fine, small and at the top of a steep flight of stairs, but clean and well-furnished and with space for him to play his horn. All his. "Better than fine. I can even see the top of the Eiffel Tower from my window! I've been dreaming about being back here for years."

"Everyone of good sense wants to be in Paris, *oui*? Everyplace else is—pah! Nothing. And that is a building full of dancers and singers, no one cares if anyone rehearses at all hours. Very useful."

Even empty and in shadows, the Club d'Or was lovely, welcoming and shimmering with red brocade-cushioned seats, gold velvet curtains, a polished dance floor in front of the stage, paintings of Parisian scenes and gold-framed mirrors gleaming. A long bar along the back wall was backed with shelves overflowing with bottles and crystal glasses. It was just as he remembered.

Monsieur Galliard led Jack to the long, polished zinc bar, lined with gold-cushioned stools and backed with a mirror that reflected the stage and dance floor into eternity. Madame Galliard stood behind it, going over an inventory list and making notes in her ledger, her bright red curls bouncing.

"Mathilde, look who has arrived! It is Monsieur Coleman at last."

"Ah, my dear *monsieur*, we are so happy to see you again! It's been much too long," she cried, leaning over the bar to give him *la bise* on both cheeks. "But how skinny you have become! You must have *déjeuner* with us, my own cassoulet. You will need all your strength if you work for my tyrant of a husband."

Jack laughed. He thought of the club owners and

band leaders in New York and knew Galliard didn't know the first thing about being a tyrant. "You sound like my ma, *madame*. Eat, eat!"

"And she is quite right. You must write and assure her we will look after you."

"She'll be glad to hear that."

Galliard caught up a bottle of wine from the bar and said, "Come, sit, let's talk."

They went to a banquette in the corner, quiet and dark, the club silent and dusty except for *madame*'s pen scratching across the paper, the clink of bottles being sorted behind the baize door. Very different from how it would be at night, all lights and noise and dancing feet.

"When should I start, *monsieur*?" Jack asked. "To-night?"

Monsieur Galliard poured out the garnet-red wine. "So eager! I'm glad to hear it, we need you."

Jack thought of those days after the war, the bands Galliard had playing every night. "You had the best music in town, from what I remember. All the cats wanted to play here."

"None as good as you, *mon ami*. I had to lure you back to Paris before anyone else could." He took a long sip of the wine. "Pierre left, went to Berlin. He'll be sorry, they say the clubs in Berlin are being raided all the time now, and there are riots in the street. Shocking stuff. And most French musicians—there are some good ones, of course, but they don't have the jazz in their blood yet, and their playing easily grows stale. They are stuck in the nineteenth century, and need time to learn the new ways. And there are more clubs in Paris, a lot more. Everyone wants to go to Bricktop's and Chez Betsy. I need to keep up, just like my musicians."

Jack studied the club, the shadowed stage. "You want me to be your band leader, *monsieur*?"

"*Oui*, the leader! You can show the others how it must be done. You are the best musician, but you are also patient and kind. That is rare, I know too well." He poured out more wine. "I want to expand one day. Open another club, maybe even closer to the Sixteenth, something elegant. Or maybe in Montparnasse. Perhaps both! Once I have this one well established again. And then, as Mathilde tells me so often, I am not getting any younger. She wants to be quiet sometimes, get a cottage in Normandy. I'll need a manager here, someone I can trust, who really knows what they're doing. Who can give my customers a splendid time, keep them returning night after night."

Jack was startled. He'd had hopes, of course, ambitions, but this was happening faster than he could have imagined. "You think I could be that manager?"

Galliard smiled broadly. "I know you can! You are a natural leader, Jacques."

"I'm flattered, *monsieur*. Really, so touched by your faith, you can't imagine. But I've never managed a place before."

"I know it is more than you were expecting to take on, Jacques, but I have given it much thought. I've built what I have by following my—how do you Americans say? Following my gut. I am sure you will be the right one for this job."

"Monsieur Galliard…"

Galliard gestured around the room with his glass. "I know this was not really what you agreed when I first wrote you. I'd increase the pay, *certainement*, and there would be plenty of time for you to see how we work here."

Jack was amazed. The pay on offer was already high, many times what he could make in New York. And to be the one in charge... "That's very generous of you, *monsieur.*"

"Just think about it, *mon ami*! Now come, see where you would be playing. I've expanded the dance floor, you see..."

Eliza swallowed hard as she studied the foyer of the Conservatoire, trying to push down her nervousness. But her stomach still fluttered, and she pressed her gloved hand hard over the blue velvet jacket of her new Chanel suit, glad she'd had only a café crème and croissant at breakfast.

The building at number fourteen Rue de Madrid was grand on the outside, all white stone, the arch leading into the cobbled courtyard announcing in gilded letters between two marble goddesses that this was the Conservatoire national des arts et métiers. Inside it was even more grand, with a sweeping staircase going down to the black-and-white-tiled foyer, students rushing past.

A woman came down the staircase, tall and slim and austere in a black-and-white frock, glasses perched on her nose, dark hair drawn sleekly back. "Mademoiselle Van Hoeven? I am Madame Vernod, I shall help you find your classes. Welcome to the Conservatoire."

"*Merci, madame.* I am most happy to be here."

Madame Vernod nodded brusquely. "Indeed. We take few new students in these days, and almost no Americans. Monsieur Faure, our esteemed director, says you have a rare talent, though, and a passion for the hard work of the true musician."

Gabriel Faure knew of *her*? Eliza gulped. "He is very kind. I do work very hard, and I hope I shall indeed find out I am a true musician here."

"We shall see, *oui*? Please, follow me." She led the way back up the staircase, to a long corridor of classrooms and practice halls. "Here you will have classes in conducting, music history, composition, voice. And here is the piano studio."

At the very end of the hall, she opened a door and led Eliza into a large room, sunny and bright, lined with tall windows, with enticing grand pianos waiting for her. Eliza studied the dark gray, mansard roofs of Paris, stretched out all around outside the window, the tip of the Eiffel Tower shimmering above it all, the golden light shimmering.

Somewhere out there was Jack. What was he doing now? Playing in his club? Whispering with a beautiful lady at a café table? Did he ever think about her, as she thought of him so often? Did he even remember those dreamlike nights on the dark deck, just the stars and the ocean and the two of them?

But she did not have much time for such bittersweet memories. The door to the studio opened, and an older man, bearded and bespectacled, looking very tall and grand in his dark suit, stepped inside.

"Mademoiselle Van Hoeven, this is Monsieur de Haviland, who I believe you met in New York," Madame Vernod said. "He will be one of your tutorial directors while you are here. He is one of the most distinguished of our faculty." She sounded rather mystified that Eliza would be worthy of that honor. Her lips pursed, reminding Eliza of her mother and Mrs. Smythe.

But Monsieur de Haviland was all affability. "Mademoiselle Van Hoeven, I am so pleased to meet you again after the New York auditions."

"And I you, *monsieur.* It's very kind of you to agree to assist me," Eliza said. "I know they say you don't usually instruct such novices to the school."

"Ah, well, I have been teaching for a very long time, and I know great promise when I hear it." He gestured to the piano. "Please, will you play for me? Whatever piece you like."

Eliza slowly sat down on the narrow bench, her hands shaking a bit with her nerves. Then she remembered playing with Jack. *Music is a feeling, a flow,* he'd said. She had to let it flow through her.

She closed her eyes for an instant, imaging him sitting there beside her, smiling at her. She smiled in return, and Monsieur de Haviland, Madame Vernod, everything was gone and there was just music. The music that bound her and Jack together even when she couldn't see him at all. She raised her hands and played the opening notes of the Chopin nocturne she had just rehearsed on the ship. And the music did indeed just flow out of her, winding out and around like the night sky itself, sparkling with ocean stars.

As the last sounds drifted away in the dusty golden bars of light from the window, she shook her head as if she woke from a dream. There was only silence in the room.

She glanced at Monsieur de Haviland, who nodded in satisfaction, and a stunned-looking Madame Vernod.

"Extraordinaire, mademoiselle," he said with a nod. "You were a wonderful talent when I heard you in New York, but now..."

"Now?" Eliza asked, nervous all over again. Had she somehow become *worse* in the last few months, her talent fading? Had she not practiced enough, not focused enough? "I'm sure I can catch up to the Conservatoire standards, I can work quickly..."

"Non, mademoiselle, no! You do misunderstand me. Now there is a—a *je ne sais quoi* about your playing. A richness, a depth of feeling I did not see before. You have advanced very quickly already."

Eliza smiled shyly, and remembered playing with Jack, remembered the way he brought life into the notes. "A freedom?"

"Freedom has no part of the perfection we seek here, *mademoiselle*," Madame Vernod said with a sniff.

Monsieur de Haviland smiled. "Ah, I quite disagree. We do not want to produce automatons here, there are player pianos enough in the world. I shall watch your progress with much interest, *mademoiselle*. We begin tomorrow morning, *oui*? Morning hours of lessons in here, then history of music in the afternoon."

Eliza felt giddy at the thought. Music, all day! No one to tell her she should leave the piano and pay attention to her social obligations. "Oh, yes. *Oui, monsieur!* I will be here."

Monsieur de Haviland departed, and Madame Vernod followed after giving Eliza her printed schedule of studies. Eliza stood at the top of the staircase and studied it all carefully—the portraits of great French composers on the walls, the marble busts, the classroom doors, listened to the notes that floated in the air. Students hurried past, mostly men of course, glancing at her curiously. "*Une femme Americaine,*" one of them said with a laugh.

Eliza refused to let any doubts make her nervous again. Not when she was so close to realizing her dreams, her plans! Not when Jack had believed she could be a real musician. Not when she could almost believe it herself.

She tucked her schedule into her handbag and fairly skipped outside into the Parisian sunshine, making her way through the busy streets as if she walked on air.

She suddenly realized, as she looked at the baguettes in the bakery windows, the well-dressed couples sipping *kir* at sidewalk cafés, the booksellers lining the Seine, men smoking Gitanes as they watched the girls stroll past, that she was in Paris. She *lived* in Paris, by herself. For herself. And she could choose what she did with her time now.

She knew she should go back to her lodgings, a flat in a house in Saint-Germain-des-Prés her mother had found. Despite it being her mother's choice, and Eliza's fears it would be a stuffy old bourgeois place with watchful chaperones around every corner, it had turned out to be quite nice. In fact, she was sure her mother wouldn't have selected it at all if she had seen it! The concierge was nice, a bit strict, but usually stayed in her ground floor flat rather than snooping about, and Eliza had a whole floor to herself where she could play the piano and be alone.

She turned into a new neighborhood, onto the Rue de la Bûcherie, and found herself standing in front of a green-painted shop with white stone floors above. A gold-painted sign proclaimed it to be Shakespeare and Company, and painted along the wide windows were the words "Lending Library" and "Books for Sale." Carts of books lined the sidewalk, with more tumbling in the windows.

Really, she should have dinner and go to bed early, she had so much work to do tomorrow. The light around her was turning amber at the edges, the day growing later as the cafés grew more crowded. But she was very tempted by those images of books spilling out the doors, the alluringly dusty window displays of such forbidden authors as James Joyce. She'd heard about Shakespeare and Company, of course—they were notorious for the racy volumes they sold, the eccentric people who gathered there, even in New York. It was surely a place her parents would hate. So she had to go in.

She stepped through the open door, enveloped by the delicious scent of leather and dust, of books. Several people were gathered on chairs and stools, reading from the overflowing shelves, a bust of Shakespeare and sketches of modern authors watching it all. One man, large, dark, shabbily dressed, was talking loudly. A woman with wavy, short brown hair, dressed in a sharply tailored black skirt and white blouse, a long gray cardigan drawn around her, worked behind the counter.

"Can I help you find something in particular?" the woman asked cheerfully. "I'm Sylvia, by the way, the owner here. If you're not sure what you want to read, we have a lending library where you can borrow anything you like, just two dollars."

"Thank you! I'm Eliza Van Hoeven, new to Paris. But I guess you could tell I'm American," Eliza said with a smile. "What a glorious shop you have. And it's true, I'm not really sure what I'm looking for." She scanned the shelves—Elizabeth Bowen, Dorothy L. Sayers' *Whose Body*, Colette, Marie Corelli, DH Lawrence, poetry, mysteries, Edith Wharton…

"That's the best way to start," Sylvia said. "The right book always lands in the right hands."

"Just like the right piece of music comes to you at the right moment," Eliza said.

"You look like a poetry sort of girl," the large, dark man in the corner boomed. "You should try this one, daughter. Yeats is always a fine place to begin. Or this!" He held out a plain, green-bound book to her. *Three Stories and Ten Poems* by E. Hemingway.

"Daughter?" Eliza asked, bewildered.

Sylvia laughed. "Don't mind Hem. He calls all the pretty young girls that. And that's his book, he's always trying to sell it. But I must say, it *is* good."

This definitely seemed like the sort of crowd who

would know about jazz clubs. "Tell me," she said, "have any of you heard of a place called Club d'Or? Where might I find it?"

An enthusiastic chorus went up, extolling the club's cocktails, dance floor—and especially their music. "I heard they had a wonderful new horn player," a woman with a sharp black bob and thick eyeliner said in a smoky voice. "American, of course. You must know him, *mademoiselle*!"

Eliza laughed. "We don't quite all know each other in America, I'm afraid." But she did hope that horn player was Jack.

"Minette, you silly fool, America is a big place," Hem boomed. "But we should all go! We can get Fitz, too, he's always up for a cocktail or ten. And you, daughter! You can see the *real* Paris there, raw and bright. No frills. Only true things. I'll tell you about the bullfights I just visited!"

Eliza smiled happily. "I would love that, thank you."

Paris was indeed wonderful, she thought—and if she could see Jack again, it would be the complete cat's pajamas.

Chapter Twelve

Eliza gasped when the doors of the Club d'Or opened and she was swept inside. The place throbbed with raw, exhilarating life, washing over her like a warm, silvery wave, carrying her forward. Hemingway held onto her arm, keeping her from falling

It didn't have the sleek glamour of the Stork Club, but it had so much more. It had a mellow elegance, a joyfulness, a whirl of fun and life. It was cozy even as it was grand, all red and gold and mirrors and life.

"Ah, *mesdames, messieurs*! A table, yes?" a woman said. Eliza looked over to see a tall, stout, smiling woman in chic black silk, her hair a flame of red curls swirled atop her head, smiling at them. "This way, this way! I am Madame Galliard, my husband owns the club, do let me know anything you might need."

She led them to a small, round, gold cloth-draped table beside the dance floor, and bustled around sliding gilded chairs closer together, waving to a waiter in a gold brocade waistcoat to bring champagne. No need

for Prohibition subterfuge there! Eliza grinned with that
sense of freedom she felt everywhere now.

"And food, *oui*?" she said. "Some oysters to start?"

Hem robustly kissed her on both cheeks, making her
turn as red as her hair and laugh loudly. "*Madame*, I
am in love with you! I have found you at last. Your establishment is the finest in all of Paris."

"Tatie, leave the lady alone or she might not bring
us those oysters," his wife said with an indulgent smile
on her pretty, freckled face.

"All are most welcome here, at any time. We always
have food and drink, *oui*!" Madame Galliard said with
a wave of her beringed hand.

"Madame," Eliza said quietly, studying the empty
stage in front of them. "Is—is Monsieur Coleman playing this evening?"

"Ah, you know Jacques?" Madame Galliard said with
a delighted little clap of her hands. Those rings sparkled
in the mellow lights.

"We met in New York," Eliza answered. "He is a
wonderful musician."

"He is a great asset to my husband's club, we're fortunate he came to Paris," *madame* said. The champagne
arrived, and she leaned over to pour generous measures
into everyone's glasses. "Any friend of Jacques is a great
friend of ours! He'll be out very soon, *mademoiselle*.
Now, drink, drink! I will send the food out, just call for
me if you need anything else."

She bustled away, disappearing into the swirling,
silken crowd, and Eliza sipped at her bubbly drink with
a secret little smile. She would see him again soon!

But what would he think when he saw *her*?

"Jacques?" the poet lady, Minette, asked.

"Jack Coleman. He plays the trumpet," Eliza told her. "He is amazingly talented."

"And handsome, too, *oui*?" Minette teased, making everyone else laugh and Eliza blush again. She would never be a sophisticated Parisian at this rate!

A musical note suddenly sounded, low and achingly sweet, and the roar of the room crested and was silent. Everyone turned to the stage.

The song was mournful at first, lazy, a sexy ballad, a bit of the blues in its rhythm. A trumpet solo, flowing as the sea, introduced the melody, then a piano came in, higher, more birdlike, drums with a high arpeggio that landed seemingly at random, in a whole different song. The trumpet played on, above it all, like the player was talking to her alone.

"Monsieur Jacques Coleman!" a stout man with a grand mustache and well-cut suit announced, filled with excitement. "All the way from Manhattan to play only here at the Club d'Or!"

Lights clicked on all around the stage, golden and sparkling like the champagne, to reveal the musicians. Eliza could see only one of them, though—Jack, sitting at the edge of the band, absorbed in his horn, wrapped in his music, as angelically handsome as she remembered, the lights glittering on his sharp cheekbones, his elegant hands flying. The song swung higher, turning merry, light, fun.

"Come on, daughter, let's dance," Hem roared, and seized Eliza's hand to twirl her out of her chair and onto the dance floor. It was packed already, everyone swirling and swaying, beaded gowns shimmering, feet flying. The air smelled of champagne and sweat and expensive perfumes, everything hot and bright.

"Ah, now, you see, *this* is a real place," he said. "This is how it should always be."

"Do you know, I think you're absolutely right," Eliza cried over the cresting beat of the music, the laughter and stomps of feet.

"Of course I am. Writers see the truth, you know, raw and real. At least they do if they're any damn good." He dipped her low, making her head spin, and she laughed. "Musicians can see it, too, I'm sure. That's what all art does. It tells us the real deal."

Eliza turned and kicked, a flick of her silver shoe, and found Jack watching her. He looked startled, his eyes wide—and then he smiled, that slow, white, sunny grin that made everything warm again. She waved at him happily, and he nodded before raising his horn back to his lips. His long, tapered fingers danced over the valves, summoning forth those glorious sounds, and she remembered how it had felt when he touched her.

The song changed to something slower, something with the easiness of a hot summer's day, and Eliza found herself with another partner. Over the loud music, the laughter, she twirled again and again, her head spinning with delight and new freedom.

Soon a female singer appeared and launched into a quieter song, only a piano to accompany her as she trilled of love and longing and summertime. Eliza spun around, and found herself landing in Jack's arms.

She couldn't help but smile, her happiness threatening to burst out of her altogether at being so close to him again. Feeling his touch around her, surrounded by the scent of his citrussy soap. For an instant, she couldn't breathe at all.

"So you're here, bird girl," he said with a slow smile.

Eliza laughed. "Yes. I met some new friends at Shakespeare and Company, and…" She waved toward their table, where a round of cocktails had just appeared. A handsome blond man, dressed as if for a regatta or something in a crisp blue jacket, a beautiful chocolate-box-blonde in pink chiffon on his arm, had just arrived and was scooping up the drinks. Probably Hem's friend Fitz. "They wanted to hear the very latest musical sensation to arrive in Paris. So here we are!"

"And how is the Conservatoire treating you?"

"Very well! I think so, anyway, I just started. Lots of classes—theory, history. I'm afraid my technique seems rather sloppy."

Yet she knew that whatever she told him, he seemed to already *know*. That tie between them seemed so strong still that she could almost see it, a shimmering cord between them. There was so much to tell him, all she had seen in Paris, all she hoped for now, but she didn't have to tell him anything at all. It was as if no time had passed since they last saw each other.

He laughed, and her heart ached at how handsome he really was. How glorious it was to be with him again. They spun and spun around the dance floor, as if they were the only people there. "I have a hard time believing you're sloppy about anything."

"I wish. But your club is gorgeous! I can see why you were so happy to work here," she said, waving around at all the velvet and gilt and laughing customers.

"It's not so bad," Jack said simply, but there was a note of contented pride in his voice, a small smile on his lips. He belonged there, so perfectly.

They danced in silence for a moment, and Eliza rested her forehead against his shoulder, inhaling him deeply, holding on tightly for as long as she could.

"Can you believe we're really here?" she whispered. "In Paris. Everything so new, so—so…"

"So free?"

She suddenly realized they had been dancing together, pressed against each other, and no one on the crowded floor cared at all. No one even looked at them. It was an astonishing feeling. "Yes."

He spun her in a circle, making her laugh. "Want to see the place?"

She glanced at the stage, where the band still played for the singer. "Can we? Do you need to play soon?"

"Colette will sing for at least two more numbers, we have some time." He gave her a teasing smile, and she had to smile back. He seemed lighter here somehow, younger. "I want to show it off a bit."

"I'd like that."

He led her through a green baize door beside the stage into a narrow corridor. It was lined with more doors, one of them open to let out clatters and shouts, the scent of roasting meats and baking bread, the air hot and steamy.

"The kitchen," Jack said, nodding toward that clamor of controlled chaos.

Eliza peeked inside at the dance of white-jacketed cooks, waiters in their gold waistcoats, flashing trays. "*Four* iceboxes? That's more than the kitchen at my parents' house!"

"The Galliards believe in the best hospitality. It's one of the best things about working here. *Madame* used to do the cooking herself, but they've become so popular they had to hire more people."

"Jacques!" cried one of the men, a tall, skinny, limp-haired cook in a stained white apron. "Just who we need. Taste this bouillabaisse, what does it need?"

Jack took her hand in his and led her into the tumult of the kitchen. He leaned over and sipped from the wooden spoon the cook held out. "More saffron! And thyme. You're French! Don't be shy about herbs, *mon ami*."

"How right you are."

"So you can cook, too?" Eliza said.

Jack gave her a sheepish grin. "My ma told me a man who can cook will get the best girls. I think she just wanted me to do more chores."

"Hmm. I think she might be right. Your mother is a wise woman," she teased, and wondered if there was truly anything this wonderful man couldn't do.

He took her hand again, and led her through another doorway, into a dim, cool room lined with tall shelves of gleaming bottles. His touch was light on hers, but she felt it all the way through her, warm and safe and delicious. "Wine cave. Pantry through there. Linens over here."

Eliza spun in a circle, drawing him with her. "It's enormous!"

"A thousand bottles at least. I'm learning about them. Wine's a bit like music, so many notes and styles!" They clambered up a winding steel staircase, higher and higher above the club. "The Galliards live on this floor."

"And do you stay here, too?" she asked shyly, wondering if she might glimpse where he lived.

"I have lodgings a couple streets over. Not bad at all, but who knows what will happen. Monsieur Galliard is talking about opening a second place, maybe even three, and he wants me to keep an eye on the Club d'Or when that happens."

Eliza gasped. "You'll be the manager?"

He shrugged. "Not for a while, if at all. Fingers crossed. But I want to show you something." He led her up and up, to a small trapdoor at the very top. He climbed the rickety ladder into the night, and reached back to help her follow.

Eliza worried she might snag the scalloped chiffon skirt of her new frock, but she certainly didn't want to miss any time alone with Jack. She hurried up the ladder, and tumbled out at the top with a gasp at the sight that greeted her. Paris was spread out all around her, the lights sparkling like a jewel box.

"Oh, Jack! How glorious," she whispered. She craned her neck one way, seeing the white wedding cake dome of Sacré-Cœur, and another to glimpse the lacy needle of the Eiffel Tower. The shining ribbon of the Champs-élysées. Jack spread his jacket out on the tiles of the roof for her to sit on, and he perched next to her, his shoulder pressed against hers. "It's like the city is all ours."

"That's how I felt when I first saw it. A dream."

They sat there in silence for a long time, letting the

night fold around them. "Jack. Why did you just disappear at Cherbourg? I looked for you to say goodbye."

He frowned as he stared out over the lights, his elbow propped on his knee. He was quiet for so long she wondered if he would answer at all. "I thought it would be for the best," he said softly. "Best for you. I'm not the sort of friend a lady like you should have, not really."

Eliza let out an exasperated sigh. "Oh, Jack. I'm sure *I* can decide who my friends are now. I'm not here with my parents to hover over me protectively. I *want* to choose my own friends. Decide what I want to do with my time."

He looked down at her, his face shadowed. "And what do you want to do?"

Eliza stared at the ribbon of the river, shining under the moon, and thought about how it would feel to just drift like that. Just see what life had to show her next. "I think I want to have a picnic by the Seine. Not a Newport kind of picnic, with tables and chairs and linen cloths and footmen to carry the baskets. One with a blanket on the quay, and cheese and bread and wine! Have you had the baguettes from the boulangeries around here?" She drew in a deep, blissful breath. "Heavenly."

"And with *macarons*? Oysters? Those little fish from the market, fried in garlic?"

"Yes, all of it. And I want you there with me, Jack. Tomorrow? I have classes in the morning, but after…"

He seemed to hesitate, to draw back from her again, and she was determined to make him stay this time. She grabbed his hand and held on to it tightly. "Oh, please! It's Paris. We have to seize every moment we are here."

At last, he smiled, that bright flash she loved so

much, and she smiled, too. "Okay. A picnic. I'll bring the wine."

"Thank you! Oh, it will be so much fun." She heard the stertorous peal of church bells nearby, and she was startled at how late it was becoming. "Should we go back?" she said, even as she dreaded losing that magical place high above the city, alone with him.

"We should. I have to play again." He kissed her hand, his lips lingering warmly on her skin, and rose to his feet, drawing her with him. They stood there, so very close to each other, wrapped in warmth and light, and it felt not like an ending at all, but a marvelous beginning.

Chapter Thirteen

"Merci, madame!" Elizabeth sang out happily as she collected the fresh baguette and tucked it into the basket with the cheese, pâté, and chocolates. The bells on the shop door jangled as she stepped out onto the street and took a deep breath of the flowers from the shop next door, perfumes of passing ladies, and sweet river tang of the Paris morning.

She slipped on a pair of tinted glasses against the bright day and turned toward the patisserie on the corner to find some *macarons*. She passed cafés, waiters sweeping the pavements outside as a few morning customers lingered over coffees, ladies rushing past in their stylish suits and summer dresses, their feathered hats, children chasing dogs and rolling their hoops toward the gardens, the elegant, pale stone houses dotted with bright flower boxes rising up above her toward the clear turquoise sky. She caught a glimpse of herself in one of the windows, and barely recognized herself in her new striped dress, the smile on her lips she couldn't suppress. It felt like something new, something strange and wonderful, was just beyond the touch of her fingertips now.

When she came out with her *macarons* in their neat little, beribboned box, she glimpsed Jack waiting at the end of the street, carrying a bottle of wine. He also wore tinted glasses, and his new gray suit that fit so well over his gorgeous shoulders, flowers in the crook of one arm. For a moment, he looked so distant, so far away from her, a beautiful mirage. She couldn't breathe as she stopped just to look at him, couldn't walk even a step, she was so stunned by him all over again.

He turned his head and saw her, and a smile burst across his face as he removed his glasses. He waved and started toward her, and Eliza felt as if she was suddenly launched into the sun. She rushed toward him, and impulsively went up on tiptoe to kiss his cheek.

He stiffened a tiny bit, his gaze darting over her head, and she shivered as she stepped back. She suddenly felt terribly embarrassed by her need to kiss him, be near him. "Did I do something wrong?" she asked.

He gave her a gentle smile. "You never could, bird girl. It's just—it's such a crowd here…"

"Oh." Like a cold wave of water washing over her, she remembered how some people at home would have reacted to seeing her touch him there on the street, the trouble they might have gotten into. She glanced around, and just saw people hurrying past them, not even looking at them. One couple even kissed under a signpost at the end of the street, entwined around each other. "But this is Paris! Look at all the couples pretending they're the only ones in the whole world. Like those people over there!" She waved toward the kissing couple. "I do think they are just about to consummate their wedding vows…"

Jack laughed, and the sweet, lilting, light sound made her relax and smile again. "You're right. Paris is a new beginning, *oui*?"

"*Oui, bien sûr, monsieur,*" she agreed firmly.

"And these are for you." He handed you the bouquet he held, fragrant dark pink roses and white lilacs bound with a creamy ribbon. "They smell a bit like your perfume." He took the heavy basket from her, tucking his wine inside.

"Do they?" she said in delight, taking a deep breath of the velvety petals. She could hardly believe the thought that he considered her, even remembered her perfume, when they weren't together.

"Shall we? We need to find the perfect spot along the river, I think." He held out his hand to her.

Eliza stared down at it, feeling the largeness, the momentousness, of that gesture. She slid her fingers into his, and they closed around her, warm and safe.

Such a tiny, tiny thing, one hand in another on a sunny day. Just for a second, it felt as if the world tilted on its axis, the sky slashing overhead, the river cresting. Then it all settled into absolute perfection.

"Shall we find that spot, then?" she said. "I'm absolutely famished! The lady at the boulangerie said if we walk this way, we can find the best view of Nôtre-Dame."

They went down the side street, past toy shops and

milliners and book stalls, past concierges staring out their doorways, and at the end climbed down slippery stone steps to the cobbled walkway along the river, still holding hands. They talked of music and art, of Paris museums they wanted to see, and laughed at small boys dashing past with their toy boats, all perfectly ordinary, perfectly wonderful. Eliza wished every day could be just like that.

Along the Seine, they did find a spot with a view of the cathedral, bridges sparkling in the sunlight, artists with their easels capturing the scene. Jack spread out the blanket and poured glasses of the sunset-pink rose wine as Eliza dished out the delicacies she'd spent the morning gathering in the shops. She tucked one of her new roses behind her ear, just under the narrow brim of her white straw hat, and pinned the other to his suit lapel. It was quite a lovely excuse to touch him again.

"*Salut*," she said, clinking her glass to his.

"*Salut*." He leaned back and studied the sunlit stones of the cathedral, a small smile on his lips. It made Eliza's heart warm to see him so relaxed, so happy, in that moment. "Have you ever seen anything so glorious in your life, Eliza?"

Only you, she thought. She tilted back her face to let the sun wash over her, listening to the echo of laughter on the water, the bark of dogs, the ringing of church bells and the splash of waves as a *bateau* glided past on the water. She dangled her feet over the edge of the embankment, and popped a bit of glorious, gooey cheese into her mouth. "Never. I could never have imagined my life would be—this. If today was a song, what do you think it would be?"

He frowned in thought. "*I'm Looking Over a Four Leafed Clover*? It's not Ireland, of course, but I do feel pretty lucky."

Eliza laughed. "Or *Blue Skies*? Hm, no, I think you would have to compose something yourself to make it feel just right."

"*Pink Roses for Elizabeth*?"

She swung her feet in delight that he might write a song for *her*. "Just so! Have you always heard songs in your head when you looked at something beautiful—or terrible, or sad, or wonderful? I have. It's the only real way to realize what I'm actually feeling."

"Of course. I must have been a teenager before I realized that's not how everyone sees things! That music doesn't really have a color, an emotion, all its own."

Eliza sighed to think someone else suddenly knew her, knew what she felt. "I see what Chopin and Liszt and Debussy saw now, when they looked at Paris. The sparkle on the water, the grace and warmth and truth of it all. Only it's so much better! No sad clouds on the horizon, not today."

He studied her for a moment, a crooked little smile on his lips, as if he could see into her very heart. "You deserve only blue skies, Eliza. Always." He glanced around and smiled. "Do you want to walk for a while? I have some time before I have to get to the club."

"Of course." She took his arm, strolling past shops and gardens, not talking of anything in particular except the sunshine and the glorious, Parisian day. In one of the squares, green and smelling of white flowers, they found a group of older men in crisp white shirts and berets tossing shining silver balls with most solemn looks on their faces.

"They look quite serious about tossing those little balls," Eliza whispered.

"It's not just 'little balls,' it's *pétanque*. A serious business," Jack whispered back.

"Oh." She had certainly heard of the game, but she's imagined it would be something like the croquet she played in Newport. She couldn't quite figure this one out. Each man seemed to just stand inside a chalked circle and toss the metal ball toward a wooden one.

"The wooden ball is the target, the *cochonnet*," Jack said. "Each game consists of several *mènes*, rounds, with two teams throwing the boules, trying to get closest to the goal. They score one point for each boule closer than the opposing teams closest boule. Could be six, but usually two or three. The first to reach thirteen wins."

They watched for a while, Eliza finding it strangely fascinating to follow the shining arc of the silvery balls, hear the thud when it met its goal. Jack stood beside her, his arms crossed as he studied the game intently.

"Ah, monsieur," he suggested, "if you held your hand like so, just turned a bit to the left, it could have more spin. More control and flexibility in the spin."

The man scowled as he looked at Jack, but Jack just kept smiling. "You play *pétanque, monsieur*?" he said suspiciously.

"A little, a long time ago, after the war," Jack said. "I liked the focus of it."

"Show us!" another man said with a laugh, holding out the ball to Jack, his face as creased as an old apple under his beret. "We want to see this American way of *pétanque*."

Jack laughed, too. "Challenge accepted, *monsieur*!" He took the man's place within the chalked circle, and as Eliza watched he took the ball onto the palm of his hand, held downwards. She barely saw his arm move, but it came up in an underarm swing that ended with a flick of his wrist. The ball landed just a breath away from the *cochonnet*. The men laughed and applauded, urging him onto their teams.

Eliza laughed, too, delighted at the moment of a small triumph, and impulsively hugged him. "You see!" she cried. "We're just like real French people now."

Jack closed the door to his little room, and found himself staring down at his hand, the hand Eliza had held as they walked, and grinning like a fool.

He'd been with beautiful women before. Emily, with her shining auburn hair and wide smile, Daisy, a dancer at the Stork Club, Lil, Mary… Girls always loved a musician. But nothing had ever felled him with such a pure, joyous thrill as Eliza taking his hand and walking down the street with him as if it was the most natural thing in the world. Nothing had made him as happy deep down inside as when she kissed his cheek, laughing giddily at the *pétanque* victory. It was like a trill of music, a song that burbled and sparkled as it wound around him.

In his experience, it was always people who limited the happiness in the world. People with their irrational ideas, their hatred and fear limiting what could be. Except for a very few, who seemed to possess happiness as easy as breathing. And Eliza Van Hoeven was like that, she was like springtime itself. It seemed he could no more stay away from her than he could that springtime sun. It was a war within himself—he craved her sweetness, her light, but he knew he would burn himself on it in the end. That he was no good for her.

It couldn't last. Paris was an interlude, not the real world, not the whole symphony. New York—that was reality, the danger and cold looks and rejection being with him would bring to Eliza. And he had to think of his own future at the Club d'Or; maybe he would be manager there one day soon. She had her own important studies, her rare talent, her dreams. But maybe, just maybe, Paris could be their *now*. Just for a little longer.

An impatient knock sounded at the door, and he spun around, startled, to open it a crack. For a second, old fears seemed to lurk inside of him, and he wondered if it was someone who'd seen him with Eliza and was furious now.

But it was just the concierge from the ground floor, her stout figure wrapped in its flowered apron, her eyes bright under the scarf tied over her graying hair. "The post came for you, *monsieur*," she said with a suspicious little frown, as if mail was a doubtful thing. She thrust out a lumpy, brown paper package and a few envelopes.

"Merci, madame," he answered, closing the door behind her retreating figure. The package was from his mother, undoubtedly a scarf and gloves she knitted in the evenings after work. She was unsure about the weather in Paris, even though he assured her it was just

as warm as at home, or the fact that French shops might not have proper scarves. He laughed, and put the package aside to sort through the letters. One from Katie, one from a friend at the Stork.

The envelope on the bottom was stained and creased, the writing smudged, but undoubtedly the messy scrawl of his cousin Leo. And where Leo went, trouble always followed. Frowning, Jack tore it open.

We were all real surprised when your ma said you'd gone to Paris. Paris! All right for some cats, I guess, and I hope you remember us who helped you way back when.

Things aren't so cool here for me. Maybe you heard about that Versailles Club thing? How should I have known who the doll was? I'm keeping my head low here, saving some money, maybe I can get to Paris soon, too...

Chapter Fourteen

Eliza held on to Jack's arm and peered up at the Comtesse's *hotel particulière* in doubt. It didn't look much like a place the free-spirited Chloe would live. It was very old, solemn, dark stone and marble, tucked away on a shady side street near the Place de Vosges. Yet she could hear music floating down from a half-open first-floor window, a discordant trombone and percussion, touched by laughter and the clatter of bottles.

She smoothed the skirt of her new gown, a dashing Poiret creation of turquoise taffeta and gold lace, and hoped she looked quite *Parisian* enough for this place.

"You look absolutely beautiful," Jack said.

Eliza glanced up at him anxiously, his gentle smile steadying her. "Really?"

"You'll be the most glamorous one there."

She smiled at him in return, and squeezed his arm. "I doubt that, but I do want to fit in. And you don't look so bad yourself, Jack Coleman."

Something flickered behind his eyes, a fleeting

shadow. "Are you sure your friend won't mind I'm here
with you? If she's a countess—these Parisian *gratin*
have some pretty strict ideas…"

Eliza laughed as she remembered Chloe urging her
to take a lover in Paris. "She will be delighted. Well,
come on, I guess we better go up before I chicken out
and run away."

Their knock on the cream-painted double doors was
answered by a butler—an actual, old-fashioned butler!
One who looked as if he'd come straight out of some
drawing room comedy musical, tall, thin, with shining
silver hair, a dark morning coat, and disapproving expression. Eliza was sure her mother would heartily approve—and suddenly really hoped she hadn't mistaken
the Comtesse. She didn't want to escape Fifth Avenue
just to land at some other stuffy party.

"Oui, madame? Monsieur?" the butler sniffed.

"Mademoiselle Van Hoeven, to see Madame la Comtesse," Eliza said, trying to sound confident.

"Certainement. If you would follow me?"

He led them through a foyer, all chilly pale blue and
snowy white, with a faded floral rug underfoot that
probably came from Versailles, a row of antique blue
and white Chinese porcelain jars as tall as Eliza, and
ancestral portraits of men in powdered hair and ladies
in court dresses several feet wide staring down at them
as they passed. They turned up a wide staircase, their
footsteps clicking on cold marble.

Eliza glanced up at Jack, who was utterly expressionless.

"I think we accidentally took a turn to Fontainebleau," she whispered, and a ghost of smile drifted over his lips.

But she needn't have worried at all. As they reached the top of the stairs, the noise of music and laughter and clinking glassware grew more raucous. The horns blasted some strange song she'd never heard before, joined with the clunk of a bass.

The carved double doors, white touched with gilt, swung open, and it was like a new planet. The vast drawing room, with large windows where red and gold brocade draperies were thrown back to reveal distant views of Sacré-Cœur, held only a few chairs and settees, just piles of embroidered pillows scattered on another faded floral rug. Several people, some in black tuxedos or silk evening dresses, some in colorful robes and turbans, sat around smoking hookahs.

Marble-topped tables lined one of the black and white-gloss-painted walls, piled with bowls of couscous, glistening pyramids of fruit and pastel iced cakes. Tall, gilded stands in the corners held more Chinese porcelain vases that contained not roses or orchids, but upright stalks of celery. Footmen lined the walls dressed in old-fashioned red livery coats, and one of them offered a tray of pink cocktails. An older man with thinning hair and a fierce frown behind his spectacles played a grand piano in the corner.

"Is that *actually* Stravinsky?" Eliza whispered to Jack, trying not to gawk.

"I think it must be," Jack answered, and she was relieved he looked almost as starstruck as she felt. She wasn't a gaping bumpkin after all—or not quite so much as she feared.

"Eliza, *ma chère*!" Chloe cried, emerging from the crowd. She wore an amazing gown of changeable purple and sea-green lamé, shining like the ocean, a train twisting behind her. The low vee of the neckline revealed a large emerald pendant on a chain of diamonds, which Eliza knew her mother would deeply envy if she could see it, even if the entertaining style was not at all Van Hoeven standard. Chloe held her long, obsidian cigarette holder out of the way as she gave Eliza *la bise* on both cheeks. "I am so glad you came to my little salon. The Conservatoire must be keeping you so busy! But you cannot stay chained to your piano all the time."

"I wouldn't mind being chained to *that* piano," Eliza said. "It's a Steinway Alma Tadema, isn't it? Gorgeous."

"Ah, yes, though I don't play myself! I'm fortunate to have such talented friends. You like Igor's *petite chansons*?"

Eliza laughed to think of something like *Firebird* being a "little song."

"Very much."

"And you brought a friend! Such a handsome one. Have we met? You do look familiar." Chloe gave Jack a considering, smoky glance from under her mascaraed lashes, and held out her hand to him. "I am Chloe. You are a musician, too, yes? From the ship? I could never forget such a face. Just like an El Greco, I think."

Jack bowed over her hand like a gallant, old-style knight, and Eliza was surprised to see he actually seemed to *blush*. She shifted on her new gold, high-heeled shoes, hating the cold little touch of—was it jealousy? "I do play the trumpet, yes, Madame la Comtesse. It's kind of you to welcome me to you home."

Chloe waved her obsidian holder. "We are not America here, I assure you, *monsieur*! There are some admirable things about your country, to be sure, but I know I am not wrong in saying our France is superior in many ways. *All* are welcome at my home—except for the boring! I will have none of them." She gestured one of the footmen closer, and took two cocktails from his silver tray to hand to Eliza and Jack. "And we have none of your silly Prohibition here! Drink, drink. Mingle! If we can persuade Igor to stop showing off, perhaps you will play something for us, Eliza?"

Eliza felt a tingle of excitement to think of getting her hands on that glorious piano. "I would enjoy that very much, Chloe."

"*Bien*! In the meantime, you must meet some of our guests. Diaghilev, you must know, *oui*?" She waved at a portly man in a paisley waistcoat. "And Leger, and Massine? They are doing glorious things at the ballet this year, you must go see them. Monsieur Picabia over there, with the Spanish painter Picasso. I expect interesting things from him. And Picabia is holding a fascinating exhibit at the Salon des Indépendants soon. His work makes me think of jazz…you should see it, Monsieur Jacques."

She led them further into the room, nodding at Hemingway, who paused in boxing with a small, cringing man to wave at them. Eliza took a gulp of her cocktail to keep from laughing.

"The Murphys, American compatriots of yours, so delightful! Gerald and Sara. Quite the leaders of society now." Chloe waved at a handsome couple who held court near the window, the golden-haired woman dressed in a draped white chiffon gown with long ropes of pearls around her neck. "And with them is Madame Goncharova, but be careful, she will try to read your palm. And Ernest, I'm sure you've met him, everyone has."

"Yes, at Shakespeare and Company." Eliza watched Hem as he tried to box with a wide-eyed, cringing, skinny man.

Chloe frowned. "He had better not break that vase, it's seventeenth century. Ah, and here is another *belle Americaine*! *Ma chère madame*, over here. This is Elizabeth Van Hoeven, *madame*, and Eliza this is Zelda Fitzgerald. You will quite like her, Eliza. Now, my handsome *monsieur*, do let me steal you away. I have another friend here who plays the trumpet..."

She took Jack firmly by the arm and led him away, as he tossed a pleading glance back at Eliza. But there was no resisting the Comtesse. Eliza gave him a little wave and a grin before she turned to the petite, chocolate-box-pretty blonde woman in a stunning, petal-pink tulle gown, the woman she had glimpsed at the Club d'Or.

"Hi, there!" Zelda said in a loamy, rich Southern accent. She left her empty glass on a footman's tray and took a full one with a flirtatious grin. "I think I've seen you before, at the Club d'Or? So you're American, too? How'd you wash up here?"

"I'm studying music at the Conservatoire," Eliza answered, almost too dazzled by this vibrant vision of blonde waves and pink ruffles.

Zelda made a little moue of her rose-painted bow lips. "You lucky ducky. I used to want to be a dancer. Or maybe a writer. Now I just keep a journal and drink. I'm good at that." She held up the sparkling golden cocktail. "You need another, too! Been in Paris long, then?"

"A few weeks. I'm from New York."

Zelda laughed, a ripple of silvery bells. "I lived in New York, too! Kicked out of all the best hotels, so we had to come here. That's my fella over there." She pointed at a man who was talking to Hem on the other side of the crowded salon, a tall, polished gold man who seemed to match her perfectly. Eliza remembered him from the Club d'Or, staggering around drunkenly, but he seemed all right tonight, nodding and talking seriously. "I'm Zelda."

Eliza suddenly remembered seeing her photo in the newspapers in New York, she and her husband the stars of a crowd Eliza's mother would never let her meet. They had indeed been thrown out of hotels—and swam in fountains, rode atop taxis, spun for hours in revolving doors. Zelda looked prettier than those grainy black and white images, with a vitality and sparkle no still photo could capture. Eliza was very envious of such an adventurous life, even if it did sound exhausting. "Zelda Fitzgerald? Who lived at the Plaza?"

"That's me! And my man is Scott. Watch out if he has another drink, he's no fun at all after two. You here with a guy, too?"

"Yes, Jack Coleman. Over there with the Comtesse." Eliza pointed out Jack, suddenly unsure. Zelda was clearly Southern, after all.

But she just laughed. "Now that's a fella who's the cat's meow! Look at those cheekbones. My daddy would just die right dead with an apoplexy if he saw that. He's a judge, in Alabama. He didn't want me marrying Scott just because he's a Yankee."

"I think my father would, too. He's an attorney in Manhattan, but mostly his job is just being a Knicker-bocker gentleman."

"Well, who cares about our parents when a fella looks like *that*! Is he a writer?"

"Musician. He plays at the Club d'Or."

Zelda sighed wistfully and reached for another cock-tail. "You *are* one lucky dame. Getting to do whatever you want. Come on, have another drinkie, let's get Olga to read our palms!"

Only after an hour could Eliza escape Zelda and the palm-reading *madame*. She found another cocktail and sat down in the corner, unable to see Jack in the grow-ing crowd. Soon Chloe joined her, lighting another cig-arette in her obsidian holder.

"Now, *ma chère*, you must forgive my bluntness, but I feel I must act as your *maman* right now! Your Jacques—so gorgeous, so sweet. But you have such a future before you! You *are* taking precautions, *oui*?" Chloe said with no preamble.

Eliza almost choked on her cocktail. "I—precau-tions?"

"Against becoming enceinte, of course. You Ameri-cans are so puritanical, I know, but one must be wise about such things."

Eliza took another sip to cover her hot cheeks. "We haven't—that is, we don't..." But she remembered very well how Jack's kisses felt, how they swept away everything else in that flood of emotion and joy, and she nodded.

Chloe took a long drag on her cigarette holder. "I see. Well, you must have fun, *ma chère*. Experience life! Just be prepared, and don't let that fun take away everything else. I will send you something, a little device. Be sure to use it!"

Zelda Fitzgerald swirled out of the crown on a pink cloud of skirt and cried, "I'm bored, everyone! Come on, let's all go to Chez Betsy, I insist..."

The Fitzgeralds' car, which they insisted everyone take to the Chez Betsy, was a gorgeous Rolls Royce Phantom, but even Eliza could see it would never fit, unless it was like a clown car she saw at a childhood circus, seemingly hundreds of Pierrots tumbling out of a Duesenberg. She stood on the pavement outside Chloe's mansion, laughing madly as she imagined what her mother would say if she could see Eliza now, watching drunken writers and artists fall around the car, feeling a little tipsy and giddy herself. Holding onto Jack's arm as if they truly, casually belonged together just like that.

"Come on, you chickens, let's just go!" Zelda cried, waving a bottle of champagne in the air. "Scott and me'll just ride on the hood...easy-peasy! Quit standing around looking stupefied!"

She held up her tulle skirt with her free hand and clambered up on the gleaming hood, reaching out to drag her husband with her. Scott followed, looking rather clammy and tousled, leaning against her. Their driver, in his green coat and peaked cap, just looked resigned, as if this happened every day.

Sara Murphy looked coolly amused, her golden hair and pearls gleaming in the streetlights. "We will just find a taxi and meet you there, Zelda darling."

Before Eliza could beg to go with the sane-looking Murphys, they vanished from under the hazy streetlights. Zelda watched as Hem and a clutch of dancers piled into the back seat and remembered she could really do whatever she wanted that night—she was there to find out who *she* was. And maybe she was someone who, well, wouldn't ride *on* a car hood, but very possibly *in* a car with crowds of people.

If one of them was Jack.

She glanced back over her shoulder at him, where he stood close behind her, reassuring and steady. They hadn't much time for talking in the salon; there were too many people, dizzying in all their color and noise, and she had played a bit on that glorious piano, danced with Serge Lifar without hugely embarrassing herself, had her palm read again. Yet every time she looked for him, he was surrounded by a crowd, laughing and at ease, and they seemed to be together even across the room.

"Shall we?" she said.

"If you don't think the car will suddenly turn into a pumpkin at midnight, Cinders," he said with a grin.

She laughed. "Too late for that, it's long past midnight. And I still have both of these." She held out her foot in its golden, strappy shoe.

Jack clambered into the car after Hem, and Eliza slid onto his lap, her legs draped over the people on his other side, her arm wrapped tightly around Jack's shoulders. Maybe it was the cocktails, the moon shining high over the Parisian slate roofs—or probably the way Jack's shoulders felt under her touch, so strong and hard—but she was sure life had never been so grand, so perfect, as it was in that moment. She'd never felt so alive, it was wonderful.

"Whee!" Zelda cried through the open windows, the breeze fresh and cool and smelling of Paris, flowers and the river. The car slid slowly through the near-empty streets, past darkened windows and the glow of lights behind curtains. The grand mansions, the carved courtyard gates, the parks and fountains, gave way to narrower, steeper lanes, to places still bright with life and noise.

"'*Non, mais c'est lui,*'" someone sang, one of Josephine Baker's famous songs, and soon everyone joined on, drunkenly off-key but full of enthusiasm. "'*Je te le dis, c'est lui!*'"

Eliza leaned her head on Jack's shoulder, holding onto him closely, and he pressed a kiss to her hair. All too soon, they came to a stop outside a building whose gilded sign read *Chez Betsy—Music, Cocktails, Dancing, All Night*. The tall windows glowed brightly, and people spilled out onto the walkway.

Just as they had packed into the car, they tumbled out again, laughing, graceless, falling over each other. Eliza stumbled a bit on the cobblestones, and her shoe slipped. Jack caught her up before she could fall, holding her high above the world, making her laugh.

"Thought you hadn't lost them, Cinders," he said.

"And I thought I was a bird girl! Flying free."

"You're both." He looked down at her with that intent, focused glow in his eyes, the one that made her feel so very seen, so understood and safe. "You're everything."

He slid her slowly to her feet, and she took his hand. "So are you."

"Come on, you two, don't miss the fun!" Zelda called, and Eliza laughed and tugged Jack into the club behind the others, just like Mamie would have done back in New York.

Chez Betsy was very grand, bigger than the Club d'Or, decorated with murals of Marie Antoinette-ish *chateaux* and milkmaids, the dance floor and pink brocade banquettes crowded with people. The band played a raucous song, led by a beautiful singer, tall and dark in shimmering copper satin, and Eliza was swept away to the bar where Gerald Murphy was already wielding a cocktail shaker as his beautiful, golden-haired wife smiled on.

"Here, my dear Miss Van Hoeven," he said, "do try one of these. My very own creation! And you, too, Mr. Coleman. It's been so very long since Sara and I were in our native land, I have no idea what American tastes might be."

"Oh, do please indulge him, Miss Van Hoeven, or he'll be impossible for the rest of the night. He does consider him to be quite the mixologist," Sara said.

"Now, my darling, do have a little faith in me," Gerald said, and handed Eliza and Jack two violet-colored drinks.

Eliza took a sip. Gin, yes, and something sweet, something tart just underneath. Strong enough to make her gasp. "I—most extraordinary, Mr. Murphy. What's in it?"

"Merely the juice of a few flowers, my dear," Gerald said airily. "And do call us Gerald and Sara. I'm sure we'll be great friends, I always sense these things when I first meet people. We're having a little party for the opening of Stravinsky's ballet. Do say you'll both come!"

Eliza glanced up at Jack. She'd never really imagined before how lovely it would feel to be a "we," invited to parties together, making friends together. "I think we would enjoy that."

"Well, as I do live and breathe! It *is* you, Baby Sweets Coleman," a rich, velvety voice purred behind them. "I couldn't believe my eyes when I saw you come in."

Eliza glanced back to see the band's singer. She was even more gorgeous up close, tall and willowy in that copper satin gown beaded in gold and bronze, her dark waves of hair swept up high under a feathered bandeau, her eyes glowing an even brighter amber.

And her smile at Jack was positively, smoothly possessive.

Eliza looked at Jack, taking in his thunderstruck expression. His arm slid out from under her hand. "Tallulah. I'd heard you were in Berlin."

"Didn't suit me. Too many bully boys marching around, no fun at all." She ran her fingertips, lacquered bright magenta, sparkling with emerald rings, along Jack's lapel. "Paris is so much more the berries. I see it agrees with you, too. You always were a beautiful one, now you look positively film star. What are you doing here, then?"

Jack took her hand in his, catching it against his lapel. "Playing at the Club d'Or."

"Galliard's place? Swanky." Tallulah glanced at Eliza, her kohl-rimmed eyes narrowed.

Jack let go of Tallulah and took Eliza's elbow in a light clasp. "Tallulah, this is Eliza Van Hoeven. A friend."

"Friend, huh?" She laughed humorlessly. "I remember when *we* were friends."

Jack glanced down at Eliza, his face unreadable. "Tallulah lived in the same building as my parents when we were kids. She and my cousin Leo and I used to get up to all sorts of pranks."

Tallulah smiled, slow and soft, like a cat before it pounced. "Oh, we did lots more than that once we grew up! And you're surely very grown-up now. Wanna dance? I don't have another number to sing for a while.

Jack took her hand and led her onto the dance floor, the two of them perfectly matched with their tall figures, their graceful way of moving. Soon they were lost to view, and Eliza was alone.

She turned back to the bar. "Some more juice of flowers, please, Gerald?"

"For you, dear girl, a double." He poured out a large drink from his shaker and handed it to her. As she sipped at it, trying to ignore the dance floor, Zelda came and climbed up on one of the high stools, her blonde hair tousled, her eyes too bright. Gerald handed her a drink, too, and she gulped it down.

"Oh, Liz," she sighed. "Love can be such a nertz, can't it? Just never get married, that's what I advise."

"Aren't you and Mr. Fitzgerald happy?" Eliza asked, remembering the newspapers that called them the Golden Couple of the Flapper Era.

"I had *so* many beaux back in Alabama," Zelda said. "Handsome, rich boys! All my jellybeans, they adored me. But then I met Scotty. He was at an army camp, you know. The war and such. Lawks, he was a gorgeous sight in that uniform! Swept me off my feet on that country club dance floor the first time I saw him. And the way he could write…" She gulped down her drink. "Life was gonna be so exciting with him."

Eliza thought of her own old life, every day the same. Until Jack came along. "Is it not exciting, then? It looks amazing."

"Sure. I've been places, met people, I never could have back in Mobile. But then a girl wants something of her own sometimes, too. You're a musician, huh? You must know that."

"Yes. I do know." And no one had ever understood what music could really mean until she met Jack. Jack, who seemed to see everything without hearing a word.

She watched him on the dance floor with Tallulah, the two of them so tall and well-matched, moving together so smoothly and elegantly, talking quietly into each other's ear. Tallulah, who knew him in ways Eliza didn't, couldn't. Was she just fooling herself with him?

"Gerry, sweetie, give us another of those what's-its," Zelda said. "And when are you going to ask us to your villa on the beach? It's in the Riviera, Liz, you should see it! Heaven. I do love to swim. I'm aching to see it again."

"In July, Zelda darling, when the renovations are finished. It's a shambles right now. And you, too, Eliza. *If* you promise to come to the show at the Salon des Indépendants and praise my new painting lavishly." He handed them fresh drinks, and gave Eliza a slow, significant nod. "Bring your young man, too. We have so many guesthouses to fill. Hem is coming, you already know him, I think, and his wife. And Picasso. He'll want to draw you, but you can put him off if he's too intense."

Eliza glanced again at Jack, and for a moment that sort of life, that dream, flashed through her mind. Swimming with him in the ocean, lounging on the beach beside him, laughing with friends together. A real couple. It seemed so wondrous, so perfectly what life *should* be. But he was laughing with Tallulah, his head thrown back. "I think he might have other plans."

Zelda snorted. "This is Paris, sweetie. We *all* have other plans. No one notices or cares about a thing."

"Quite," Gerald said. "Look at my sister-in-law…"

"Sapphic, in with the Natalie Barney set," Zelda whispered. "They dance naked under the full moon and call out to the goddesses."

Eliza had to giggle into her drink. How wide the world was away from Fifth Avenue. Yet could it ever be really wide enough for all she desired?

"Would you care to dance?" one of the artists asked, and she nodded, glad of the distraction.

She twirled into the dance, changing partners again and again, laughing and spinning, until she finally found herself in Jack's arms. "There you are," she said happily, leaning against him as they moved into the steps. Over his shoulder, she glimpsed that beautiful singer, Tallulah, her expression solemn, her lips frowning as she watched Eliza and Jack. "I think your friend doesn't approve," she whispered.

"My friend?" he asked quizzically.

"That gorgeous singer. Miss Tallulah."

He nodded. "She just worries about everything."

Eliza knew how that felt. It was only when she came to Paris that she could lay down some of the anxiety that had always seemed to plague her. But what did Tallulah worry about? Jack, getting mixed up with a Fifth Avenue girl? "I—maybe she has a point."

Jack glanced around, and took her hand to spin her through a nearby door, away from the raucous crowd. Eliza found herself in a silent alley, along with Jack, and she took a deep breath.

"Eliza," he said. "She's just a friend. And I don't worry when I'm with you. I just—just…"

"I just *feel* when I'm with you," she said, daring to let the truth out. She didn't think, worry with him—she just felt like she was sinking down into a warm blanket, able to be herself, to laugh and talk and kiss and feel *right*. Feel like for once she belonged somewhere. She wrapped her arms around his neck and held on tightly.

He seemed to know exactly what she meant. He

turned his face to kiss the inner pulse of her wrist, and it beat so frantically at the nearness of him. His breath was so warm and vital and delicious against her bare skin, a fantasy she could hardly believe was true. If only she could do the same for him, hold him safe above the world. She feared she could not, not forever; he needed someone like Tallulah for that, someone wise in the world. But Eliza was the one there right at that moment. The moment was hers.

And they were not parted yet. She wanted to seize onto everything she had right then, make it her own and never forget it. She closed her eyes, inhaling the warm scent of him. "Oh, Jack," she whispered. "I wish—I wish…"

But she couldn't say anything else. His lips claimed hers, and she went up on tiptoe to meet him, putting all she had into that kiss. It was full of desperation, passion, need, everything she couldn't say aloud.

"Eliza," he whispered back, his kiss tracing over her cheek, her temple. "Eliza, I know what—that is…"

"You don't need to talk, Jack," she said, scared of what he might say. "I know. I really do."

He nodded, and just held her close as the night fell softly around them and time slipped away from her like a silk scarf through her hands. But she knew she would always have this moment, no matter what.

"So, Baby Sweets, what are you really doing with that little blonde?" Tallulah asked as she waved to the bartender for two whiskies. Just like it was back in Harlem, when they had played in the same clubs.

Jack glanced over his shoulder. Eliza had left with her friends once they snuck back into the club, swept off in their tipsy whirlwind, but he was half afraid she would come back and overhear, that those doubts would creep back into her eyes. Doubts he understood, because he shared them. "We're just friends. We can do that here—to an extent."

"You still need to be careful," Tallulah said sternly. "Remember what happened to Pete? And to your cousin Leo."

Jack nodded grimly, and tossed back his whiskey. Leo had been arrested in that Versailles Club raid; Pete, a childhood friend, had been beaten on the street for talking to white girl. "It won't happen to me."

"Because you're here? New York isn't so far away."

"Because I'm careful." But was he? When he was with Eliza, she was all he could see. All he could think about.

"You didn't look so *careful* dancing with her." She put a gentle hand on his arm, her smile full of sympathy. "You have a rare talent, Jack. That should always come first."

He nodded. He knew she was right, really. Hadn't he told himself that a million times? His music was the most important thing, the key to the future. He didn't forget his music when he was with her, talking to her, laughing with her. Music, like everything else, felt so much more intense with her. Made the world brighter.

He nodded at Tallulah, who smiled again. He really should be with someone like her. Someone of his own world, who knew things about him, his past, without a word. Eliza did that, too, but with her it was different, more fundamental, not part of the real world but only what was inside of them.

"Let's dance again, then," Tallulah said, her smile turning mischievous. "You used to be the best bunny-hugger in Harlem…"

Chapter Fifteen

Eliza was exhausted when she finally got back to her lodgings from a long day of classes. Early music, composition, analysis. She kicked off her shoes, tossed her hat on a table, and fell into a brocade chair by the window where the light was turning bronzy pink at the edges. The sunset hour, when Paris glowed at its most glorious. The *cinq à sept*, Chloe said, when lovers met before going home to their spouses.

Except Eliza expected no lover to appear. She hadn't seen Jack since their night at Chez Betsy, the night he found his old friend Tallulah. She'd been buried in studying, but even so she'd been so tempted to go to the Club d'Or, to find him, talk to him. To make a fool of herself all over again.

She sighed, and reached for the pile of mail left on the table beside her hat. Invitations, including one to the Murphy's bateau party for Stravinsky's ballet, letters from a few friends in New York, a scribbled note from Mamie.

And a letter from her mother... Margaret Van Hoeven's oh-so-perfect handwriting neatly slanted on the creamy stationery. Eliza didn't want to read it, not without some of Gerald Murphy's "juice of a few flowers" to bolster her. But she knew she had to, she hadn't written to her parents in too long and the last thing she wanted in this newfound freedom was their suspicions.

She opened it, and quickly scanned the copperplate lines.

> *My dear Elizabeth*
> *How encouraging is your news from the Conservatoire! You will surely be finished very soon and home again where you truly belong.*
>
> *My dear friend Mrs. Smythe tells me she has invited you to have tea with her and her delightful nephew Henry, and you are much too busy to meet them at the Ritz. I am sure that cannot be so! A Van Hoeven never neglects her social duties. It is vital that you maintain a good name among the people who matter.*
>
> *I insist you write her very soon and give her a date for your meeting. Or I shall be forced to take other measures to remind you of your upbringing.*
>
> *Do not disappoint me.*
> *Love, Mother*

Eliza tossed the letter down and shuddered as she remembered Henry Smythe's hands slithering over her on the dance floor. And Jack rescuing her. If only Jack would show up at the Ritz for tea, too, and whisk her away!

She almost laughed to picture it. Jack in a swirling

cape, sweeping into the glittering restaurant to catch her up in his arms and sweep her out of there! Yet surely, even if she could lure him there, he was much too busy at the Club d'Or—or with the beautiful Tallulah.

She shook her head. Probably Henry could not get too handsy with his aunt right there, and afternoon tea was a small price to pay to keep her parents away. She'd had to do things like that every day in New York.

And would have to do it again when Paris was finished. There would be no more piling into cars to go to middle-of-the-night clubs for cocktails then, no racy salons and art shows and bateau parties.

There was a knock at the door, and Eliza quickly shot up and put her shoes back on, as if her mother could somehow see her. *"Oui?"*

"Le téléphone, mademoiselle," the concierge said, sounding slightly put out. The phone, Eliza had been told when she moved in, was strictly for emergencies. She felt a jolt of fear that something terrible had happened.

"My dear Miss Van Hoeven," the laughing voice said on the other end of the phone, definitely *not* her mother. "This is Sara Murphy. We met at Chloe's? My husband was the lout who insisted on mixing up his drinks for everyone."

Eliza laughed in relief, and in the memory of that gloriously lovely couple with the Riviera villa. "Yes, of course, how lovely to hear from you!"

"I wanted to remind you about our little party this weekend. For darling Igor, his new ballet is debuting at the Théâtre de la Gaîté Lyrique. *Les Noces*, perhaps you have seen articles about it?"

"Not yet, and I'm so eager to see it when it opens. I love his work. And I would love to come to your party." Anything but tea with Mrs. Smythe.

"I'm afraid it's nothing grand, I couldn't find a proper venue at such short notice, but a lovely friend found a barge for me, so amusing. Sunday evening! And do bring your handsome friend. The more the merrier…"

By the time Sunday evening came, Eliza was so very excited she couldn't wait inside her flat a moment longer, pacing around, worrying about her new gown of carmine silk edged with gold beading. She grabbed up her gloves and handbag and hurried down the stairs to stand outside the foyer doors where she could watch for Jack. She ignored the curious glances of the passersby, the frowns of the concierge from the window behind her. He had said he would come when she wrote to him. What if he had changed his mind?

At last she glimpsed him through the crowd, tall and distinguished in his evening suit, his hat slouched over one eye. She waved in excitement, bouncing on her toes. He laughed and kissed her cheek, handing her a single rose he'd bought from one of the carts. "You seem to be looking forward to the evening, bird girl."

"Oh, I am! Let's take that bus," she said, as the green and white vehicle slid to a stop across the lane.

Jack laughed. "A bus for Miss Van Hoeven?"

"I've never tried one before."

"Never?"

"My mother would never allow such a thing." She squeezed his arm. "But she isn't here to lecture me now. Come on!"

He still laughed doubtfully, but he followed her up the steps and onto a seat at the center of the bus. Eliza was so filled with wonder at the people around them, the smell of gasoline and perfumes, the streets outside the window, that she bounced a bit on the leatherette seat. "Isn't it marvelous? You can see all the sights. I can't believe I've never tried it before. I'm always going to ride the bus now."

Jack gazed out the window, his expression unreadable. "If we were in New York, bird girl, we wouldn't be able to sit beside each other."

She glanced up at him, startled. "What?"

"I would sit in the back, you would sit in the front." He held up their entwined hands. "We definitely couldn't do this. I'd go straight to jail."

Absolutely appalled, Eliza studied the other passengers. No one paid any attention to them at all, except one prune-faced Mrs. Smythe lookalike. Everyone else read their *Paris Match*, kissed their partners, scolded their children, or just stared out the window.

She felt her cheeks turn hot. "I'm so embarrassed," she murmured, unable to believe her own thoughtlessness. "I never even noticed…"

He smiled at her gently. "How could you, if you don't ride the bus?"

Eliza swallowed hard. He was right; she didn't ride the bus. She didn't see past her own piano bench sometimes. It made her want to hold on to Paris, to that moment, even harder, and never come back to earth. "I—I'm not sure I've ever been a party for a ballet before, either. Not a ballet like Stravinsky's. You must think me such a greenhorn about everything." She'd heard that the ballet, *Les Noces*, was quite daring, much like riding a public bus. A primitivist wedding fable scored with piano, drums, bells, even a xylophone to show off the social forces that drowned the human wishes of the bride and groom.

She couldn't wait to see it, but now she wondered if it would be too sharp.

"Now, no buses I can believe," Jack teased. "But no ballet parties for a Conservatoire girl like you?"

She laughed, and leaned her head on his shoulder. "Only little cocktail receptions after a *Swan Lake* first night. Sipping warm champagne and muttering things like 'such lovely tutus.' I doubt the Murphys ever gave a dull party like that in their lives. I heard their food and music and conversation are always perfect! So several firsts for me today. Who do you think will be there?"

"Your friend Stravinsky, of course…"

"My friend!" If only. But when she was with Jack, anything seemed possible.

"All the people from the Comtesse's salon. And Princess de Polignac, that Singer sewing machine heiress— I've heard she's underwriting this ballet, like she does a lot of the arts. I guess she's someone we should know."

Eliza smiled, feeling a silly little thrill at the idea that she and Jack could be a "we," partners in their musical lives. And she had to admit she was also a little thrillingly scandalized at the thought of meeting the

American *princesse*, who Zelda Fitzgerald said was in with Natalie Barney's "sapphic set", like Gerald's sister. "How fascinating! Tell me more, all the gossip..."

Once the bus reached their stop, they found their way not to a hotel or ballroom, but to a two-story barge tied up on the river in front of the Chambre des Députés, just as Sara Murphy had directed. It glowed with lights from tip to tail, the red and white striped awnings catching the wind as fashionably dressed couples teetered up the gangplank and music hung in the air. Eliza was very glad of her stylish new gown, of Jack to hold her hand.

The Murphys waited to greet everyone on the deck, Gerald handing out his "juice of flowers" cocktails in vivid purples and pinks, Sara elegant in a simple silver gown and her pearls. "My dears! Welcome to our little dinner and flowers gala. I'm afraid I made a terrible error," Sara said, airily kissing their cheeks. "This is usually the only day the deputies don't use this barge as a restaurant, Sunday, so I could have it—but I forgot the flower markets are also closed Sundays! I had to rush to the Montparnasse market and improvise. Forgive the eccentricity. But go, dance, have fun! Don't feel you have to drink Gerald's concoctions, there's champagne at the bar."

Eliza kissed her in return, and took Jack's arm to carefully make their way along the narrow deck to the lower salon. As they stepped inside, she laughed. Rather than lilies and carnations, toys were heaped in pyramids and hillocks on the tables, dolls, trucks, tops, stuffed bears. They lined the buffet tables between the silver dishes and the zinc bar where champagne fountains flowed. Suspended from the ceiling was a laurel wreath spelling out *Les Noces—Homages*. Stravinsky himself, his spectacles gleaming, hurried between the tables studying the name cards, switching some around.

Jack handed her a bear, and a glass of champagne. "Here's to lots of firsts, bird girl."

"And to us! Oh, look, do you think that lady over there is the *Princesse*? She certainly has enough diamonds for such a grand title…"

They made their way up to the upper deck, open to the night air and the pink sunset light, pointing out everyone they knew to each other, speculating on all the graceful figures who could only be dancers. The portly Diaghilev with handsome men like Lifar around him, dark-haired Vera Nemchinova, said to be the most beautiful woman in the world.

"But you're much more beautiful," Jack whispered, making Eliza giggle.

Madame Goncharova reading palms again. Chloe waved her cigarette holder at them from the stern, surrounded by waiters eager to bring her more champagne.

As the sun set, and the champagne flowed on, Eliza was swept into the dance. She whirled through foxtrots and waltzes, even a blurry Charleston with Jack, their arms and legs moving together, spinning around each other. She had her palm read by Madame Goncharova…

"Danger, *ma petite*! I see much danger, but much fulfillment. And a voyage across the seas…"

The night was a wonderful, dizzy swirl, like nothing she could have imagined back in her parents' home. And when the hours wound down, everyone scattered when Monsieur Stravinsky himself took a flying leap across the chaos of the dining room and jumped through the wreath spelling out his name.

After the wreath came down, there didn't seem any reason to stay at the party. Yet Eliza was in no hurry to go home as she took Jack's arm and left the barge, waving to the sleepy Murphys. They crossed the river into the shadow of Nôtre-Dame, its lacy spire gleaming with the first rosy hints of dawn. She cradled her stuffed bear in one elbow, and sighed to remember everything that had happened that night. The party seemed like a lifetime's memories in one evening!

"I'll never forget this," she said softly, and she knew she wouldn't.

"Neither will I, bird girl." He took her into his arms and held her so close, so very close they couldn't possibly be parted, not yet. She wrapped her arm around his neck and closed her eyes, drawing the essence of him into her, the spirit of him and Paris and the party and everything good in life. She knew those scents, the rosy smell of Paris, would always make her think only of him.

His lips claimed hers, desperate, full of need, of everything they felt and yearned for in that moment, and she knew she didn't want anything else but him. The one thing that couldn't be hers forever.

Chapter Sixteen

On an ordinary day, if Mamie was with her maybe, or even her mother, Eliza would have loved the Ritz. She followed a red-jacketed maître d' through the lobby, past ladies in exquisite gowns and hats, flashing jewels and glowing pearls, past potted palms and velvet banquettes, maids hurrying by with elaborate bouquets destined for guest rooms, paintings and sculptures and rich, velvety carpets underfoot. It was every inch elegance and luxury, modernity, and it begged to be admired.

It was no ordinary day, though. She was there, on her mother's orders, to have tea with Mrs. Smythe. She couldn't imagine a scene more different from the Murphys' glorious party.

She was led to an inner garden courtyard, a serene oasis of elaborately trimmed topiaries in majolica pots, a fountain burbling softly at the center, surrounded by white-draped tables and green wicker chairs, where ladies in pastel chiffons and large organdy hats sipped tea and champagne. A harpist played behind the potted palms, and the air smelled of carnations.

Eliza glimpsed Mrs. Smythe at one of those tables, stern and solid in impeccable gray silk and pearls, so much like her mother. She self-consciously smoothed the embroidered cuffs of her cream linen coat, feeling like an unruly child all over again. Nothing like at the Club d'Or, where everything was easy and comfortable and full of laughter. Where Jack was with her.

"Elizabeth, my dear," Mrs. Smythe said, rising to kiss Eliza's cheek before a waiter held out a chair for Eliza. Mrs. Smythe smelled of rose powder and Guerlain perfume, just like Eliza's mother, and the feather from her hat drooped down and tickled. It was like being catapulted straight back to Fifth Avenue. "How thin you are looking! They must drive you terribly hard at that Conservatoire. I shall never understand why your parents allowed you to go there."

"I'm enjoying my classes very much," Eliza said. "My professor of composition says I should be able to perform in a student concert quite soon."

"Hmm, well. Indeed." She waved her hand to the waiter and ordered tea sandwiches, "no onions at all," strawberry cakes, and Darjeeling. "Now, my dear, I promised your dear mother I would help look after you while I am in Paris. To be a substitute mother, if you will."

Eliza much preferred Chloe's way of being a "new *maman*," who sent her birth control devices "just in case." She pressed her napkin to her lips to hold back a sigh. "That is very kind of you."

"Not at all! I would do anything for my friends. And quite frankly, my dear, I am rather worried about you."

"Worried? About me?"

"The Van Hoevens are one of the oldest, most respectable families in New York. Our two clans have been close for hundreds of years, I am sure! It is a rather small world, and if *I* had a daughter..." She sniffed, as if overcome by the thought. "It can be so perilously easy to make a misstep in a strange country. A young lady must always be mindful of the future." She paused as the waiter served the tiered tray of sandwiches and cakes, poured out the tea. "Do have an eclair, my dear. I know thin is chic now, but young men do prefer something different!"

Eliza thought of Chloe and Zelda, of the beautiful Tallulah, thin as willows in their stylish gowns. Their men didn't seem to mind. "Thank you, Mrs. Smythe. I assure you I am always thinking of the future. It's why I'm here, after all. For my studies."

Mrs. Smythe ate one of the salmon sandwiches before answering. "Music is all very well, of course. My mother was a constant supporter of the Academy of Music! Yet it cannot be the full work of a lady's life. She needs a home, a proper position, an establishment—the right husband."

Eliza knew all about the "right sort of husband" her mother wished for her—an old name, a good fortune, a brownstone mansion, a nursery. "I do see a French *duc* over there. Very proper husband material, maybe?"

Mrs. Smythe gasped in horror. "Oh, no! A title is all very well, but—you do remember, I'm sure, what happened to poor Anna Gould when she married a French title. Dreadful business! A Van Hoeven needs a good *American* husband."

"One day, yes." Though of course she did not. Eliza had long thought she didn't want any husband at all. Now there was Jack...

"None of us get any younger, my dear. And your mother tells me she is so concerned."

That was exactly what Eliza feared—her mother becoming alarmed, finding out all about her daring new Paris life. "Concerned?"

"Yes. Associating with that scandalous Comtesse on the ship! Visiting her home, too. She is not a proper friend for a Van Hoeven."

Eliza blinked hard, trying to conceal her dismay that gossip had already reached her mother, that people were chattering about her. How did they know she had gone to Chloe's salon? "Madame la Comtesse has a very popular salon. Many people attend, great artists and musicians! Poets and novelists..."

"Art is all very well, but only in its place. Your mother is worried that you are too young to be left on your own."

"I spend most of my time studying."

"Of course, my dear, but surely not all of it. Not that you need fear! I am here to help, at least until I travel on to Vienna soon." She glanced up, and a smile spread over her powdered face. "Ah, my dearest Henry! What a great surprise."

Eliza froze, a fight-or-flight sensation flooding through her. This was surely no "surprise"! She remembered Henry on the *Baltimore*, his aunt pushing them together, his grabbing, clammy hands as they danced, his arrogant assumption that she would welcome his "eligible" attentions. She twisted her fists into the napkin over her lap as Mrs. Smythe rose to embrace Henry.

"Miss Van Hoeven and I were just talking of the future, Henry," Mrs. Smythe said as she urged Henry to sit down next to Eliza, much too close. She could smell the cloying sweetness of his cologne, the hint of gin, see the oil on his blond hair, the fine linen of his suit. He smiled at her, confident and smug, sure she would be overjoyed at his presence beside her.

Mrs. Smythe poured him a cup of tea and went on talking. "I was going to tell dear Elizabeth all about your job at the law office, the finest firm in New York, of course, Elizabeth. It's just waiting for him after his graduation from Yale, they were so eager to employ him. How very splendid it would be, for Margaret and me, to see the two of you dancing together in New York. The world just as it should be."

"Quite right you are, auntie," Henry said, smiling at Eliza over the gold rim of his cup. His foot swept along her stockinged leg, making her jump, and he grinned when she slid away. "But surely we don't have to wait until New York! Come dancing with me at the Palm Court, Eliza. Next week, maybe?"

Mrs. Smythe beamed. "Such a splendid idea! I am sure it would quite put dear Margaret's worries at ease to know you were looked after, Elizabeth. Now, let me tell you about what I heard about the Van Allens' new house on Madison Avenue..."

At the end of the seemingly interminable tea, Mrs. Smythe insisted on Henry walking Eliza to the foyer and finding her a cab. That was the last thing Eliza wanted, but she wanted the afternoon to end as soon as possible, with no fuss, and so she went along with it. She half listened to Henry as he talked on about his studies, his new job, how he was climbing the ladder so quickly, blah blah. But near the doors, just as she saw escape so close, he took her hand tightly in his, so tight the bones in her wrist ached, and he leaned down to kiss her.

It was so sudden she couldn't back away before his lips slid over hers, damp and insistent, grinding against her teeth. It was as unlike Jack's wondrous kisses as anything she could imagine, and cold revulsion swept over her. She pushed him away and stepped back, touching her aching lips with her gloved hand.

Henry smiled smugly. "You see how well we go together, Elizabeth? Our families would love to see us together. I shall see you soon."

Without answering, without daring to let herself know how hideous such a life, such a future, would be, she spun around and rand outside. The doorman seemed to have seen what happened, for he smiled sympathetically. "A car, *mademoiselle*?"

Eliza found she didn't want to go back to her lodgings yet, to be alone and think and brood. "Non, merci." She walked as quickly as she could, past all the sparkling shop windows, the perfumiers and jewelers and chocolatiers, until she came to the river. She crossed to the middle of the Pont Neuf, the sun golden over the gray roofs, and leaned her elbows on the old stone balustrade to stare down at the rippling waters, the boats floating past, the couples strolling by arm in arm, ladies hurrying toward home with their shopping baskets.

Home. That was what Mrs. Smythe said about New York. One of the first families of Manhattan; where Eliza belonged. Yet Eliza knew as she stood there, watching the mellow glow of Paris spread out before her, standing in a spot where millions of people over hundreds of years came to watch that very river, that she had never belonged in her parents' house. Never belonged anywhere at all, until now, here in a city that seemed to wrap her tightly in its perfumed arms.

She had never belonged with *anyone*, until she met Jack. Until she looked into his eyes, and knew they truly saw each other's souls because they were the same.

But that was just a fairy tale, wasn't it? One day she would have to close this beautiful book and go "home," To find an *establishment* and a *position.* To marry someone like Henry Smythe, move into her own brownstone, sit on charity committees, plan dinner parties. Be proper.

She thought of the Murphys, beautiful, serene Sara, and Gerald, with his paintings and his "juice of a few flowers." They were wealthy, they were from old families, and they had made their own life here. They were the center of a sparkling world of art and friends and merriment. Surely she could find a way to do the same, somehow?

Eliza sighed. Yet how could she find her way, with her mother spying on her, Mrs. Smythe lurking around every corner? It was all infuriating beyond words. She had to learn to hide better.

The sun was sinking lower now, turning grayish amber, and she wiped at her eyes and turned toward her lodgings. She had to study, to be ready for composition class in the morning. She couldn't let Mrs. Smythe distract her.

The day's mail was waiting under her door, and on top was a scrawled note that instantly made the annoying day all bright and sparkling again.

Galliard loaned me a car for tomorrow, bird girl! I warn you, I'm a hinky driver, but can you have lunch in the country with me?

I heard about an old inn, great cheese and pâté, lots of sunshine. What is it that pretty Mrs. Murphy calls it? Dinner and Flowers Gala.

Pick you up at nine?
Jack.

Eliza couldn't help herself, she pressed the note to her lips and smiled.

Chapter Seventeen

"I love driving!" Eliza cried as the car, an old Peugeot, jounced over the country lanes. After the crowds of Paris were left behind, they found green hedgerows, towering horse chestnuts casting shade over the bumpy lanes, peeks of old villages, chimneys and church towers, over the meadows. It was sunny and blue sky, the air wonderfully clear and green-sharp. Best of all, she was alone with Jack.

Now, as she hung her head out the passenger window, the wind catching at her hair, the smell of the earth and the grass and the flowers all around her, New York and Henry Smythe and the dismal future seemed to just blow away. There was just France, and Jack, sitting so close to her their legs pressed together and it was wonderful.

He laughed, and shifted the gears with a grind. "It's not the Fitzgeralds' Rolls."

"It's better! It's all ours. For today, anyway." She sat back on the cracked leather seat and kicked off her shoes, tucking her stockinged feet under the hem of her white muslin dress. She'd tossed off her straw hat earlier, and it sat on the floor with its cherry-red ribbons fluttering in the wind. She felt so very light and free. "Tell me about the club. Have you been terribly busy?" She wouldn't ask if he'd been busy with his friend Tallulah. It was too glorious a day to ruin.

"Very. It's even better than I imagined it." He shifted again, and shot her a wide smile, brighter than the country sunshine. She was struck again by how very handsome he really was, his face all sharp planes and angles, his eyes glowing gold. "Galliard wants me to play some of my own compositions."

"Jack! That's wonderful. Of course, he'd be a fool not to. You're the best musician in all of Paris. *And* all of New York!"

He laughed. "Not Berlin or Madrid?"

"Those, too. Will you play your bird song?"

He glanced out the window, looking almost shy. "I have a new bit I've been working on, too."

"What's it like?"

"Not jazzy. More like a—a ballad. Something soft and sweet, warm. I call it…" He broke off, a faint pink blush touching his sharp cheekbones.

"What do you call it?" she asked, afraid it would be titled *Tallulah, the most beautiful woman ever.*

"I call it *Eliza.* But I haven't finished it yet."

She gasped. "You named it after me?" She didn't want to feel too hopeful, too delighted—yet she couldn't stop it. She couldn't stop the silly smile that took her over.

They passed through another village, a cluster of

pale yellow cottages with faded red tiled roofs around a square dominated by an ancient church, a large fountain, and found the inn they were looking for tucked along a side lane. It was two story old building, the same yellow stone, blue shutters thrown aside at the windows. White-covered tables were clustered under the towering, shady trees, and a large dog slept in the doorway, unmoving when they car screeched to a halt. An old man snoozed under the shade just like his dog.

The inn's luncheon was just as good as they were told. They sat at a small table under the shade of the trees in a back garden, watched by an old, dozing man under a grape arbor and served by a red-cheeked woman in a lavender-printed apron, who clucked at them to eat more and admonished her old father not to be so lazy, to stop snoozing and help in the kitchen. He didn't answer, but she kept bringing out plates of the delicious food, pate and fresh-baked baguette, *boeuf bourguignon* with rosemary potatoes, *salade landaise*, wonderfully gooey cheeses, and a lighter-than-air soufflé.

They laughed and talked as they ate, letting the warmth of the day soak into them, the scent of flowers all around, until at last Eliza couldn't help herself a moment longer. She leaned over and kissed Jack, letting the perfection of the moment linger.

"Ah, young love," the old man said with a cackle of laughter. "I don't mind if you kiss in the garden all day. If I was just thirty years younger! But we do have rooms to rent. Lovely feather beds."

Eliza dared not look directly at Jack as she drew away, for fear he would laugh at her bright red face.

Yet under her embarrassment, she felt a brilliant sun flare thrill. To see Jack—*really* see him, feel him, be his completely. For as long as she could have him, as long as she could cling onto these wonderful feelings. To have this time to hold onto for the rest of her years...

But what if *he* did not want *her*? What if everything they'd done together, felt, their laughter and delight and bone-deep understanding, was all on her part? Her own romantic naivety?

She peeked up at him, and suddenly she knew, she was *sure*, it was not all her. He felt for her, too, wanted her, even if perhaps he didn't love her as she did him. She could see it in the intense depths of his eyes, the sudden solemn stillness about him.

She impulsively wound her arms around his neck and felt him press against her, lean and strong and so, so wonderful. And she felt something else, too, hard through his trousers. *Oh, yes,* she thought with a delighted laugh. He did want her. And he was so beautiful, so wonderful. He was everything she could ever, ever want.

And it would be a shame to put Chloe's gift, tucked secretly into her handbag, to waste...

"A feather bed does sound like the bee's knees," she said.

"Eliza..." he said hoarsely, warningly. "You haven't... done this before? I know you haven't."

"Well—no," she said, flustered. She had begun to rather fancy herself a sophisticated Parisian lady, but she knew now she certainly was not. "I'm sure I won't be *that* bad at it, though. With a little practice."

"Oh, Eliza," he said, laughing helplessly, the sound flowing against her, through her, like a song. "No one in the history of the world has ever been as adorable as you."

"Adorable?" she said, putting on a little pout. "I'd rather be *glamorous*. Or a vamp!"

"But you just can't help it. You are adorable, no two ways about it." He bent his head and kissed the tip of her nose, her cheek, a soft, fleeting, teasing movement over her lips. "Your first time should be with someone you care about. Someone you—you…"

"Care about?" she cried. "Jack, you are the man who showed me how to really fly on music! How to see the world in new and beautiful ways. How to be true to myself. You—you…" *I love you*, she wanted to shout for all the world to hear. But mostly she just wanted *him*, all of him, desperately. Wildly. "Do you care about me?"

He smoothed his palm over her hair, so tender and gentle, his eyes gazing deeply into hers. "You are the sun and the stars and everything good and lovely and bright in all the world, Eliza Van Hoeven," he said roughly. "You're everything I never thought could be true."

Eliza feared she would burst into tears at those words. "Then let's rent that room. Please?"

In answer, he took her hand. That one gesture, their two hands meeting, clasping tight, the two of them together in the bright light of day for everyone to see—it was everything, she saw that now. It was love and freedom, and not being alone against the cold world anymore. It was all of that, and so much more.

The old man pointed them up the stairs at the back of the foyer to a chamber at the top, shadowy landing. It was a very small room, with a sloping ceiling and one window looking down to the garden, but it had the only important thing—a large bed spread with fluffy quilts. And the most handsome man in all the world with her.

Without a word, Jack took her in his arms and kissed her, and the sweetest music imaginable rang out in her mind, closing out everything else.

They fell back slowly to the mattress, the soft blankets and cool sheets billowing around them, enveloping them. He rolled onto his side next to her and reached out his palm to cradle her cheek. His long fingers loosened her hair from its pins, wrapping the curls around his wrist, binding them together. Slowly, ever so slowly, *too* slowly for her quickening blood, he cupped his fingers around the nape of her neck and drew her closer.

Her eyes closed tightly as he kissed her, his lips sliding softly over hers, and she tasted the honey-sweetness of their sunlit lunch. And beneath there was just Jack, and he tasted full of life itself.

Their tongues tangled, all artifice and hesitation and shyness melting away in sheer need and raw desire that washed away everything else. Who he was, who she was, their past and future—none of it mattered when he kissed her.

Through the shimmery, blurry haze of lust and tenderness, she felt his hands in her hair, combing free the last of the pins until it fell around them in a bright cloud. With a deep groan, his lips slid from hers and he buried his face in her hair, to the soft curve where her shoulder met her neck, nuzzling there. He drew her dress and chemise away from her, letting them drift to the floor.

"Eliza,'" he whispered against her bare skin. "You're so very beautiful."

"Not as beautiful as you," she whispered back. She reached out hungrily for him, pulling him on top of her so she could kiss him again, could press her starving lips to his cheek, his bare throat, to the smooth, dark skin revealed by his loosened shirt. He tasted of salt, sunshine, mint and wine. She held on to him so tightly, closing her eyes, to absorb all of him. His heartbeat, her breath, the vibrant strength of him.

He *was* beautiful, she thought, every part of him, body and soul. She needed him beyond all words, all rational thought.

"Eliza," he muttered. He quickly removed her dress, her camiknickers until she was trembling before him, completely bare. His lips trailed down her bare neck, the tip of his tongue swirling in the hollow at its base. He kissed the soft swell of her breast. She gasped at the warm waves of pleasure that followed his mouth, his touch.

She wove her fingers into his hair, holding him close.

"I just want to see all of you," he said.

She nodded mutely, arching her back. For a long, still moment, he stared at her avidly, and she couldn't breathe. Did she look…all right? Were her breasts too small, too large? Would he find her pretty?

"So beautiful," he said roughly, erasing all her doubts. "Eliza, you are perfect."

She laughed and drew him back down to her. His

lips closed over her tender nipple, drawing, licking, so shocking, until she moaned in sheer delight.

Her eyes closed and she pushed back his dressing gown until he was as bare as she was. She closed her arms around him, sliding her palms down the groove of his spine, feeling the taut muscles of his shoulders. But it wasn't nearly enough.

She wanted him in every way she had ever read about in forbidden books, or heard whispers of among married ladies. *Only* him.

"Please, Jack," she whispered. "Please, make love to me."

He raised himself to his elbows on either side of her. His eyes were burning with a desire to match hers. And she knew, in that moment, they belonged to one another.

"Yes,' he said. "Oh, Eliza. My darling." He pushed away his shirt and trousers to join her clothes, abandoned on the floor, and took her in his arms again.

At last, they lay together, she wearing only her white silk stockings. He knelt above her, tracing his fingertips over her knees, her thighs, to the bare skin just above. Lily thought she might snap from the ache, the tension. She felt so damp at her very core, so heavy with need.

Then, at last, at last, he touched her *there*. His fingers combed through the wet curls and then pressed forward to circle that one aching, throbbing point.

She cried out, shocked and delighted. So this was what those books were talking about! "Now, Jack, please!"

He lowered himself over her, bracing his palms to either side of her, holding her his willing captive. His lips caught hers in a passionate kiss, a kiss that blotted out everything else. There was no doubt or fear, just the knowledge that tonight they belonged only to each other.

She wrapped her legs around his lean hips, arching up into him, her naked skin sliding against his and making her sob with need.

His moans aroused her, his warm breath on her ear making her shiver.

"I'm so sorry,' he gasped. "I have to..."

She nodded and tilted back her head as she felt his manhood press against her, sliding slowly, so slowly, deep inside of her. She bit her lip against the sudden, stinging pain.

'I'm sorry,' he whispered again.

'No, no, I...' But already the sting was fading away. As they lay still together, that pain curled away, leaving only bright pleasure.

He pulled slowly back and drove forward again, a bit deeper still, and that pleasure burst free like a bright comet. Every thrust, every movement, every moan and sigh, drove that pleasure higher and higher. She was blinded by the burst of light.

He suddenly arched taut above her, shouting her name, and something in her mind exploded into blue, white and red flames that seemed to consume her from within.

Then all was darkness. When she opened her eyes, she found herself curled in the crumpled sheets, Aidan stretched beside her, his chest heaving for breath. His arm was heavy around her waist, holding her close. His eyes were closed, his hair tumbled over his brow.

"Jack..." she whispered.

"Shh…' he said, not opening his eyes. He just drew her even closer, until they were curled together. "Just sleep for a minute, bird girl."

Eliza closed her eyes and happily snuggled into the curves and angles of his body. She wished she could stay there, for ever and ever.

In the gleam of twilight, navy-blue and gold in the little room, Eliza came suddenly awake as she heard Jack shout. She rolled over, panicked, to see that he seemed to dream, his face creased in his sleep. She shook him gently, calling his name until his eyes flew open. For an instant, he seemed not to see where he was, remember her. Then he shook all over, and ran his hand over his eyes.

"I'm sorry, bird girl," he said roughly. "Sometimes I have these nightmares, you see, and they…"

She nodded. "Maybe it's the war?"

"Um-hm," was all he said.

"Was it—horribly, horribly bad for you?" she asked. She'd never felt such pain before, as if it came from him and soaked into her, into her very heart. She couldn't bear that he had been so hurt.

He was very quiet for a moment, his face turned from her on the pillow. "Yes. Not nearly as bad as for some. I came back whole. But sometimes now it just feels—unreal. Like a story, an anecdote to tell people about at parties."

"You don't have to tell me. I know. You disappear into it, like you're not even there for a moment sometimes. Like music. A pause, a stutter in the requiem."

"Music is better than anything else for making a person forget the ugliness of the world," Jack said. "Except for you. Nothing could ever make a man forget like you can, Eliza Van Hoeven."

"I feel just the same," she said, and snuggled close to him as the night fell outside their window. "Nothing can make everything better like you can."

Chapter Eighteen

The art show at the Salon des Indépendants at the Grand Palais was crowded as Eliza and Jack made their way through the rooms, up the grand, sweeping staircase where Gerald Murphy's giant *Boatdeck* was displayed. She liked the close-cropped view of the smokestacks, the rigging, the simple juxtaposition of red, black, beige, and white, as it reminded her of the time with Jack on the *Baltimore*. But she wasn't exactly certain what she should be seeing in the painting before them now, a scene of brown and yellow squares amid streaks of pink and blue. She sipped her champagne and tilted her head back and forth.

"So tell me, bird girl. What do you think this one means? What do you see in it?" Jack asked, tugging on her hand to show her another scene, a smaller canvas made up of interlocking squares of bright colors on a blue ground.

She tilted her head back, trying to see it differently. Just as the last few weeks had made her see life so very differently. "I like it, but I'm not sure why…"

Then she saw it. Just as when a piece of music clicked under her fingers, in her brain, and she *knew* it. Like when Jack kissed her, and everything went right side up. "It's a bird in flight!" she said happily.

"Singing its soul out," Jack said, his face glowing with awe as he looked at the image.

"It all feels so—so *now*," she said, spinning around to take it all in, the paintings and sculptures and people. "New, different. Nothing like my parents' world." Nothing like Mrs. Smythe and her "position." It was motion and color and raw feeling. It was flight. Music.

It was being with Jack. The sense that everything was made new and bright when they were together.

"Lizzie!" she heard a woman call, and Zelda Fitzgerald rushed toward her from the crowd, the silver lace of her skirt swirling, a cocktail in her hand. "There you are! Come see this painting over here, I just love it. If only I could paint this way…"

Laughing, Jack waved Eliza away, and went to look at Gerald Murphy's giant boat deck again. Eliza was caught in the whirl of Zelda's enthusiasm over the art, her chatter about what she herself would one day paint or write. Until she glimpsed a golden head through the crowd, heard a drunken laugh, and glimpsed Henry Smythe across the room. All the fun and newness of the night seemed to fade under the force of her old world, old expectations.

When Zelda went to fetch another cocktail, Eliza found Jack again. She took his arm, and didn't say a word, but he took one look at her and whispered, "Wanna get out of here?"

Eliza drew in a deep breath, feeling as if she'd landed in a safe harbor. "Yes, please."

"This is where you live?" Eliza said, taking in the small room of Jack's lodgings after they'd tiptoed, laughing, past the concierge's dark apartment. A bright blanket was spread on the bed, a stack of music and magazines on the desk, clothes piled on the one chair. It was tiny, but the window looked down onto the glowing city, a bird's aerie.

He tossed his coat across the rest of the clothes and smiled ruefully. "Not big, but…"

"Cozy. And look at that view!" She went to the window, gazing at Paris all around them, sparkling points of light in the night. The quiet was like a fur wrap, comforting and perfect after the noisy party.

Just like being with Jack always was. It felt so right. She heard his soft footsteps on the scuffed wooden floor, and his arms slid around her waist and drew her back against his warm, strong body.

Her eyes fluttered closed as she felt his hand slide over her stomach, the swish of her silk gown and his touch over her skin. His breath was hot and quick against her ear, and she thought she could feel his heart pounding through her, echoing her own. He held her so close, and they were all alone, the only two people in the world.

She'd never felt more wonderfully alive than she did in that moment. Everything sparkled like those lights outside, and it was a beautiful night.

The tip of his tongue lightly touched the nape of her

neck, just below the twist of her hair, and she shivered. His kiss slid ever so slowly to the curve of her shoulder just where it was bared by the beaded strap of her gown. He nudged it out of the way and it drifted down her arm.

"So beautiful," he whispered hoarsely, and in his words she *felt* beautiful, as she never had before.

She spun around in his embrace to wind her arms around his neck. He pulled her up against him, and their lips met in a hot rush of desire. She held onto him tightly, and felt his tongue trace the curve of her lower lip, lightly, teasing, before he pressed inside to taste her fully. She opened eagerly to meet him, any shyness, any doubt, vanished.

Through the blurry, hot haze of their kiss, she felt him lift her up. The room tilted and swayed as he spun around, and they landed on the bed. The quilts were soft under her, the small room enclosing them together in that warm, intimate space.

Jack pulled back from her, breaking their kiss, and she cried out with need. But he didn't leave her; he just rose above the bed to shed his jacket and tug his tie free before coming back into her waiting, eager arms.

Their mouths met again in a hungry kiss, full of that vital need built up for so long. That hunger for love and belonging, for each other. He tasted of champagne and mint, of that sweetness that was only his and which she loved so much, which she grew drunk on.

He slid her gown away from her skin, slowly easing it down as he kissed each inch he bared. His lips and tongue touched every curve as if she was some beautiful goddess, and even as she knew she was far from that she felt his emotions in every embrace. She cried out with pleasure, and reached to unfasten his shirt until he was bare against her. He slid slowly down the length of her body as she traced a light caress over his bare shoulders, his chest, the skin so warm and smooth over lean muscles. He was so beautiful—and he was hers, all hers, even if it was just for a night.

It was still dark outside the window of Jack's room, the night still wrapped safely around them, the lights of Paris sparkling like tiny direction markers leading her forward. Eliza laid back on the pillows of the rumpled bed, wearing only Jack's shirt as she listened to him play his horn. A sweet, sad line of melody that drifted into the night itself. She felt surrounded by the song, by the smell of him on the soft cotton fabric, the lingering glow of their lovemaking. It felt safe there, perfect.

"Should I bob my hair?" she said lazily, wrapping a long strand of wavy gold around her wrist as she thought of the stylish women at the art gallery.

Jack laughed as he lowered his horn. He sat back, the lights from the window gilding him in the night. "I don't want you to change a single thing, bird girl. Not your hair, not your sky eyes, not this freckle right here…" He leaned toward her and kissed her shoulder, making her sigh.

"You wouldn't wish I was more like your friend Tallulah?" Eliza whispered, thinking of that gloriously elegant woman.

He went very still, and leaned back in his chair again. "Black, you mean?"

Eliza sat up, wrapping her arms around herself. She'd known they would have to confront it sooner or later, that one ineffable truth in their dream world. "I suppose so. She is very beautiful, and she knows your world. Knows *you* in a way I can't."

"You know me better than anyone else ever has, Eliza. Our souls—they're the same thing."

She couldn't help but smile. "I know. I feel it, too. No one knows me as you do. Nobody else sees me with just one glance. But that means I want you to be happy."

He carefully laid his trumpet back in its case, and sat down beside her on the bed. She curled against him. "I can't deny it would be easier if you were from Harlem, or I was from Fifth Avenue. Of course it would be."

"Here we're just us."

"Eliza and Jack. Here we can hold hands walking by the river, ride a bus, dance in a club. Back where we're from…"

"I'm a Van Hoeven," she whispered, hearing it in her mother's voice.

He looked terribly solemn. "We can't quite get away from that, Eliza. Who we are."

"But I don't want that! I never, ever did," she cried, feeling desperate as if something infinitely precious was sliding away, slowly but inexorably, like a silk scarf through her hands. She reached for him, holding on. "Even when I was a little girl, I only wanted to be me. *Me* was never good enough, though. Never right. I couldn't belong. Only with you can I do that."

"And only with *you* can I be myself. Only you see

me, Eliza. You see everything. You *are* everything. But you're also a white girl from Fifth Avenue."

"Jack, that doesn't matter…" But even as she said it, she knew she was wrong.

"It does matter. No matter how much we want it to change. Back home, if we held hands on the street, you know what would happen."

She closed her eyes tightly. "I'm strong enough for anything, Jack, if I'm with you. I never thought I was strong before, I was weak, shy, quiet. Not now. Not with you."

He framed her face gently between his hands, gazing deep into her eyes. "You have never been weak. My sunshine, my bird girl. You're the strongest person I know. The kindest, the most honest. But it doesn't change everything else. You think I would let you be cast out, laughed at, or worse? I thought I was in love with a white girl once, a nurse in the war. Emily. But she couldn't take what that meant, she left, and she was right to do that. Even though I was angry and hurt then, I see she was right now."

He had loved someone else once, someone like her. But she knew it couldn't be the same, couldn't end the same. Eliza felt cold numbness rise up in her throat, choking her, tearing at the beauty of what she and Jack had. She wouldn't let it, though. That ugliness couldn't, wouldn't, destroy something lovelier than she had ever dreamed.

And she would give anything at all to take that haunted look from Jack's beautiful eyes.

"Just kiss me, Jack," she whispered. "Kiss me right now…"

He took her into his arms again, holding her against him, and for those moments their kiss held everything else at bay. How long could it hold out, though? How long could she push it back?

Jack held Eliza close as she slept, her golden hair on his shoulder, her peaceful face dappled with moonlight from the window, a small smile on her face as if she had sweet dreams. That was all he ever wanted for her— sweetness and peace. It was what she deserved, what he feared he could never give her. This moment was the most perfect he'd ever known, but he knew it couldn't last. He had to do what was right for her, sooner or later.

He took a deep breath and cradled her even closer. He knew so well that not being with her any more would be the most painful thing he ever knew. She was like the sunshine, bright and life-giving and joyful. And he loved her—he could admit that to himself now. Loved her so much, far too much to make her life difficult or dangerous in any way.

He ached inside as he held her, memorizing everything about that moment to cling to later. The scent of her perfume, the feeling of her soft skin under his touch, the little sounds she made in her sleep. It was perfect. Like the most wonderful piece of music ever heard.

"I'm sorry, bird girl," he whispered. He never should have let himself live in such a dream world, thinking somehow he could be with her. Surely he'd learned better in his life. People like them couldn't belong together.

But, just for that one flashing instant in the Parisian night, she was his—and he was hers forever.

Chapter Nineteen

"*Monsieur*, I must speak to you," the concierge called as Jack started to dash up the stairs to his rooms, his horn case under his arm. He was late for rehearsal, and he wanted everything to be extra-perfect for that night's performance, since Eliza promised to be at the club. He couldn't remember when he'd felt so full of fizzing excitement. Every day seemed full of light and warmth now! Every precious day he had left with Eliza, no matter what might happen after. But that stern voice was not to be ignored.

He paused with his foot on the lowest step, and turned to give her what he hoped was a charming smile. *"Bonjour, madame."*

"Humph," she exhaled, her round, lined face creased with that perpetual irritation she seemed to have. "Now, *monsieur*, there are a few house rules here. Not many, but we must have standards."

"I quite agree, *madame*." Jack ran quickly through everything he might have done wrong. Music too loud?

Left hair in the basin when he shaved? He couldn't afford to get kicked out now, the Club d'Or was busier every night and there was no time to find new digs.

"Your lady friend," she said with a sniff. "Your— your *chère amie*..."

"Oh." Jack's heart seemed to sink under cold waves, his earlier exuberance fading. No one should ever talk about Eliza like that.

She gave an elaborate shrug. "I am not like some people. I don't care what sort of girl she is, what color she might be, only that she does not live here. One person to a room, *monsieur*!"

"I do know that, *madame*. She has her own apartment."

"Then who is it that arrived today with *suitcases*!" she said, her voice rising in indignation.

Jack was baffled. He certainly wasn't expecting anyone. "Suitcases, *madame*?"

"Many cases! And a guitar—thing. I would not have let him upstairs, but he knew your name. I couldn't let him stay down here cluttering up the space, you musicians keep such odd hours who knows when you would be back."

Jack was even more confused. "He, *madame*?" he asked, feeling a bit like a parrot repeating the same few words over and over and understanding nothing.

She scowled at him. "Tall, like you, *monsieur*. And a coat with a fur collar! It is much too warm for such a thing. You Americans dress so foolishly."

"Whoever it is, *madame*, I'll make sure he doesn't stay long," Jack assured her, as he ran through all his friends in his mind to see who might have come there. It was true that musicians often fell on hard times unexpectedly, but who would move in with him? He wasn't that close to anyone in Paris yet.

"He can't live here!" she shouted behind him as he dashed up the stairs.

He threw open his door, and found his small room really was piled high with "many cases," battered old suitcases, a cracked leather valise, a musical case leaning in the corner.

And casually sorting through Jack's pile of sheet music was his cousin Leo, flopped down across the bed, his "foolish" fur-collared coat draped on the brass bed knob.

"Jack! My cat," he said happily, pushing himself lazily to his feet to unfold his full tall, lanky height. "You're looking like the berries, man."

For an instant, Jack just saw his beloved cousin, his old friend, again. The boy he pulled pranks with on their apartment building roof; the young man who improvised songs with him until the neighbors pounded irately on the thin walls; the one who gave him that silver flask. But then he remembered what came after— the mobsters, the police, the danger. His mother had written that Leo had lost his latest job and vanished, much to his father's despair. Trouble always followed Leo everywhere now.

"Leo," he said, closing the door firmly behind him, hoping the concierge hadn't followed to eavesdrop. He put down his horn case. "What are you doing in Paris?

Ma said you'd gone off somewhere, but no one would have thought it was here."

"Uh—yeah. I lost that last job, at the Plantation Club. No one can forget what happened at the Versailles Club." He sat down on the bed again, smiling sheepishly. "New York got too hot for me. I had to find somewhere to sit tight for a while. Paris is a long way from Harlem."

"And those brunos you were such buddies with have long arms."

Leo glanced away. "I'm just small stuff to them! What's a few dollars to people like that? I was good at the jobs they gave me, I deserved more."

Jack ran his hand over his face. "They broke knee-caps for a 'few dollars'! They just lynch men like us and forget about us. You could get deported from here just like a snap, you know." And get Jack deported, too. All his hard work for nothing at all.

"They'll forget all about me, out of sight out of mind," Leo insisted. "It's just—well, there was this girl."

Jack shook his head, and sat down hard on his one chair. Of course there was a girl—a dangerous one, no doubt, probably even a mobster's girlfriend, knowing Leo. Leo never went for anyone suitable. "A bruno's doll? Or maybe a politician's daughter?"

Leo frowned. "Not like that, man. She's a real lady. Elegant. A—well, a lady."

A lady like Eliza? "Leo…"

"I met her at the Versailles. Remember?"

"How could I forget?" Jack muttered. He helped Leo get that job at the Versailles, and it all went nertz in the end. It usually did for Leo, but this time it ended up in the newspapers.

Jack certainly couldn't fault him for falling for a lady. He'd done just the same, and what he had with Eliza was certainly dangerous enough. Yet with Leo there was always something extra perilous in everything he did. "A married lady?"

"No! But a really good family. There was a raid, and she got caught with me."

Jack nodded shortly, remembering the scandalized headlines, screaming across the city in bold black ink. "So her family is after you now?"

Leo wouldn't look at Jack, just dragged his toe over the worn planks of the floor, staring down. "A guy I worked for once, just running some numbers. I had to find a way to see her again, so I might have just—borrowed a little from him."

"Borrowed?" Jack said tightly.

"I thought I'd find some work here. Pay it all back before he notices. Start fresh, yeah? Like you did."

Jack pushed himself to his feet and poured out a measure of gin from the bottle on the rickety kitchen table. He thought about the old days with Leo, about their family ties. How could he turn him out, even with this dangerous situation Leo had gotten into again?

But with Leo there, that old life crowding in again on the Paris idyll he'd made, Jack could feel the danger all around, closing in tight. Closing in on Eliza. He couldn't let it touch her, not a shining hair on her beautiful head.

Yet he couldn't just turn his back on his family.

"I'll help you," he said shortly. "Just this once. We'll

get you out of here, maybe to London. In the meantime you can play a bit at the Club d'Or."

He handed Leo a drink, and a relieved smile spread over his cousin's lean face. "You won't be sorry, Jack. I swear it this time. It's going to be different now."

Jack was already plenty sorry. "We'll see."

Leo gulped down his drink. "I was reading this book…"

Despite everything, Jack couldn't help but laugh. "You? A book?"

"You might be the smart one of the Colemans, but I'm figuring out how not to be a Dumb Dora of a guy. By Booker T. Washington. You know of him?"

"Sure."

"He says we do best when we just keep the white folks out of our lives. Let 'em be—we don't need their help." He drank the last of his gin and held his glass out for a refill. "Wish I knew that back when I met *her*."

Jack nodded. He had heard people saying such things all around him, ever since he was a kid, and he'd reckoned they were probably right. White people just seemed to mess everything up, whether they were actively harming or trying to help. Keeping to himself had seemed the way to go. Yet now he wanted so much more—wanted to live where he chose, love who he wanted. Love Eliza.

Heaven help him, but he couldn't deny that any more. He'd loved her from that moment he saw her walking toward him at the Stork Club, all the light in the world gathered only on her. Her radiance, her beauty and goodness and rare talent.

"Every race has good and bad people," Jack said. "We're *all* just people. I learned that here in Paris."

Leo looked at Jack like he'd suddenly gone insane. "Guess you'd better stay here in Paris, then. There's no 'just people' in New York."

Before Jack could answer, he heard the light patter of shoes on the stairs and landing outside his door, too light to be the concierge. A quick knock sounded at the door, and it opened to reveal Eliza. She wore a pale blue muslin day dress and white straw cloche hat, a bunch of pink flowers in her arms that matched the glow in her cheeks, all bright and light and summery.

"Oh, Jack," she cried, and tossed the flowers onto the table to run forward and throw her arms around his neck. "You'll never guess the amazing thing that happened at the Conservatoire today…"

Jack stiffened, and she stepped back, a puzzled crease flashing between her eyes. Then she saw Leo.

"You…" she whispered. "You were the one with Mamie at the Versailles Club!"

Chapter Twenty

Earlier that day

Eliza slowly raised her fingers from the keys as the dying notes of the Schubert faded in the dusty air of the classroom. The piece had bedeviled her for too long, the notes too quick, too tangled, too intense and then soft. Hopefully now she had managed to capture its essence, after she remembered Jack's advice that music was just a flow, a feeling. She'd gotten underneath it and let it help her soar, let her deepest feelings come out in the cadenzas.

"Brava, mademoiselle," Monsieur de Haviland said, with a single clap of his hands. A clap from him was like a standing ovation from anyone else, she had found, and she smiled in relief and tucked a vagrant blond curl back into its pins. "You have come a very long way in your technique. Your interpretation was always superb."

"Thank you, *monsieur.*"

"Now, I have a bit of news," he said. "The Société des

Concerts is having a student showcase in a few weeks, and we need a bit of Schubert on the program. I would like you to play this piece for the performance. And Monsieur Faure himself would like to meet you! It is a very great honor for such a new student."

Eliza was so overcome with joy she could barely speak. She'd been invited to play with the Société des Concerts performance! And to meet Monsieur Faure. She couldn't *wait* to tell Jack all about it. Somehow, things never seemed real any more until she shared it with him.

When she floated out of the school, she stopped at a boulangerie for a baguette, a wine shop for some of that lovely Pinot Gris, and impulsively bought some flowers at the fragrant florist shop on the corner. Jack would be practicing at his lodgings before he went to rehearsal at the club, and she could put together a little picnic for them to celebrate. Then afterwards, if there was time, maybe even a tiny bit of hanky-panky...

Eliza laughed aloud as she dashed up the stairs to Jack's landing. *What a hoyden you've become, Elizabeth Van Hoeven*, she thought gleefully, but really no one had ever told her how much *fun* hoydenism was before. No wonder her mother tried so hard to hide all the books like *The Sheikh*.

Not that it was like that with Jack. It was much nicer, more delightful, lighter, natural—fun. She was determined to hold onto it with all her might as long as she could.

His door was ajar, and she knocked and pushed it open, dropping her flowers and market bag on the little table. How domestic she felt! All cozy and home-like, dreamy and wonderful.

"Oh, Jack!" she said, and ran over to hug him. "You'll never guess…"

But rather than hug her back, lift her off her feet twirl her around as he did sometimes, kiss her until she was dizzy, she felt his shoulders stiffen under her touch. His silence felt like a wall, not the comforting place it usually was. She stepped back and studied his face carefully. He was expressionless.

A flutter of movement, a blue shirt, came from the corner of the room, and she glanced over there, distracted. A man was standing there, very tall and thin, his long oval face handsome. He looked familiar somehow. She frowned as she tried to remember…

Old newspaper headlines flashed through her mine, Mamie's face in grainy black and white as she was hauled out of a club in a raid.

"You were the one with Mamie at the Versailles Club!" she gasped. She felt so bewildered at her old life suddenly coming into the new. It all hardly seemed real anymore.

The man looked shocked. "You know Mamie?"

"She's my cousin."

"How—how is she?" he said, almost shyly. "It's been so long. I never meant for…"

"She got into a lot of trouble after that," Eliza said sternly, propping her hands on her hips like her old nanny when she was cross. "And then you never wrote to her! She was very unhappy about that."

"How could I? After what happened?" he said. "But I thought about her a lot…"

Eliza glanced between him and Jack's tense face, and she saw traces of resemblance there, the same eyes, the same cheekbones. "Who are you, anyway? How are you here in Paris with Jack?"

"Eliza," Jack said cautiously. "This is *my* cousin, Leo. It seems New York got a little hot for him, so he's come here for a little while. Leo, this is Eliza Van Hoeven."

Leo's eyes widened. "Miss Van Hoeven, is it? Well, I see you brought some wine with you. Let's all have a glass and have a little chat about all this business…"

"I still don't understand how he's here, your cousin," Eliza said, as Jack walked her back toward her apartment along their favorite riverside path. The afternoon was growing late, the air warm and still as they walked by sunbathers, couples whispering, children playing with their hoops and marbles, the light shimmering on the windows and rooftops. "He's the one who gave you that silver flask? The one you said was always in trouble now."

Jack shoved his fists deep into his jacket pockets, looking straight ahead. "That's Leo. It seems he, er, borrowed some money from a dangerous person. Without asking."

Eliza stopped to stare down at the water, the way the sunlight caught on the waves stirred up as a barge glided past. "No wonder he didn't write to Mamie. She tries to act all careless, but I do think she felt sad about it all. That Versailles Club mess."

Jack kicked at a loose cobblestone. "You know how it is, Eliza. Back home. It's not like here in Paris. That stuff means real trouble there."

Eliza nodded slowly, feeling that new distance between them, that chilly atmosphere. Jack would hardly look at her. "I know it does."

"Your cousin is better off without Leo, anyway. My ma says he's trailed trouble behind him since he could walk."

"And he came here to get away from trouble?"

Jack frowned. "So he says. Make a new start, find some new cats to run with. I'm not really sure."

"But you're sure you'll help him if you can." Because that was the kind of man Jack was, kind and generous. Even when it wasn't easy.

He sighed, staring across the river at a church just there, the sun bouncing off its stained glass, casting the walkway in blue and red. "Yeah. Again. As if it's gonna be *different* this time."

"Maybe it will! Mamie used to be a complete rebel—now it's only maybe one-third." She could sense how much Jack cared about his cousin, and she longed to reach out to him, to make it all better somehow. Yet something about him, about the tension in that moment, held her back. She wrapped her arms around herself to guard against the cold distance.

"I would settle for half trouble with Leo," he said, trying to smile. "But what were you going to tell me back there, when you first came in?"

"Oh!" How could she have forgotten something so momentous? It had seemed so urgent to share it with him then. Now she wondered if it could matter. "I was asked to perform in a student concert, with the Société des Concerts. Schubert. Already! I haven't been there long at all."

He smiled again, this time for real, the radiant white grin she loved so much. "Get out of here! That's wonderful, bird girl. They'd be stupid not to have you perform all the time."

"Do you think so? I'm terribly excited, but worried, too. What if I sit down on that stage, and all the notes just fly right out of my head? Maybe..." she hesitated. "Well, maybe we could practice together before then? You could listen to the piece, give me some advice?"

He went very quiet again, staring at that church. "You don't need my advice, Eliza. And it's going to be pretty busy at the club for a while."

"Of course," she said quietly, and turned to walk on. "Shall I come by the club one night this week? You said there's that new song you've been working on."

"Sure, if a future concert pianist can stand our jazz squawking," he said with a laugh.

Eliza laughed, too, and put up her nose like her mother would. "Well, it's not *Mozart*, but I find it bearable sometimes."

"Glad you can bear us. But really, Eliza—I know you'll have a lot of work to do with the other students, even though you'll be miles above all of them."

Eliza thought of the people she'd met in her classes, stupendous musicians with so much knowledge of the classical repertoire, but she had never learned more about music from anyone than she had from Jack. She certainly valued no one's opinion more. But she still felt that new distance between them, and she didn't want to push.

"Not so much as all that," she murmured, and they walked on in silence as the city swirled around them.

Chapter Twenty-One

Two weeks later

Jack didn't have a good feeling about this at all.

He glanced up from the sheets of music he was going over with some of the other musicians, waiting for the club to open, to see the door open and a group of three men stroll in. They were dressed in long coats and hats pulled low, and tried to seem casual, just looking around, but their eyes darted too quickly from one area of the room to the other, their hands shoved too deep in their pockets. Jack automatically stood up straighter, his senses on alert as they had been so often at the Stork Club.

The men waved away Madame Galliard, and made a beeline to Leo at the bar. Even across the room, Jack could see his cousin's face turn ashen. It looked like trouble had reached out for them already even across the Atlantic, or maybe Leo already found time to get into a whole new Parisian stew. Either way, it didn't look good.

He carefully put down the music and his horn, and made his way across the club. The others on the dais also watched, eyes narrowed.

"…by the end of the day tomorrow," one of the men was saying in English. "Our boss doesn't like people who don't deal with him honestly, or who run away. You see what I mean?"

"I have to make the money before I can pay it back, don't I?" Leo said. He tried to sound casual, laughing, but Jack could hear the tension beneath. That debt, then, and obviously to someone who didn't let stuff like that slide.

"Is there some difficulty here, messieurs?" Jack said in French, watching them carefully but keeping a cool head. A man had to stay watchful with people like that.

The men turned to him, and he saw the gleaming butts of pistols tucked into their belts beneath the coats. From the corner of his eye, he glimpsed Monsieur Galliard coming behind the bar and reaching for the old army gun he kept there. Time seemed to slow down, grow fuzzy and cold at the edges.

"None of your business, boy," one of the men said with a dismissive sneer. "Just trying to collect a little debt."

Jack studied Leo. Leo had said when he showed up in Paris he had to stay low for a while; so this must have been what he meant. Trouble followed men like Leo, men like them, everywhere. "I don't think this is the place for that."

"This is where the debt is, aint' it?"

The door to the club opened and a few early customers came in, bringing laughter and daylight. They would be open properly soon, crowds pouring in, and they couldn't see this. Some of the waiters moved closer, and Jack held out his hand to keep them back. He'd had lots of practice in the New York clubs on how to keep things cool; the Galliards couldn't have a fight in their place. He'd lost the knack for defusing hot heads in Paris, gotten too peaceful, but the instinct came back.

"You're in France now, gentlemen, and the people here do not take kindly to that way of doing things," Jack said. "There are plenty of folks in this club won't let you interrupt their business. And business is always foremost for all of us, isn't it?"

The men suddenly seemed to notice where they really were, that no New York cops were there to ignore uproars, and they studied the room with a flicker of nervousness behind their cold eyes. Leo stepped back.

"I'm sure that if this man owes a debt, that can be taken care of in the right way, the right time," Jack said in his hardest, calmest voice. "This is not that place. You have the chance now to leave."

For one long, tense, sizzling moment, Jack didn't know how it would all end. Flying fists, gunfire, the ruin of everything. But finally, one of the men nodded, and they turned toward the door. "This isn't over," he hissed at Leo. Then they were gone, the only sound in the club the usual clatter of opening.

"What was that all about?" Jack muttered to Leo, reaching out to grad his cousin's arm before he could flee.

"I—well, I made a bet back in New York. You know,

I told you," Leo stammered. "That's why I had to come here. That, and the dame at the Versailles Club. I guess those guys came to collect. How could I know they would come all the way to Paris, man?"

Jack sucked in an impatient breath, and spun away from Leo before he could punch the fool. "We'll talk about this later. Get ready to play for now." Leo nodded tersely, his face tense and filled with fear. Jack couldn't stop himself from saying, "You don't have to do that anymore, Leo. You can make a new start, like I have."

"That's easy for you, Jackie. You have a rare talent," Leo said sadly. "You're special, always have been. Me, now—I gotta make a life somehow." He ran off toward the dais.

Monsieur Galliard, his usually affable face solemn and hard, put his gun back behind the bar. "Jacques. Who were those men?"

"Just someone my cousin had some business with," Jack said.

Monsieur Galliard shook his head. "I can't have 'business' like that in here. The club, our reputation…"

"I understand. It won't happen again." And it wouldn't. It couldn't. Jack had come so far, worked so hard to build this new start. Was it going to crumble now, brought down by the past? He'd known he would have to leave Eliza, for her own sake, her own future, but he had hoped it wouldn't be so soon. Now it had come, and he had to be strong. Had to do what he'd known would be right.

As he made his way back toward the band, he saw Eliza standing near the door. From her wide eyes, her pale face, he knew she had seen at least some of what happened. Suspected trouble. He wanted more than he'd ever wanted anything to go to her. Hold her, tell her she was safe. But she turned away, and he knew he had to focus, had to keep her out of danger. Being in Paris had made him soft. All the parties and museums, the walks hand in hand along the river, they'd made him forget how the world really worked. Leo and his thugs made him remember all too well.

He had to remember that real world now. Being with him, near him, would put her in danger, and he wouldn't ever let that happen. He'd resolved on that before, that he would let her go when the time came. And it was sweeping down on him now.

Chapter Twenty-Two

Eliza stared at the book open in front of her, but she couldn't focus on her studies. The words just blurred in front of her eyes, and she saw the Club d'Or again, those strange men, Jack's blank look as he watched her. How could she prepare for her concert when she didn't know what had happened? She'd conquered her own doubts in life, her own need to be on her own, to think being with *him* mattered. Now she didn't know at all.

Had she really been a fool all those weeks, drifting around in a shimmering sort of dreamworld with Jack? It all felt so real—their picnics, the parties, the dances and music, the country inn where they were truly together at last. She knew Paris was different from New York, that her freedom here was so new and fragile, and her trust in herself delicate. Yet Jack made her feel so strong, so happy, so *right*.

She'd dared to hope she did something of the same for him. She could never erase his past, ease what he'd been through, what he still faced. But she hoped to just be by his side, to see him, *really* see him, as he'd always seen her. She'd been sure his heart was like hers; that their souls were made up of the same music.

She—well, she loved him. That was all. She loved him, more than she'd ever imagined she could love anything, more than any heroine in a book ever loved her hero. She wanted his life, his whole world, to be only a happy place where his sublime music could take flight.

She'd dared to dream, as they played music together, walked the city, went to parties, talked and laughed and kissed, that she could be a part of that happiness. Her new friends made her see how life could really be. Now she saw, like a sudden freezing wind cutting through a summer's day, that maybe she stood in the way of his happiness after all. That she held him back from everything he could achieve.

Eliza rubbed hard at her eyes, her head aching from the sleepless nights without Jack, the tears she couldn't always contain.

She got up from her desk, the piles of books and musical manuscripts she couldn't even see, and went to the window. She swung the panes open and sat on the edge of the sill, staring out at the city around her, the rooftops and chimneys, the ribbon of the river in the distance. Its beauty soothed her, even reassured her. *This* was the world she knew now, the place where she and Jack were together. Still fragile, still unsure, but it gave her more than she'd ever imagined before.

Jack was more than she could have imagined. Handsome, kind, strong, filled with the most sublime music.

A knock sounded at her door, startling her so much

she nearly tumbled off the sill to the floor. Maybe it was Jack? Her heart pounded at the thought.

"*Une moment*," she called, and brushed off her blue pleated skirt, smoothed her hair. She hurried to the door, trying to tidy a bit as she went, straightening pillows, sweeping some papers into desk drawers, nudging her shoes under a table. Restoring order to the mess was hopeless, though, and she sighed to think of her always immaculate room at home, with its tulle-draped dressing table and brocade bedspread.

She couldn't hold back her delighted smile, her anticipation at seeing Jack again at last. But it was not him who stood outside her door. It was her mother.

Eliza gasped before she could stop it, her heart sinking down as if she'd been suddenly tossed into a freezing pool. For an instant, she wondered if staring out at the sunny day had blinded her, made her hallucinate. She blinked hard—and saw her mother still stood there.

Margaret Van Hoeven hadn't changed a bit, still slim and stylish in a dark blue suit and tilted, feather-edged hat, a small net veil floating above her icy blue eyes. She smiled, a small stretch of her pink-painted lips. "Elizabeth, darling. Has France quite erased all your manners? Aren't you going to invite me in, or shall I hover on this landing?"

Eliza swallowed past her dry throat, struggling to find her voice. "Mother. Yes, of course, come in. But what are you—? I didn't expect…" She glanced toward a pile of neglected mail on top of her desk, half hidden by a Debussy score, and wondered frantically if she had missed a letter that would have warned her.

As Margaret swept into the apartment, taking off her embroidered kid gloves, Eliza saw that her mother wasn't alone. Mamie was coming up the stairs, a flash of bright yellow chiffon and bouncing, bobbed curls.

"*I'm so sorry*," Mamie whispered as she hugged Eliza. Eliza squeezed her back, thinking of how Leo was in town, too, and they couldn't meet at all.

"I am sorry, darling, for my own sad lapse in manners," Margaret said as she studied the clutter of the room, her lips pursed. She glimpsed the small, stuffed bear from the Murphy's bateau party, and picked it up with a frown. "There simply wasn't time to write, we had to catch the next sailing of the *Normandie* so quickly."

Eliza wondered if her mother had ever heard of a telegram. She remembered that her "gift" from Chloe, of the precious device, was hidden in her bedside table, and her mother had penetrating vision. She carefully shut the bedroom door.

Mamie squeezed her arm and gave a reassuring smile. She looked rather pale and drawn, her eyes wary, and Eliza could only imagine how her cousin must be feeling after an Atlantic crossing with Margaret Van Hoeven.

"Your brother wanted to come…" Mamie began.

Margaret waved her hand, her sapphire and pearl rings catching the light. "He has so much to do with his studies, so I asked Mamie to come instead. Getting away from New York will do her some good, I'm sure, and give her poor father a rest."

Mamie grimaced.

"You're both so welcome, of course, and I'm dying to hear all the news from home," Eliza said. "But—why…"

Margaret sat down on the desk chair. "I received a letter. No, more than *one* letter, from Mrs. Smythe."

Eliza groaned inwardly. She should have guessed she hadn't heard the last of that busybody! "Oh, yes? I did see her on the *Baltimore* coming over, and then for tea at the Ritz."

Margaret frowned. "She said you and her nephew Henry—such a promising young man—got along so very well on the voyage."

Eliza shivered to remember Henry Smythe grabbing at her. "I wouldn't quite say that."

"She was sure she would see you again here in Paris, after your delightful tea. That you would let Henry escort you to the ballet, perhaps."

"I've been too busy with my studies to socialize very much, Mother." And she would rather stick a pin under her fingernail than sit at the ballet with Henry.

Margaret glanced up at her, her eyes narrowed. "Yes? Well, Mrs. Smythe also told me you have been seen around town in jazz clubs. And at a wild party on a barge, with people who call themselves artists and merely splash a bit of paint on a canvas before going about getting drunk."

Eliza bit back a smile as she remembered that glorious party. "It was a soiree given by the Murphys, Mother. You know them. She was a Wieborg, and his family owns Mark Cross."

Margaret sniffed. "Their families were once very fine, that is true, but now they live here all the time, associating with such scandalous people. And they are friends with those Fitzgeralds! They were drunken vandals when they lived in New York, you know, tossed out of every hotel in town. Van Hoevens must maintain standards."

"I think that party sounds like the bee's knees," Mamie piped up from where she lounged on the settee. "I wish I had been there."

Margaret gave her a cold glance. "Elizabeth is not you, Mamie."

Wasn't that the truth? Eliza thought wryly. Mamie had always been braver than her, bolder, uncaring of what anyone thought, while Eliza had always been shy, cautious. Only here, in Paris, with Jack, had she found her own boldness.

Now she felt it leaking away, like a sad helium balloon after the bright circus was over.

"Is that why you've come, Mother?" she asked. "To lecture me on the proper Van Hoeven manners again?"

Margaret turned her icy glare onto Eliza. "Really, Elizabeth. I hope I never *lecture*, merely instill the correct values for your position in life. And I have come here to make sure everything is going as it should, that Mrs. Smythe was quite mistaken. We were not at all sure you should study here in the first place. If there is gossip, then surely the experiment was a failure and you must be where we can watch you carefully again."

Eliza felt a surge of raw desperation, terror that she would be yanked away from Paris so very soon. "Oh, no, Mother! My studies are going so well. I've been asked to perform with the Société des Concerts, and I met Monsieur Faure himself. He said he had such fine reports of my talents."

Margaret tapped her buffed fingernails on the edge of the desk. "Your music has always been exceptional, I admit. Yet I am very concerned about all the other things a mother of a daughter must naturally worry about. Your future…"

"The Conservatoire seems to think my future could be secure at the piano."

Margaret's eyes widened. "A musical career, on the stage, for a Van Hoeven? Oh, my dear Elizabeth. Paris has turned your head, most unfortunate. Music is a most worthwhile pastime, and has gained you much admiration. Yet you know it cannot be a woman's life, not a woman in your position. Only a suitable marriage can do that."

Eliza glanced frantically at Mamie, who gave her a sympathetic grimace. Eliza could feel the box closing in around her, catching her up again. "Mother, please. Let me tell you how I feel, what I've been doing, studying, here in Paris."

"How you *feel*?" Margaret said with a little laugh. "Elizabeth, it hardly matters how you feel, this is simply how it is. How the world must be."

And yet Eliza had seen that the world didn't have to be like that at all. It could be free and light, as she had found beside Jack, among their new friends. There were people who found their true fulfillment, who worked to achieve it, and she wanted to be one of them. "Have you come to take me back to New York, then?" she said tightly. She would soon come into her inheritance from her grandmother, which would pay for her studies if she needed it; she could work hard to make a career in the future. But not yet.

"Not at present. I shall see for myself how you are living here, and decide what changes should be made." She looked around the untidy apartment, and shook her head. "You should hire a maid, for a start."

"I like being alone here, Mother."

Margaret sighed. "Exactly so. Your standards are slipping, my dear, but I am here to help now." She rose to her feet and reached for her gloves and handbag. "Now, I must go, I am staying at the Ritz. You will join me there for dinner, yes?"

Eliza had planned to toast a cheese sandwich and keep studying, but she knew that implacable expression of her mother's too well. "Of course."

"Very good. We can talk further about all of this then. And I have arranged for Henry Smythe to take you to the *dansant* at the palm court tomorrow. You will enjoy that, I'm sure. I am not against all fun."

Eliza felt that cold dread seize hold again. "Mother! I can't do that. He..." But how could she tell her mother what had happened on the ship? Her revulsion toward that "promising young man"? Her mother would never believe her.

"His aunt was most kind in helping to arrange all this. Henry is a very suitable escort for you, and he admires you a great deal." She gently touched Eliza's cheek. "Remember what I said, darling—you must consider your future. I insist upon it." She kissed her lightly on the cheek and wafted off in a cloud of violet scent. "Until dinner, then! Mamie, are you coming?"

"I'll just stay here for a while, Aunt Margaret, and catch up with Liz," Mamie said, stretching lazily on the settee.

Margaret shook her head. "Oh, very well, but do not stay too long. Elizabeth must rest. She is looking rather pale."

At last her mother was gone, the door clicking shut tightly behind her, and Eliza was alone with her cousin—and all her whirlwind thoughts of confusion, shock, and anger.

"Whew," Mamie cried, collapsing back onto the cushions again. Even after a long voyage with Margaret, she looked beautiful and modern in her yellow dress, her tousled short hair. "I thought I would never be free of her. It was the longest ocean crossing of my life, Liz, I swear."

"I perfectly understand," Eliza said. She sat down next to Mamie and leaned on her cousin's lace-draped shoulder. "I am glad to see you, though, even though Mother is part of the package."

"I'm very glad to see you, too. And I'm sorry I couldn't stop her from coming here. I'm sure your parents are terrified you're going to turn into me, racing around all alone here!"

"I doubt anyone could ever stop my mother once she makes a plan. I can only hope she'll decide everything is perfectly proper and go home soon." Eliza sighed as she tried to think about how to persuade her mother she was living like an absolute nun in Paris, especially if she caught a whiff of rumor about Jack, about all her new friends and their independent ways.

Mamie dug around in her beaded handbag and lit a cigarette. "So, tell me, Liz, what are you *really* up to here in Paris? Not actually being perfectly proper, I hope."

Eliza laughed, thinking of all she'd seen and done. The party on the barge, the art shows, the nightclubs—the wonderful country inn with its beautiful feather beds. "Well, I really do study a great deal. I have to do well at the Conservatoire if I want to have my own future, and the classes there are heavenly. Composition, history, even maybe conducting, if I do practice enough."

Mamie leaned her head back on the settee cushions and grinned. "So you just study night and day, huh?"

Eliza kicked her feet up, trying to cover up her hot blush. "Er—not exactly, no."

"I knew it! Tell me all. Have you met someone? A *real* someone, not that callow lizard Henry Smythe."

Eliza thought about her feelings for Jack, the wonderful joy, the dark doubts, the beautiful moments she'd found in his arms. "Well—yes. I rather have. He's a musician, the best one I've ever heard. You wouldn't believe his arpeggios…"

Mamie sat up straight, her eyes wide with interest. "Who cares about his—his musical whatsit? Is he handsome?"

Eliza sighed. "Terribly. Like a film star."

"Where does he work?"

"A club in Montmartre. The Club d'Or, you'd love it there. He might be the manager soon."

"He sounds dreamy."

That was rather what Eliza started to fear—that Jack was just a dream, and all too soon he would slip away into the light. "There is more, I'm afraid, Mamie," she whispered.

"Oh, yes?"

"He's—well, he's from Harlem, you see."

Mamie's jaw dropped. "He's black, you mean? Oh, Liz."

She nodded. "He was here in France during the war, and always wanted to come back. I can see why, they adore him here. They really appreciate his art."

Mamie lit another cigarette, her hand trembling. "You know I'm the very last person to ever judge someone's romantic choices, darling, and I do know it's different here than at home, but—are you really, really sure? Are you prepared for…?" She waved her hand in an arc of silvery smoke. "For everything, if this becomes serious?"

"I thought I was. I am! I only want to be with him." She was quiet for a long moment, a feeling of disquiet creeping over her. "You won't tell my mother, will you?"

"Certainly not! I'm no snitch. But what if she finds out anyway? What will you do then?"

"I—I don't know. At all. It's all been so wonderful here, so lovely and perfect, I didn't think about that sort of thing at all."

Mamie nodded solemnly. "Just don't get caught like I did."

Eliza bit her lip. "That's another thing, Mamie…"

"Another thing? This isn't enough? Did you set fire to the Louvre or something?"

Eliza laughed. "Not yet, but the *Mona Lisa* was a little disappointing. But, well, I met Leo. Your Leo. Here in Paris."

Mamie's powdered face went even whiter. "Leo?" she murmured.

"He's Jack's cousin. He came here to get away from some kind of trouble in New York, I think." And it looked like *trouble* had instead come to him. To all of them.

Mamie slumped back on the settee, the cigarette forgotten between her fingers. "Oh, Liz. What a sad pair we are. What are we going to do?

Eliza leaned her head on Mamie's shoulder again and closed her eyes. "I only wish I knew."

Eliza followed the waiter across the lobby of the Hotel Majestic, toward the bright, glass-domed Palm Court. She nervously straightened her gloves, glad that at least the place was light and crowded—no chance of Henry Smythe's wandering hands again.

She wondered again exactly why she was there, why she agreed to meet with a toad like Henry. Somehow, when faced with her mother and no warning at all, she went right back to being the Elizabeth she was in her parents' house, quiet, shy, obedient because that just made things so much easier. The Eliza she'd become in Paris, the giddy, sunlit beginnings of the true self she wanted to be, with Jack, just flew away.

She sighed, and glanced at herself in one of the tall, gilt-framed mirrors. She looked like a ghost in her pale green and cream lace frock, the wide-brimmed green hat on her upswept hair. She had to find that real Eliza again, and hold on to her ever so tightly. Once she got rid of Henry Smythe.

"This way, *mademoiselle*," the waiter said, and led her down the short flight of marble steps into the Palm Court. It was quite lovely, the music from a string quartet delightful, the dancers' chic dresses and feathered hats enviable. She would have reveled in it all, if Jack was the one waiting for her. Jack who would sweep her into a swirling, dipping tango.

Alas, Jack was far away, and Henry waited for her at their table near one of the marble, ivy-twined pillars. He rose as she approached, and she could see why her mother liked him; why any lady of New York Society who only saw the facade would like him. His tall figure was set off well by a perfectly tailored pale gray suit, his blond hair gleaming.

Her mother's world, the world she wanted Eliza to stay locked inside of, was all façade. Nothing was real, nothing true, nothing deeply felt. Jack had shown her the hollowness of all that, shown her another, better way to live.

"Elizabeth," Henry said, swaying a bit as he reached for her hand. She noticed two champagne bottles on the table, along with the tea service. He kissed her fingers before she could snatch them back, and she was enveloped in the sickly-sweet scent of wine and bayberry hair oil. Thankfully, she wore her gloves. "How pretty you look! My aunt and your mother are absolutely right."

Eliza sat down on the edge of the cushioned wrought iron chair, and the waiter unfolded an embossed linen napkin across her lap. "Right about what, Mr. Smythe?"

"Call me Henry! We're good friends now, aren't we?"

He winked at her as he took the bottle of champagne from a silver bucket. "And a great deal more soon, I'm sure."

How very confident he was, she realized, despite the utter disaster of their past meetings. Not confident like Jack was, not just quietly sure of what he was, what he should be doing, but confident that he could have whatever he wanted by snapping his fingers. Probably because it had always been that way for men like Henry Smythe.

"Friends?" she said, watching as he poured her a glass of the champagne. She usually loved those golden bubbles, they were like sunshine, but today she just longed for the pot of Earl Grey. A bit of the liquid slopped down the side of the glass.

"Certainly! Our meeting on the ship, it must have been fate. And then here in Paris." He leaned closer, and she saw that his gray eyes were bloodshot. "You must see, as I do, as everyone does, how well-suited we are, Elizabeth. How connecting our two families would be so useful to everyone."

Eliza's hand froze as she reached for her teacup. "Useful?"

"Yes, it's obvious. I have a good position lined up at the law firm, a house my parents have promised me on Madison Avenue. Maybe I will go into politics one day! Who knows how high I could go? And I need the right kind of wife to help me, one to run the house and organize social connections."

She took a slow sip of the tea. "And who might this "right wife" be?"

He sat back, a smug smile on his face. "Why, you,

of course. You're perfect! Pretty, fine manners, a Van Hoeven. You could play the piano for our guests, show them how cultured our families are. And, as my aunt says, a little Parisian polish for a lady is always a good thing. Your mother tells us you don't have to finish the full Conservatoire course, which is good." He laughed, a sound that reminded her of a braying mule. "Such a thing as *too much* polish, right?"

The cup clattered in her saucer. "I am not finishing the course?"

His smile thinned. "Mrs. Van Hoeven said you're coming back to New York at Christmas. Very wise. A lady should marry before twenty-four, I think, and after Christmas there would enough time to plan for a summer Newport wedding."

"My mother was mistaken." Eliza carefully folded her napkin and placed it beside her cup. "I have no intention of marrying any time soon." Especially not to someone like Henry Smythe. "And I am definitely finishing my studies. I will be too busy as a concert pianist to entertain anyone's political friends. Now do excuse me, I have an important appointment."

Henry frowned, his smugness vanishing in a most satisfying manner. "What do you mean? This is insane!"

On the contrary, she finally felt fully sane indeed. She rose to her feet, gathering up her handbag. He shot up, as well, reaching across the table to grab her wrist in a hard grip. The people at nearby tables stared at them, startled. "This is not at all what your mother told us," he muttered through gritted teeth.

"I am not my mother. You should have asked *me*

what my plans are." She twisted her arm and snatched back her wrist, stepping back out of his reach. She felt something moving through her she never had before—strength, her own strength. The strength Jack had told her she held all along.

She turned and hurried out of the hotel, Henry spluttering behind her until she stepped outside and was alone on the Paris street. She walked blindly toward the river, toward her safe spot by the water, and smiled as she saw those glorious buildings, gleaming with their overflowing flowerboxes, the crowded cafés, the artists with their easels, the booksellers. It was all so wonderful, so glorious. It was like home.

She laughed, and realized that soon enough she would have her inheritance from her grandmother, she would have her Conservatoire education, she could find ways to stand on her two feet, make her own future. And it was Jack, her wonderful, sweet Jack, who had shown her the way. Now she just had to reach for it.

Chapter Twenty-Three

This had to be the place.

Mamie Van Hoeven glanced from the scribbled address in her hand to the building across the cobbled street. It was closed so early in the day, the shutters drawn over the windows, the sidewalk bare, but the dark red and gold awnings were there, the painted sign swaying in the breeze declaring this the Club d'Or.

She looked back over her shoulder, uncharacteristically uncertain. Leo was working there, Eliza had heard. *Leo*—in Paris. She'd thought she had forgotten all that, left it behind, and now just hearing his name had brought it all back. The giddiness, the fun, the dark sadness. The trouble after they were caught.

Mamie frowned as she watched the sunshine gleam on the upstairs windows. She'd certainly never been one to run from trouble. Too much the opposite. But Leo was trouble like she'd never known.

She had to go inside that club, though. Eliza's Jack was there, and needed to talk to him without Eliza knowing. Eliza was all the things Mamie was not—

serious, talented at her music, kind, unselfish. She had a bright future ahead of her, a successful career, even, if she wanted it. Something no Van Hoeven lady ever had before. She couldn't throw it all away on men who were no good for her, as Mamie did.

The thought of her sweet cousin stiffened Mamie's resolve. She stuffed the address back into her handbag, straightened her Lelong hat, and marched into the club.

It wasn't open so early in the day, but the door was unlocked. The interior was dim, cool, the touches of gold and red velvet glinting in the shadows. She could hear the echo of music, snatches of a dance song, and it led her toward the stage where the musicians rehearsed.

Several men in their white, ghost-like shirtsleeves, a lady in a blue day dress at the piano, a portly, mustachioed Frenchman polishing glasses at the bar. And, at the edge of the stage half behind a bass, just as she'd feared, was Leo.

And he was every bit as handsome as he'd been in New York, tall and lanky, amber eyes in a long oval face, laughing as he played, his head tilted to one side.

She tore her gaze from him and scanned the others, wondering which was Eliza's Jack. The trumpet, Eliza had said, and she saw just the one he had to be. He looked like someone Eliza would like, definitely. And her cousin had excellent taste, Mamie had to admit, because he was utterly gorgeous. The smile he flashed at one of the other men was wide and gleaming white, a beam of sunlight breaking through a gray day. And he looked sweet, just like Eliza. Gentle, despite the breadth of his shoulders, the length of his stretched-out legs.

Mamie frowned. It didn't matter how handsome, sweet, talented he was, he couldn't be any good for Eliza. A white lady married to a black man...how could she get ahead in her career anywhere outside Paris? How could Eliza bear a break with her family? She wasn't a rebel like Mamie.

"*Mademoiselle*, may I be of assistance?" the portly man asked. "I am Monsieur Galliard, owner of the Club d'Or."

"*Bonjour, monsieur.* I'm Mamie Van Hoeven, Eliza Van Hoeven is my cousin."

He beamed, and came from behind the bar to shake her hand. "Ah, yes, Mademoiselle Elizabeth! She plays the piano most exquisitely. She graced us with a song here once or twice."

"She did say your club is wonderful. I see she was right." She glanced around, at the dance floor, the tables, the array of glittering bottles behind the bar. "I'd like to speak to Monsieur Coleman, if he has a moment."

"Of course. Jacques! A lady to see you," Monsieur Galliard called, bringing attention to her just as Mamie hadn't wanted. She'd wanted to slip in, discreetly speak to Jack, and sneak out again.

But now she had Leo's attention, too. His expression was shocked, frozen, as he stared down at her.

"Mamie," he said slowly, in that rough voice that once so excited her.

"Leo," she answered flatly, not daring to look at him. But then she *did* peek, and saw a long cut on his cheekbone, a blackened eye, and she gasped. "What happened to you?"

He gave her a wry, crooked grin, that smile that had drawn her too close before. Burned her. "A little disagreement, that's all, darlin'."

"You seem to have those a lot," she said, remembering the rough characters he'd hung around with in New York.

"Not anymore. I'm turning over a new leaf."

"Hmm. Me, too." Only she found that she, like Leo, wasn't really one to make new leaves stick. Not when the old ones were so much fun.

"You wanted to see me, *mademoiselle*?" Jack said, coming down off the stage, and Mamie turned to him gratefully. His horn hung loosely from his hand, and his face was polite, faintly curious as he looked at her.

"Yes, if you have a moment. I'm Mamie, Eliza's cousin." She held out her hand to him, deeply sorry she had to be harsh with such a lovely man.

He put down his horn and shook it, his grip warm, slightly rough. "And you want to talk to me about her? I have a break from rehearsal due, should we go someplace quiet?"

Yes, indeed, somewhere far away from Leo. "That would be splendid, thank you."

Jack led Eliza's cousin across the empty club to a banquette at the back, sharply aware of Leo watching them at every step. He wondered what had brought her there, what she wanted from them. She didn't beat around the bush.

"Jack. What do you really want from Eliza? She's so sweet, so protected from life. She couldn't bear up under

some cat taking what he wants and then just leaving."
Mamie crossed her arms over her waist. "She's not me."

Jack was shocked. "I would never do that. I'm Eliza's
friend." *Friend*, what a weak word for the multitude of
things he felt for her. "She's an incredible musician and
a good person."

"Mmm-hmm. She certainly is that." Mamie took
a cigarette from her handbag. "I've met men like you
before. Like your cousin. Eliza isn't for you. She never
will be. If you're her friend, you should stay away from
her." She gave him a pitying look over the glowing end
of her cigarette. "It's hard, I really know that, but it's
for the best. For everyone."

Jack rubbed his hand over his eyes. He'd never imagined someone like Eliza could walk into his life, that
what happened between them could ever occur at all.
Sir Galahad indeed—selfishly taking up with a well-
bred white lady. Just because she made him feel so alive,
so glorious, so—perfect. Because she was like molten
gold magic. He knew now his next step would have to
be a very, very careful one. He had to make sure Eliza
was safe from men like the ones who'd come looking
for Leo. Safe from all the trouble he could bring her.
He'd known that all along; Mamie Van Hoeven didn't
tell him anything he didn't believe. And she was right.
The time had come to end things.

He probably never should have dared to spend time
with her in this beautiful bubble of Paris. He'd fallen
for her so hard. He'd forgotten his family, his ambitions,
the real world. How could she ever really understand
those things? How could he understand her?

Yet every moment he was with her, he *did* understand her, deep down, without even a word. And when she looked at him with her wide, blue-sky eyes, he was sure she saw him, too. Knew him. It was always shockingly easy to be with her, after a lifetime spent on his guard.

But he knew, stronger than he'd ever known anything, that he did love her far too much to ever let her get hurt. He had to protect her, but from afar. He should have had more self-control all along.

"You're right, Miss Mamie," he said, and his chest ached as if precious bonds with Eliza were snapping. As if nothing would ever be the same again. "I'll send her a note asking to see her, and then I'll break things off."

She gave him a sympathetic nod. "It's not an easy world we live in, is it, Mr. Coleman?"

"No, indeed. Truer words were never spoken."

Chapter Twenty-Four

Eliza glanced in the mirror above her bookshelf and smoothed her hair. She didn't know why she was so nervous about seeing Jack. Usually knowing she would soon be with him filled her with joy! Yet there was something about that note.

She picked it up and read it again.

Hope to see you...there's so much to talk about...

It didn't quite sound like her Jack, and she frowned as she wondered what he meant. What they needed to talk about.

A soft knock sounded at the door, and she hurried to open it. She smiled at him, but he didn't smile back.

"C-come in," she said, feeling suddenly cold, as if an icy room blew through her warm sitting room. She told herself she was being silly, seeing trouble where surely there was none, but deep down there was the discomfiting feeling all was not right. That the distance she'd sensed lately between them was about to grow wider, deeper.

His expression didn't make her feel better, it was so wary, closed.

"Sit down, Jack, please," she said, waving toward the settee. "Should I make some tea? Or champagne? Or we could go to the café…" She was suddenly quite desperate to get out from those closing-in walls.

But Jack sat down on the straight-backed chair by the table. "No, Eliza, please. It won't take long. You must be busy, with your family in Paris and everything."

Eliza carefully perched on the edge of the settee. She thought of how little she'd really had to see her mother, after she had walked out on Henry Smythe, had refused to go shopping all day with Margaret, refused to discuss going home to New York. "Not really. I'm just getting ready for the concert. How is your cousin after—after what happened at the club. Those men."

"Galliard found him a job in Marseilles. Just for a while, until things cool down and he can decide what to do next. I don't think seeing Mamie again helped his state of mind."

Eliza fidgeted remembering how he'd said Mamie came to see him at the Club d'Or. "I suppose not. That thing at the Versailles Club, it did cause a lot of arguments with Mamie's father."

"I can imagine," he said quietly.

She suddenly realized perhaps that was the trouble— Jack saw the trouble that happened when people like them mixed. Yet she and Jack, they weren't like Mamie, surely. It wasn't just parties, rebellions, it was real and true and deep. "Jack, I think—that is..." She broke off, unsure of how to put her swirling thoughts and fears into words. She wished she could play it in music, and from the look on Jack's face she imagined he wished that, too. "Are you having regrets about what has happened between us? At that country inn?

Jack grimaced, and shook his head. "I should, but I can't regret it. It was the best thing that ever happened to me, Eliza, it really was. But..." He broke off, spreading his hands apart as it to let that memory go.

She shivered all over again. "But what? Oh, Jack. Just tell me."

A heavy silence fell in the room, as suffocating as a mink cloak on a hot day. "It was wonderful. You know, though, that I'm no good for a lady like you. You have a great future ahead of you, your cousin was absolutely right about that. You're beautiful, talented, you deserve so much more."

So that was it. Eliza folded her hands tightly in her lap to keep from reaching out to him, bit her lip to stop its trembling. She felt like she was caught in a sticky, horrible web she couldn't escape. "Jack. How can you do this to me, now? How can you be someone else who tells me what I need to do for my own good?"

He was expressionless, as if carved from stone. "I have to do what's right. I won't hurt you any more. I won't get in the way of your career, your family."

She laughed hoarsely. "What's right? I *chose* to make love with you, chose my own course for the first time in my life. And now you want to take those choices away? Just like my parents."

Jack was quiet, and when Eliza glanced at him she

saw he stared at the floor. He was so far away from her already, like a stranger, not the wonderful man she had come to love.

"I did think for a while we could remake the world just for us," he said softly, kindly, and somehow that was worse than any shouting could be. "But the world won't change for us. After what happened at the club, what happened between Leo and Mamie, I see that clearly now."

"I wanted to make *our* world, for the two of us," she said, and she suddenly realized how very true that was. The outside world was a long way from catching up to them, but she could be strong, could be true to her feelings, if only she could be with Jack. He was the only thing that mattered; what they had together, their soul-meeting rightness, was all that mattered. "I'm stronger than I seem, *you* showed me that. I wanted—wanted…" She broke off, choked by tears caught in her throat.

"I wanted so much, too. I can't be selfish, though. Eliza, I care about you too much. I want you to be happy."

She couldn't bear it anymore. She jumped up and hurried to the window, turning her back to him. The scene outside was blurry with the tears she refused to let fall. "Well, I am not your problem now, am I? You want me out of your way, so I will be. You don't have to think about me any longer."

She heard him move, felt the warmth of him come near. It made her heart twist, made her want to scream with the pain. And when his fingertips lightly brushed her arm…

She tore away, her skin on fire, and raised her hand to warn him away.

"I'm sorry, Eliza," he said gently, so horribly gentle. "So sorry. I never meant for things to go this way."

He stepped away, and there was only that coldness in the air again. She waited until the door clicked shut behind him before she let her weak knees buckle and she fell to the floor. She buried her face in her hands and let out the sob that choked her. She'd never felt so very alone in her life.

Chapter Twenty-Five

"Are you going to read *all* day?" Mamie said. She lounged on Eliza's settee, flipping through a stack of fashion magazines while Eliza pretended to study.

She just wanted to be alone, as she had in the days that slowly ticked past since Jack left. She'd tried to go to her classes, play the piano, avoid her mother, avoiding thinking or feeling at all. She managed it most of the time during the day, pouring out her pushed-down emotions and anger on the piano keys, nodding through the dinners with her mother she couldn't manage to avoid.

"Probably," she said, turning a page.

Mamie tossed down the magazine. "Oh, Liz. Are you still angry with me for going to talk to Jack?"

Eliza frowned as she remembered when Mamie confessed that she had gone to Jack, told him he should leave her alone for her "own good," just like everyone else. She *had* been angry then, furious, but now she just felt numb. "No. I know you meant well, darling, that you were trying to help me."

"I was! I don't want you to go through what I did."

Eliza sighed. She looked at her table, where a vase of roses from Henry Smythe rested. They never gave up. "That's the trouble. You, Jack, Mother—you all think you know what's best for me. No one ever asks me what I think."

Mamie went very quiet. Eliza glanced at her, and saw something like shock written on her cousin's beautiful face. "I—I didn't want you to go through what I did with Leo. You're too *good* for that, you deserve…"

Mamie did sound like Jack. "What do I deserve?"

"All beautiful things. That's all."

"I thought I had that." With Jack. Despite all her intentions of forgetting, when the darkness and silence of night came, she sat awake and remembered everything she and Jack did together like a series of photographs. Dancing at the club, laughing at the Murphys' party, picnics by the Seine, lying entwined in bed as they whispered of hopes and dreams. She'd never felt as she did with him, as if she was just where she should be.

Now those memories were fading, burned at the edges, and she had to find a way to make a new start. Alone.

"I am sorry, Liz. Really I am. But surely you see that such a match could never work. You and Jack—you're too different, too…"

"I know it would have been hard. I can't deny that." But this, this being without him, was so much harder than facing a disapproving world together would have been. If only she could have made Jack believe that.

"Well—what are you doing tonight?" Mamie said, determined to be cheerful.

"Mother wants me to have dinner with her at the

hotel, but I told her I have to study. She just talks on and on about Henry Smythe, about the duties that wait for me at home." That life that had always been laid out for her waited like a net, a trap.

"That won't do. We should go out! I won't be here in Paris much longer. We could dance, have some champagne."

"Not to the Club d'Or!" Eliza said. Once, that place had felt like home, especially when Jack took her to the roof and showed her Paris laid out before them, waiting for them. Now she felt cast out. Cold.

"Of course not! There's lots of other clubs. Or we could just sit at a café, watch all the lovely poets walk past."

Eliza smiled as she remembered those evenings dancing with the Fitzgeralds, laughing at poets and painters swinging from the chandeliers of the Murphys' bateau party. It *had* been glorious. "I guess I am a little tired of looking at these walls."

"Sure you are. We're in Paris! We should enjoy it while we can."

Eliza nodded. Her mother had been urging her to return to New York, too. How could she, though? Despite her heart lying around in broken little pieces, Paris had become a sort of home. A place to hide, but also to be herself. "Okay," she said, and snapped the book closed. "Maybe Chez Betsy's? Just for a few songs."

Mamie clapped her hands. "You won't be sorry, Liz! It will be so much fun."

And yet somehow they ended up at the Club d'Or after all, pulled there by the Fitzgeralds when they

saw them at Chez Betsy's. Eliza sighed as she glanced
around, seeing how it all looked just the same, cozy and
filled with fizzy fun, the dance floor crowded as Mamie
vanished into a Charleston. There were no strange men
threatening anyone, no Leo, not even a Jack on the dais.

But one person who *was* there was Henry Smythe,
shouting loudly at the bar as Monsieur Galliard ignored
his demands for another drink. Hemingway, sitting further down with a notebook open in front of him, gave
Henry a disgusted look.

Henry's eyes widened when he saw her, and he took
a staggering step toward her. She managed to dodge into
the crowd, avoiding him and the menace of his grabby
hands—and the reach of her family and past, the different future she'd glimpsed all too briefly with Jack. She
made her roundabout way to the bar, and sat down next
to Hem. She knew Henry wouldn't dare mess with *him*.

"Daughter!" he shouted. "Haven't seen you in a
while. Busy with your piano?"

"Too busy." Clearly not busy enough, though, when
Jack still haunted all her thoughts. "What are you drinking? That looks yummy."

"A daiquiri. You should try one. *Monsieur!*" he
called. "A drink for the lady *ici! Ici.*"

Eliza sipped at the sweet drink, and talked with
Hem about things like the idea of true freedom, finding the real soul under a world that moved too fast,
and other things she couldn't quite follow, but which
took her mind off romance for a while. Finally, feeling
a bit giddy on the daiquiris, she agreed to dance with
a young Frenchman and swept out onto the floor in a

quick two-step that led into a foxtrot with someone else. She whirled through the cloud of perfume and cigarette smoke and music, laughing helplessly.

Until she found herself pulled into Henry's arms, and held so tightly, so close to his damp body, she couldn't get free. "Let me go…" she gasped, sure she would suffocate. The crowd pressed tight around them, and Henry laughed.

"Come along now, Elizabeth, you've played hard to get long enough," he said, his lips trailing over her cheek as he stumbled into her. "I don't need games like that!"

He leaned down to kiss her lips, and she gagged, panic sweeping over her. She tried to twist away, but she was trapped, unable even to scream…

Jack couldn't let Eliza look so scared, not even for a second. He'd come from the back room to find the club crowded, noisy—and Eliza caught in that drunkard's arms just like on the ship, her face defiant but vulnerable. She tried to twist away, but the pig held her too tight.

He put down his horn and wound into the crowd to grab her hand, spin her away from the man's tight grasp. "I think this is my dance," he said.

Eliza stared up at him, wide-eyed, and said, "Yes. Right. Always."

"Hey!" the man shouted. Up close, he was even more unpleasant than on the *Baltimore*, red-faced, sweaty. But he was also tall and broad-shouldered, some Yaley who boxed, probably. And drunk as a skunk. "That's my girl!"

"Doesn't look like she agrees," Jack said, trying to get Eliza away through the crowd.

"She certainly does *not* agree," Eliza said stoutly. Despite what had happened between them, their break-up, the hurt and the lies, she pressed close to Jack. And it felt so right, so just the way things should be. They spun away in a dance that was more running than real dancing.

But Henry wouldn't let them get away so easily. His face was purple now with rage, and he roughly grabbed at Eliza. She screamed and kicked out at him, missing and tripping, falling into another couple. They in turn fell into someone else, and soon there was a melee on the dance floor. Monsieur Galliard shouted for calm.

Jack tugged at Eliza's arm, dragging her out of the roiling crowd, the fists and kicks. She reached for him with her other hand, and he glanced down at her pale face, her wide, frightened eyes.

"You floozy! Hanging around with men like him…" That drunkard—Henry—grabbed for Eliza, and she screamed. Jack saw a metallic flash and glimpsed a knife in the man's fist. Aimed right at him.

"No!" Eliza cried, and tried to push Jack away. He shoved her behind him and faced Henry square-on, his instincts raised, a fighting urge burning inside of him like he hadn't known since the War. He was enraged by this man's treatment of Eliza, raging for a battle.

Jack hit the man, feeling a hot, red tide of fury rising up inside of him. Henry reeled around, the drink catching at his balance, but then he spun back towards Jack, and there was a flash of something silver, the agonizing pierce of pain in his side. Henry shouted, the sound dim and faraway, and Jack saw him dragged away by his equally drunk friends as he tumbled to the floor.

"He—he stabbed me," he whispered, startled. The pain grew and grew, like a wave, before it broke over him.

"Jack," Eliza sobbed, falling to her knees beside him. The chaos and din of the club faded, and he saw only her. Her sky eyes, bright with tears, the golden hair falling to her shoulders in a tangle. "Help! Help us!" she cried, and cradled his face gently in her beautiful hands. "Hold on, my darling, we'll get you out of here."

The room turned dark at the edges, and Jack found that death wasn't quite what he'd expected. It was chilly, serene, slow. He reached up carefully, painfully, and traced his fingertips over her cheek, feeling her tears against his skin. His angel. That's what she'd always been, what she'd always be. "I'm sorry," he whispered. "I love you, Eliza, I always have. I shouldn't have left you. I love you…"

And then it all went dark.

Chapter Twenty-Six

He was back on the battlefield, choking on smoke and the coppery tang of blood as he huddled down in a trench, hearing the shriek of shells bursting overhead, screams and shouts. The fear, the cold still center of it all, the chaos—he couldn't breathe, couldn't scream, couldn't do anything.

Then he smelled it—flowers on a clear, springtime breeze, washing away the old memories and fears. It was so sweet, and it had nothing to do with mud and smoke and blood. It was all goodness, and cleanness and joy. It was Eliza, washing away the past.

It was just a dream.

He forced his gritty eyes open, half afraid *she* was the dream, and he would find himself catapulted back onto a muddy battlefield. And, for an instant, he was sure she was. Sunlight from tall windows pierced his aching head, and he blinked hard to see that she sat nearby, that light turning her hair to liquid gold. Her dress was blue, sky blue, and she held a magazine in her hands, frowning slightly as she turned the pages. She was surrounded by white, so much sparkling, blinding white from tiled walls and sheer curtains.

Was he dead? He remembered in a lightning flash what happened. The man harassing Eliza, the knife, the burning flash of pain, the darkness. Was he really dead now, paying for his mistake? His mistake in leaving her—or for being with her. He'd tried to let her go, to do what was best for her, but he found he couldn't in the end. The cords that bound them together, and had ever since he first saw her in that snow-dusted tree, were too tight and wouldn't let him go.

He knew then that life was so short, love too precious, and he couldn't deny it. There was nothing in the world more precious than her.

"Eliza," he tried to whisper, yet nothing came out from his dry throat. She seemed so very far away. *Eliza.* He closed his eyes, gathered all his strength— and vowed never to let her go again.

Eliza knelt by Jack's bed, staring at him, willing him with all her power to open his eyes and look at her. She didn't know if it was still night, or if the daylight had broken outside, didn't know anything but the feeling of his hand in hers. She was surrounded by the cold white of the hospital, by antiseptic smells and chilly air. The doctors said they would just have to wait, to be patient, to see, but she couldn't bear it. He had saved her in that fight, but what if she lost him now?

"Wake up, darling," she whispered. "I have to tell you—I love you, too. You need to know that."

But he didn't stir. She sat back in the chair a nurse had left for her, and reached for a stack of magazines. She found what she'd been reading, over and over, for the last day, a review of the band at the Club d'Or.

"'An exceptional work by a gifted new man of the horn; something fresh and exciting, pushing Paris into the new decade...' Come on, you have to wake up and hear all this!" she said, trying so hard to be cheerful. One of the nurses had told her he might be able to hear her. She might be able to summon him back to her. "You'll be famous! The new King Oliver, remember? You can't let that go now."

"B-better," a hoarse whisper said. "Eliza."

"Jack!" she cried. She turned back to the bed, and saw to her soaring joy that his eyes, his beautiful golden eyes, were open at last. She knelt down beside him, reaching for his hand to kiss it, over and over. "You're awake."

"I'll be much better than King Oliver ever dreamed," he said with a trace of a smile. "I'm sorry, my love."

"Sorry for what? You saved me!"

"No, before. I'm sorry I left you, that I hurt you. That I hurt us both."

Eliza bent her head over his hand, trying to hide the flood of tears she couldn't let free, not yet. "I know you were trying to help me."

"I was. Or at least, I thought I was. You deserve so much, Eliza, you deserve the perfect life. Not me and my crazy cousin, not—not a man like *me*."

She sucked in a deep breath. "How can my life ever be perfect, ever be anything at all, without you? We are the same. The same heart, the same soul." She kissed his fingertips, one after the other, softly. "It's not an easy choice, to be together in this rough world, but it's my *only* choice. You are my only choice. I could never be happy without you."

"My bird girl. My angel. I thought you were like the summer sunshine that night at the Stork Club. So sweet, so warm. You, me, our music—it's all I could want."

"It's all I want, too. So don't make me chase after you again."

A smile whispered over his lips. "I'm standing still now, aren't I? Galliard will give me that club manager job, I'm sure, especially after that review you're reading. We can live here in Paris on that."

Eliza nodded, choked with so much joy and tears, everything so shining perfect in that moment. It would carry her through anything they faced in the future. "And I'll have my grandmother's inheritance soon, it's not much but I can finish at the Conservatoire and make a living. *We* will make a living together. Just us."

"Just us." His hand closed tight over hers. "Marry me, Eliza?"

Eliza held on to him, sure she'd fallen down into some glorious dream. "Yes, Jack Coleman. Of course I will marry you. This is forever, you know. You and me."

"Forever," he said, and kissed her like he would never let her go.

Epilogue

Eliza drew in a deep breath, trying to steady herself and stop shaking. This was her big moment, and she couldn't ruin it. Couldn't let it fly away.

She patted at her newly bobbed hair, smoothing the short, blonde waves under her beaded headband, and made sure the lace cap sleeves of her blue silk dress were straight. Mamie had helped her choose the frock at Doucet before Mamie left for the Riviera in search of sun and sand and "handsome film stars."

"It's your very first Paris concert, Liz!" she had declared as she watched Eliza twirl before the atelier mirror. "You have to look perfect. And remember I'll be there in spirit, cheering you on! In everything."

Eliza's mother's parting words were not nearly so peachy keen. "We have tried to give you every advantage, Elizabeth," she had said coldly as the porter carried her luggage out of the hotel, bound for the boat train. "And now you have thrown it all away. So very shameful."

But there was no room for sadness now, no regrets, not on this day. Her hard work was about to come to fruition. As she adjusted the pearl-beaded sash of her dress, the light caught on the new ring on her left hand. A small sapphire flanked by pavé diamonds, gleaming and bright as summer afternoon by the Seine.

She smiled to remember the moment Jack slipped on her finger, as they stood on the Pont Neuf, the water sparkling beneath them.

"We'll get a bigger sapphire," he said. "When I'm the new and improved King Oliver."

Eliza had no doubts at all that fame and fortune would land on Jack sooner rather than later. The Club d'Or was packed every night now, and there was talk of a recording. But she never wanted a different ring. This one was *hers*, a reminder of all that she had now, all the love and joy and strength and laughter her Jack gave her. The future that laid before them, unknown, different, glorious.

A door opened along the corridor, and she heard the last notes of a Mozart concerto played by the student before her on the program. It was almost time.

Nervousness fluttered low in her stomach again, and she pressed her hand hard against her silk skirt. "Nothing to fear," she whispered.

"Mademoiselle Van Hoeven, five minutes, *s'il vous-plaît*," the usher called, and she nodded.

She thought of what Jack always said. "It's a feeling you build, and keep building inside of you—that feeling of music. You have it, Eliza, and when you have it it's simple. Whole, natural. Flow. Just flow with the sound."

She held her head high, pasted on a bright smile, and followed the usher through the winding corridors of dressing rooms and props onto the stage.

For an instant, she was blinded by the glow of the lights, but then she saw the grand piano waiting at the center of the space, glowing in its spotlight, waiting just for her.

The footlights were still bright as she stepped forward, yet when she peered beyond them, she saw Jack sitting right where she could see him, in the middle of the third row next to the Galliards and Chloe, his smile filled with pride and happiness.

Beside the Comtesse was one of her salon friends, a man Eliza recognized as a director of the Palais Garnier, a man who could hire her for the ballet orchestra, the opera. Yet even knowing someone like that, someone who could help her begin her career, was listening couldn't make her frightened now. Not with Jack smiling at her. Not with that ring on her finger, and the future unfurling before them, shining like the Seine.

She sat down at the piano, raised her fingers above the keys, and let those wondrous feelings flow through her like the light of Paris itself. Like love, and all its promises.

* * * * *

*If you enjoyed this story, why not check out
Amanda McCabe's Dollar Duchesses miniseries*

His Unlikely Duchess
Playing the Duke's Fiancé
Winning Back His Duchess

And be sure to read her Debutante's in Paris trilogy

Secrets of a Wallflower
The Governess's Convenient Marriage
Miss Fortescue's Protector in Paris

Author Note

I'm so excited to share Jack and Eliza's story with you, and I hope you enjoy their romance as much as I loved writing it.

A Manhattan Heiress in Paris includes so many of my loves in life—Paris, music, and especially passionate soulmates who overcome all else to be together. Watching Jack and Eliza find each other made me cry a bit—maybe even more than once!

Thankfully only my dogs witnessed the ugly-cry, LOL!

It was also fun to incorporate a bit of real history in the story. The great love the French had for jazz music, the new art of the Salon des Indépendants, Hemingway and his drinking and inconvenient boxing at parties, the glamorous Murphys and their party on the barge.

Paris in the nineteen-twenties always seems like a magical time of artistic experiments, a remaking of the world after the horrors of the war and the flu epidemic. But of course it was also a very complicated time, particularly for matters such as race relations, and I didn't have the space to delve nearly as deeply into these very important issues as I would have liked.

Eliza and Jack will face many large challenges in their lives together, but love is very powerful, too, and they have that together in abundance.

Here are just a few of the many sources I used in my research, if you'd like to dive deeper into the times.

Mackrell, Judith (2013), *Flappers: Six Women of a Dangerous Generation* Picador

Mercer, Jeremy (2005), *Time Was Soft There: A Paris Season at Shakespeare and Company* Picador USA

Morgenstern, Dan (2004), *Living With Jazz* Pantheon

Chinen, Nate (2018), *Playing Changes: Jazz for the New Century* Vintage

Sandke, Randall (2010), *Where the Dark and the Light Folk Meet: Race and the Mythology, Politics, and Business of Jazz* Scarecrow Press

Kofsky, Paul (1998), *Black Music, White Business: Illuminating the History and Political Economy of Jazz* Pathfinder Books Ltd

Pryor Dodge, Roger (1995), *Hot Jazz and Jazz Dance* Oxford University Press

Duke Ellington (1974), *Music is My Mistress* W. H. Allen/Virgin Books

Anversa, David Anversa (2020), *The History of Racism in the United States and the World* Independently Published

Floyd, Samuel A Jr (1996), *The Power of Black Music* Oxford University Press USA

Carr, Ian (2016), *Miles Davis: The Definitive Biography* HarperCollins

Kahn, Ashley (2000), *Kind of Blue: Miles Davis and the Making of a Masterpiece* Granta

Lees, Gene (1994), *Cats of Any Color: Jazz Black and White* Oxford University Press

Ward, Geoffrey C. & Burns, Ken (2001), *Jazz: A History of America's Music* Knopf Publishing Group

Roe, Sue (2014), *In Montmartre: Picasso, Matisse and Modernism in Paris, 1900-1910* Penguin

Roe, Sue (2018), *In Montparnasse: The Emergence of Surrealism in Paris, from Duchamp to Dali* Penguin

Charters, Jimmie (1937), *This Must Be the Place: Memories of Montparnasse* Collier Books

Hemingway, Ernest Hemingway (1936), *A Moveable Feast*

Johnson, Diane (2007), *Into a Paris Quartier: Reine Margot's Chapel & Other Haunts of St.-Germain* National Geographic

Green, Nancy L. (2015), *The Other Americans in Paris: Businessmen, Countesses, Wayward Youth, 1880–1941* The University of Chicago Press

Downie, David (2015), *A Passion for Paris: Romanticism and Romance in the City of Light* St Martin's Griffin

McAuliffe, Mary (2019), *When Paris Sizzled: The 1920s Paris of Hemingway, Chanel, Cocteau, Cole Porter, Josephine Baker, and Their Friends* Roman & Littlefield

Riley Fitch, Noel (1985), *Sylvia Beach and the Lost Generation A History of Literary Paris in the Twenties and Thirties* W.W. Norton & Co

Hansen, Alrlen J. (2013), *Expatriate Paris: A Cultural and Literary Guide to the Paris of the 1920s* Arcade Publishing

Putnam, Samuel (1947), *Paris Was Our Mistress: Memoirs of a Lost and Found Generation* Viking Press

Evans, Sian (2020), *Maiden Voyages: Women and the Golden Age of Transatlantic Travel* Two Roads

Maxton-Graham, John (1997), *The Only Way To Cross: The Golden Era of the Great Atlantic Express Liners* Barnes & Noble

Kern Holoman, D. (2004), *The Société des Concerts du Conservatoire 1828-1967* University of California Press

Simeone, Nigel (2000), *Paris: A Musical Gazetteer* Yale University Press

Vaill, Amanda (1998), *Everyone Was So Young: Gerald and Sara Murphy, a Lost Generation Love Story* Houghton Mifflin

Dearborn, Mary V. (2017), *Ernest Hemingway: A Biography* Knopf Publishing Group

Brody, Paul (2014), *Hemingway in Paris: A Biography of Ernest Hemingway's Formative Paris Years* Independently Published

Milford, Nancy (1970), *Zelda: A Biography* Harper & Row

THE NIGHT SHE MET THE DUKE (Regency)
by Sarah Mallory
After hearing herself described as "dull," Prudence escapes London to
Bath, where her new life is anything but dull when one night she finds an
uninvited, devastatingly handsome duke in her kitchen!

THE HOUSEKEEPER'S FORBIDDEN EARL (Regency)
by Laura Martin
Kate's finally found peace working in a grand house, until her new
employer, Lord Henderson, returns. Soon, it's not just the allure of the
home that Kate's falling for...but its owner, too!

FALLING FOR HIS PRETEND COUNTESS (Victorian)
Southern Belles in London • by Lauri Robinson
Henry, Earl of Beaufort and London's most eligible bachelor, is being
framed for murder! When his neighbor Suzanne offers to help prove his
innocence, a fake engagement provides the perfect cover...

THE VISCOUNT'S DARING MISS (1830s)
by Lotte R. James
When groom Roberta "Bobby" Kinsley comes face-to-face with her horse
racing opponent—infuriatingly charismatic Viscount Hayes—it's clear that it
won't just be the competition that has her heart racing!

A KNIGHT FOR THE DEFIANT LADY (Medieval)
Convent Brides • by Carol Townend
Attraction sparks when Sir Leon retrieves brave, beautiful Lady Allis from
a convent and they journey back to her castle. Only for Allis's father to
demand she marry a nobleman!

ALLIANCE WITH HIS STOLEN HEIRESS (1900s)
by Lydia San Andres
Rebellious Julián doesn't mind masquerading as a bandit to help Amalia
claim her inheritance—he's enjoying spending time with the bold heiress.
But how can he reveal the truth of his identity?

Get 4 FREE REWARDS!

We'll send you 2 FREE Books plus 2 FREE Mystery Gifts.

FREE
Value Over
$20

Both the **Romance** and **Suspense** collections feature compelling novels written by many of today's bestselling authors.

YES! Please send me 2 FREE novels from the Essential Romance or Essential Suspense Collection and my 2 FREE gifts (gifts are worth about $10 retail). After receiving them, if I don't wish to receive any more books, I can return the shipping statement marked "cancel." If I don't cancel, I will receive 4 brand-new novels every month and be billed just $7.49 each in the U.S. or $7.74 each in Canada. That's a savings of at least 17% off the cover price. It's quite a bargain! Shipping and handling is just 50¢ per book in the U.S. and $1.25 per book in Canada.* I understand that accepting the 2 free books and gifts places me under no obligation to buy anything. I can always return a shipment and cancel at any time by calling the number below. The free books and gifts are mine to keep no matter what I decide.

Choose one: ☐ **Essential Romance**   ☐ **Essential Suspense**
                     (194/394 MDN GRHV)   (191/391 MDN GRHV)

Name (please print)

Address   Apt. #

City   State/Province   Zip/Postal Code

Email: Please check this box ☐ if you would like to receive newsletters and promotional emails from Harlequin Enterprises ULC and its affiliates. You can unsubscribe anytime.

Mail to the **Harlequin Reader Service:**
IN U.S.A.: P.O. Box 1341, Buffalo, NY 14240-8531
IN CANADA: P.O. Box 603, Fort Erie, Ontario L2A 5X3

Want to try 2 free books from another series? Call 1-800-873-8635 or visit www.ReaderService.com.

---

*Terms and prices subject to change without notice. Prices do not include sales taxes, which will be charged (if applicable) based on your state or country of residence. Canadian residents will be charged applicable taxes. Offer not valid in Quebec. This offer is limited to one order per household. Books received may not be as shown. Not valid for current subscribers to the Essential Romance or Essential Suspense Collection. All orders subject to approval. Credit or debit balances in a customer's account(s) may be offset by any other outstanding balance owed by or to the customer. Please allow 4 to 6 weeks for delivery. Offer available while quantities last.

Your Privacy—Your information is being collected by Harlequin Enterprises ULC, operating as Harlequin Reader Service. For a complete summary of the information we collect, how we use this information and to whom it is disclosed, please visit our privacy notice located at corporate.harlequin.com/privacy-notice. From time to time we may also exchange your personal information with reputable third parties. If you wish to opt out of this sharing of your personal information, please visit readerservice.com/consumerschoice or call 1-800-873-8635. **Notice to California Residents**—Under California law, you have specific rights to control and access your data. For more information on these rights and how to exercise them, visit corporate.harlequin.com/california-privacy.

STRS22R3

HARLEQUIN
PLUS

Try the best multimedia subscription service for romance readers like you!

Read, Watch and Play.

Experience the easiest way to get the romance content you crave.

Start your **FREE TRIAL** at
<u>www.harlequinplus.com/freetrial</u>.